ENDGAME

CSI Reilly Steel #7

CASEY HILL

CSI REILLY STEEL SERIES

CHAPTER ONE

There was nothing quite like the stench of fresh vomit.

Standing in the early morning sunshine just outside the tidy four-bedroom house, Reilly Steel could smell the potent sickly odor from the front entrance.

Her sensitive nose caught it coming through the windows, opened in an attempt to air the place, and she'd picked up the distinctive funk almost as soon as she emerged from the Garda Forensic Unit van.

The detached house sported an elaborate red brick facade and a neatly trimmed front garden, though a few empty beer cans littered the lawn and were strewn through the hedges bordering the grass.

Neighbors had gathered in their pajamas up and down the road of the small housing estate in Churchtown - a staunchly middle class Dublin suburb - to watch the police and investigators at work, and though Reilly knew it was doubtful they could smell anything, she almost expected them to have their hands over their mouths and noses in disgust.

She made her way into the house, donning gloves and a mask that would in all likelihood end up being worn as head-covering. Face masks at a crime scene were like wearing sunglasses in a dark room; they dulled the senses.

She preferred to take in a scene fully, though lately she was unsure if she could depend on her usually trusty nose. Her blonde hair was already pulled back from her face in a tight ponytail she had fastened it into when she'd got the call earlier.

The night before had been one with which Reilly had recently become all too acquainted – she'd tossed and turned in her bed, trying every method she knew to fall asleep, but to no avail.

In the war against her insomnia, she could only claim to have won a few battles, so in the end the eight AM call had proved a welcome distraction.

The heads-up had come from Detective Chris Delaney, informing her that a high school kid (or secondary school as they called it in Ireland) had been attacked and killed in his bedroom following a party the night before. She heard the scratchy undertone of Chris's deep voice and knew that her colleague hadn't been awake long. The lucky bastard actually got to sleep at night.

The smell of vomit inside the house was even stronger, and while Reilly commended the first responders' efforts to air the space out, the open windows were really doing little to alleviate the woeful stench.

Crossing the doorway, she readily took in the scene; the interior of the house was in a state of chaos. Reilly could easily visualize these kinds of teenage parties - she'd been witness to many back home in California growing up, and immediately recognized the disarray such gatherings caused.

And in the meantime of course, she had seen plenty of this kind of thing portrayed in the movies or on TV. Though in her experience, the depictions of real life situations, such as forensic work, on TV shows weren't all that accurate, to say the least.

As she moved inside, the carpeted hallway soaked with spilled beer gave a little under her feet, and she had to step over the offending pile of vomit and a broken beer bottle to get to the stairs.

Lucy, her fellow GFU technician, was already in a room to the left swabbing surfaces, and the younger tech gave Reilly a smile in greeting as she passed by.

She made her way up the stairs, studying the framed pictures of the house's inhabitants as she went. She noted that they depicted a happy and respectable-looking Irish family, professional parents and two ruddy faced boys - all bright eyes and happy smiles at the camera. From the look of the house and the occupants, this family was firmly middle class; there was money, but not too much.

As she came to the top of the steps, she was met by Gary, another forensic tech, who was doing the same thing his colleague had been on the floor below.

He looked up at Reilly and while he normally would have smiled broadly in typical jocular fashion, today Gary just managed a welcoming nod, his mouth and nose concealed by his face mask as he focused on his work.

Detective Pete Kennedy was also standing on the landing, speaking to someone on the phone. The heavyset middle-aged detective apologized once, twice, and then again. Judging by his tone, if Reilly had to take a guess to save her life at the person on the other end of that line, it was his wife Josie.

He was still apologizing as Reilly passed him. He looked at her with jaded eyes and shook his head before she made her way into the bedroom.

"Morning Goldilocks," he murmured, looking speculatively at her, his gaze inevitably skipping down to her burgeoning stomach as it always did these days, before finding her face again.

Reilly's 'blob' could no longer be called that; now in the middle of her second trimester, she was carrying a full-on Bumpasaurus.

"Ah sure, she's used to it," Kennedy was saying to his wife, and Reilly guessed that Josie was telling her husband off for his by now customary greeting. She smiled indulgently. He was right; she was used to it and it never bothered her - far from being offensive, the older detective's predictable bluster was now almost endearing. Almost.

Pausing a little before she entered the bedroom - the primary crime scene - Reilly steeled herself for what she would see when she went in. When Chris had called her that morning, he'd used the word *kid*, something that instinctively made her stomach turn.

This was indeed a male teenager's bedroom, that much was clear as soon as she walked in. The walls were painted a dark gray, and posters depicting various sports stars hung on the walls, intermingled with 'come hither' poses from busty models or whichever reality TV or Instagram star was in vogue these days.

The bed was messily unmade and a pile of laundry in the corner was threatening to break free and flood the rest of the room.

Reilly inhaled and was immediately assaulted with another odor of an altogether different kind; the metallic stench of blood, which was spattered across the wall as well as on the heavy oak desk and some of the laundry. She also detected the faint whiff lingering in a room when cologne or perfume was sprayed often, the kind of generic alcohol that stuck in the carpet and cloth surfaces like curtains, near wherever the person got ready.

Finally, she moved to take in the victim himself. She always waited a little until resting her gaze upon the corpse, as she didn't want the victim's state to influence her initial observations at the crime scene.

With so many years in CSI, Reilly was by now pretty much hardened to the harsh truths of the world - one of them being that people died in horrific and heinous ways.

So, when she finally looked down at Graham Hackett, the seventeen year-old boy who had been beaten to death in his own bedroom, she hoped to remain calm and composed. But the sudden spike of nausea and all out revulsion that shot through her stomach made her take a step backward.

She stared at the boy; thrown a little by the angelic expression on his youthful face and how the blood surrounding his caved-in skull was caked into his sandy brown hair. He was on his side, arms curled under him almost like he was sleeping. His eyes were closed, and despite the violent way he'd died, he looked calm and content.

He really was just a kid.

This boy had met his end before he'd had a chance to do anything with his life, hadn't gotten a chance to experience the best of what the world had to offer. Someone had stolen that from him.

But as she stepped backwards into a man's hard chest, none of those logical thoughts were running through Reilly's head. In fact, little tangible thought could be isolated - instead, she was overcome by fear and revulsion at the pitiful sight before her.

Detective Chris Delaney caught her, startled by the look on her face. He had seen that same look on countless newbie faces, freshly-trained uniforms who thought they would be grand the first time they saw a dead body, only to feel complete helplessness when they gazed down on someone who'd had their life brutally ended. Hence, the welcoming pile at the bottom of the stairs.

Chris felt it every time he showed up at a crime scene actually. The feeling followed him around and there were only a few places in the world he could forget about what he'd seen for a while. Also, only a few people in the world that could help him forget.

Reilly Steel was one of them.

"Hey," he said, gently grabbing her shoulders and stepping round her. "Are you okay?"

She quickly composed herself; nodded and set her gaze on the detective, catching a full whiff of his equally distinctive scent: a sharp, woody aftershave that lingered after him in an almost palpable wave to her sensitive nose.

"I'm fine, Chris," she said, moving away from him to look at the body again. "It's just...he's so young."

"I know. Barely out of school - finished his state exams only this week apparently."

Reilly looked around again, at the walls and the blood spattered across them, trying to get a sense of what had happened.

The victim had been bludgeoned to death; that much was obvious. She frowned then, as looking at the surrounding walls, she noticed some strange circular marks beneath the blood spatter. All roughly the same shape and the circumference of a baseball, the marks seemed to occur in a rough pattern all the way up the wall as far as the ceiling.

"What the hell is that?" she asked, her eyes narrowing as she moved towards the wall.

Chris followed her gaze. "I can't be sure, but I'd hazard a guess they're ball marks - *sliotar* marks probably." He nodded at a couple of sports trophies on a nearby shelf.

"*Sliotar?*" she repeated, baffled.

"Irish word for the ball used in hurling - a GAA sport," he told her.

"Right." Reilly knew next to nothing about traditional Irish sport but had caught a clip of the game Chris was talking about one time on TV. Hurling was fast-moving and shockingly violent, sort of a cross between hockey and street fighting.

And this kid had won trophies for it.

"Looks like he might have been practicing against

the wall," Chris explained, indicating the markings, and while Reilly still didn't quite understand, she agreed that the markings did indeed look consistent with someone aiming a spherical object at the plaster. She'd keep an eye out for this 'sliotar' Chris had mentioned.

"Chris..." The sound of the other detective's weathered voice made Reilly jump again, only disproving her assertion that she was fine. Pete Kennedy glanced at the two of them for the briefest moment before addressing Chris again. "The kid who called this in is outside - was at the party last night apparently. We'd better grill him while everything is still fresh in his mind."

Chris took another glance around the room, before turning to his partner. "OK, be with you now."

As he walked from the room, moving carefully so as not to contaminate any evidence, Kennedy commented to Reilly. "Looks like you've got your work cut out for you."

CHAPTER TWO

The aforementioned kid who'd called in the incident was outside the house on the front step, leaning against one of the pillars beneath a canopy that sheltered the front door from the elements. He looked to be a year or two older than the victim, and his hair was the same sandy brown color. His eyes were closed, but there were definitive bags under them, like he had gone days without sleep.

His clothes were wrinkled beyond redemption, as if he had just grabbed something off the floor and pulled it on, dirty or clean. The detectives could just about make out a high tempo rock song blaring through the earbuds snaking up to the boy's ears.

Chris was about to ask his partner if the kid was sleeping off a bad hangover, and that they should maybe leave him to it for the moment until he came to, but

Kennedy unceremoniously nudged the boy's thigh with his heavy black shoe.

"Hey, mate. Detectives. We need to talk to you."

The teen opened one eye and looked up at the men casting a shadow over his rumpled form. His eyes were bloodshot and his lids were heavy as he slowly pulled one earbud from his ear and raised an eyebrow at them.

"You're the guy who called this in?" Chris affirmed.

The boy looked back and forth between the two detectives, before sighing and taking the other earbud out. After taking his sweet time in wrapping the cord up around the MP3 player and placing it securely back in his pocket, he said simply, "Yeah."

Opening his notebook, Chris cleared his throat at his offhand demeanor given the gravity of the situation. Didn't Kennedy say this guy knew the victim? "First up, can you please state your name as well as your relation to the deceased?"

The teenager yawned and looked over the bottle-littered lawn, scratching his head and running his hand through his hair a couple of times before settling against the pillar again. Running his hand through his hair didn't help, Chris thought, because it now stood crazily on end and matched the rest of his bedraggled form.

He set a lazy gaze on the detectives and said in a highly insolent tone, "Someone already asked me this stuff. Twice. Do I really have to go through it all again?"

Chris gripped his pen, trying to level his voice out. Someone had died in this house last night - presumably a friend - and this cocky asshole was more concerned with his personal inconvenience? "Yes, but we need to hear it coming out of your own mouth. Because you called this in, you're now a part of our investigation."

Another deep sigh. "Name's Simon Hackett. Graham's my brother."

Chris's shock might not have been apparent on his face, but it was patently obvious on Kennedy's, who looked just as surprised at the guy's admission. He knew, sure as you like, that if *his* brother had been murdered, he certainly wouldn't be sitting outside the house, listening to rock tunes.

People displayed grief in all sorts of different ways though, he had to remind himself, as he looked at the kid's impassive face. Still, Simon looked back at them as though he and Kennedy were nothing but an imposition.

"We're very sorry about your brother, bud," Kennedy intoned sympathetically before getting right back to the point. "According to the report, you found the vic...your brother earlier? Can you tell us now in your own words what happened, exactly, from the moment you woke up?"

"Like I said before, I got out of bed, saw the

trashed-up house, went to look for Graham, and found him...like that, in his bedroom."

Chris bristled. Again, for a guy who just found his own flesh and blood beaten and battered to death in their own home, Simon Hackett seemed spectacularly unfazed. Was he simply in shock, maybe still too drunk or maybe doped to appreciate that this was actually happening? It was the only way to explain how he could be so unaffected by such a deeply traumatizing experience.

"That's everything that happened, exactly, from the moment you woke up?" Chris pressed scornfully. "As detailed as you can be?"

Simon scowled at the two of them. "Okay, I woke up, scratched me hole, pulled on my jocks, drank a glass of water, pissed, blinked...What more do you want from me?"

"To start, how about a little respect - if not for us, then for your own brother?"

"Chris," his partner warned in a low tone, and he took a breath.

The kid's attitude was grating, yet it would do them no good to get into a verbal spat with a witness - asshole or not. Chris tried to put himself in the brother's shoes for a second. Last night, he'd had a few drinks and the craic with his mates and went to bed like any other night. But when he woke up, his brother was dead.

Assuming of course, that the guy had nothing to do with the attack.

He approached the situation from another angle, trying to keep his impatience out of his voice. "Simon, how about you describe to us bit by bit what happened, but maybe leave the hole-scratching out of it."

Simon sighed again. "I got up around seven, because like I said, I needed a slash. The house was trashed after last night, but it was Graham's party and I sure as feck wasn't cleaning it up, so I went upstairs to wake him after I had something to eat. When he wouldn't answer the door, I went in and found him...on the floor. Then I came back out and called the guards."

Kennedy jumped back into the questioning then after Simon opened up a little.

Chris glanced up at the bedroom window, then back at Simon, who was regarding him with the same apathetic stare. "Did you hear or see anything suspicious last night?" he asked, already not expecting a straightforward, simple answer. "Maybe overheard an argument or sounds of a struggle coming from your brother's room?"

"Look, there were about ten or fifteen people here, so you tell me what I should've seen. Graham had a party to celebrate the end of his exams. People were in and out of the house all night and most of them were his friends, but strangers to me. I was here with some of my own mates, but we left at about midnight to go to a club in town. The last time I saw my brother, he was out in the back with some girl, looking cozy. And before you ask, no, I don't know who she was. I think they went out at some stage, maybe? Anyway, when I got back home ... sometime after half-two or three, I crashed just after and was zonked until this morning, like I already told you."

"And you heard nothing suspicious that could have woken you or roused your attention? Signs of a struggle in the bedroom or raised voices from an argument?" Chris was trying to get a handle on the timing, though the ME would soon be able to give them a ballpark as to time of death.

But given the fact that Simon hadn't heard anything - and it would have taken quite a ruckus to cause the mess upstairs - it was reasonable to assume that the attack on the younger Hackett brother happened while the elder was out at the nightclub. Again, assuming he was being upfront and telling the truth. Chris studied the brother's hands and face looking for any telltale injuries that might contradict his story.

"I told you already, I conked out. The next thing that happened was my morning piss, unless you want to know about my dreams too?"

"Where are your parents?" Kennedy asked then, while Chris had to bite his tongue. By now, this kid's attitude was getting right up his nose.

Simon was quick to answer that one. "Spain," he

said, with a little more vigor than he'd possessed for the previous questions, like this was one he hadn't been asked yet. "We have an apartment over there and Graham and I were supposed to fly down there and meet them this weekend once his exams were finished." He looked away. "I guess that won't be happening now."

Kennedy scribbled this down in his notepad. "And have you spoken to them today?"

"Not yet."

The detectives shared a look. Someone, likely one of the first responders would have no doubt already contacted the parents, but the fact that their own son had neglected to do so was strange - considering the distraught circumstances. Though perhaps Simon was merely the kind of guy who didn't react well to grief?

"We strongly encourage you to get in touch with your folks, son," said Kennedy gently. "I'm sure they're desperate to talk to you."

The detectives kept up their questioning until Simon grew so irritable and uncooperative it was no longer advantageous to continue. Chris had to wonder what kind of parents would raise a kid so disrespectful to law enforcement, not to mention blatantly insensitive to his own brother's murder. Though obviously the kind that took off to Spain on holidays rather than stayed around to encourage their son during his final exams.

Yet he tried not to make too many assumptions at

this early stage and eventually he and Kennedy walked away from the kid in silence.

The interview hadn't revealed much. In fact, the only thing the questioning of Simon Hackett had managed to do was set Chris's suspicions of the kid on high alert. He took note of the nightclub Simon supposedly attended last night, fully intending to check it out; grief-stricken or not, they weren't taking anything for granted and the older brother's reaction was just plain weird.

From their position out front, the two men could see a couple of neighbors - some still dressed in their nightclothes - watching the uniforms and forensics moving around and through the Hackett house. They were all straining to see over the tops of their respective hedges or fences, which Chris thought was ironic, considering all the trouble they must have gone to putting them up.

The detectives shared a look, then made their way to the house next door.

A middle-aged couple was standing beneath their porch observing, and when the detectives approached, the woman quickly disappeared into the house, while the man took a few steps forward to greet them.

"Good morning," Chris said, "I'm Detective Chris Delaney from the Serious Crimes Unit, and this is my partner, Detective Pete Kennedy. We'd like to ask you a few questions about your neighbors and anything you might have witnessed last night, if that's okay."

The man nodded and put his hands on his hips, glancing over at the house next door before focusing his gaze back on the detectives. "Of course. Anything I can do to help. That poor boy … I heard the terrible news from one of the other officers earlier. Who would have … ? Though I might as well warn you, I doubt I can be of much help."

Just then the door behind him opened and the woman he'd been standing on the porch with bustled out, two cups of coffee in her hands. She hurried up to the detectives and handed them each a cup.

Kennedy politely refused. "Thanks, but we've just had some. Your names?" he asked, opening his notebook up.

Chris knew better however and gratefully accepted, even though he had indeed just finished a coffee. But you never refused an offer of hospitality from a potential witness. "You're very kind, thank you," he smiled at the wife, turning on the charm.

"I'm Emily Green and this is my husband, Thomas," the woman told Chris, as she took a spot next to her husband, facing the detectives. She shook her head. "I still can't believe it … poor Graham. Who'd believe that something like that could happen around here? These are very quiet parts, this kind of stuff never happens."

Addressing the couple together, Chris asked, "So did you hear or see anything suspicious last night?"

Thomas Green placed his arm protectively around his wife's shoulders, pulling her closer to him. "No – other than the usual."

Kennedy raised an eyebrow which encouraged the man to keep going. "Well, the older Hackett boy throws a party every few months, whenever the parents go abroad. Sometime around midnight the noise gets to be a bit much, loud music, shouting, whatever."

"And did this noise ever bother you and your family?"

Green shrugged, "It was a bit annoying at times, but our houses are far enough apart that it doesn't really affect us too much. The first couple of times the ruckus got a bit over the top, we called it in to the local station who came over to caution them, but it didn't do a lot of good. Ah sure, you know yourself how kids are."

After discussing a little further the Hackett children's party exploits, the detectives were very quickly put to rest about any suspicions concerning this couple. Feuding Irish neighbors were surprisingly notorious for getting out of hand and escalating quickly, but it was obvious the Greens' qualms about the party noise were nowhere severe enough to warrant the violence that had occurred next door.

"OK," Kennedy said in conclusion, "thanks for that - we'll get outta your hair."

The detectives made their way through the rest of the neighboring households, gathering information that almost matched the Greens' word for word. Most of the families stayed out on their lawns to watch the drama unfold at the house in their midst.

The lights of a TV news crew caught Chris's eye. A blond journo he recognized held a microphone up to an older lady who was being interviewed. He was too far away to hear what was being said, but he could guess without being able to lip-read. Much like the Greens just now, the local reaction was always the same.

Words and expressions like 'shocked', 'terrible', 'who would have thought this would happen round here?' always seemed to roll from people's tongues. Chris was always surprised by how surprised people were. But then again, most people didn't get to see what he did day in day out.

The detectives made their way back to the Hackett residence and walked around the back.

The rear garden was something to behold – a good sized lawn of rolling greenery, as well as extensive and elaborate bedding featuring vibrant plants and a beautiful gazebo.

A wooden decking area to the rear just off the kitchen looked to have been the preferred spot for last night's gathering; there was a table full of empty beer bottles and cans, but mostly sickly smelling alco-pops that suggested a younger crowd. Blasted sugary crap had a lot to answer for.

Back in Chris's day, teens didn't tend to get so out-of-their-heads drunk because alcohol tasted like alcohol, and you could only take so much of it. Whereas now it tasted like gummy bears and they were all knocking it back like there was no tomorrow.

Which in the case of poor Graham Hackett, there wasn't.

He and Kennedy surveyed through the debris, keeping most of their initial observations to themselves. They were both aware that the upcoming investigation would bring a never ending workload involving bereaved parents, a whole host of witnesses and a lot of dead ends, before eventually (hopefully) they found their killer. With this thought in mind, and knowing how much talking and surmising they would have to do to reach the point before they even had a suspect in custody, the detectives let the air around them fall silent, as if soaking up the calm before the impending storm.

CHAPTER THREE

Back inside the house, which was now clear of first responders, Reilly and her team had taken full charge of the since isolated crime scene, and secured the property while Dr. Thompson the medical examiner, prepared Graham Hackett's body for removal to the morgue.

She watched for a moment as Gary moved through the room, photographing and cataloguing the scene, then turned to Karen Thompson, who was just finishing up her preliminary examination of the body. "Does he have anything to tell us?"

The ME looked up from the victim's battered form. Her gaze caught on the impact blood spatter on the wall before she met Reilly's. "Blunt head trauma and shoulder lacerations aside, there's also a broken shoulder and multiple finger fractures - defensive injuries - suggesting a defensive posture during the struggle. Based on lividity, we're looking at time of death somewhere between two and five am. Really can't say much more until I get him on the table."

Reilly nodded, suspecting as much.

If only the dead could speak ...

Having just rolled the victim and his clothes for trace evidence, she removed her gloves and donned new ones, before moving over to the desk at the bottom of Graham Hackett's bed.

She stood there for a moment cataloguing the items on top. Just some exam papers, flotsam and jetsam and what looked like flyers and informational material from universities, as well as being littered with gum wrappers and stray pens. She remembered what Chris had said about last night's party being related to the end of state examinations. To think of all the time the poor kid had spent between these four walls studying for exams.

And all for nothing.

She pulled the drawers open and looked through them. They were mostly older school assignments and blank sheets of A4 paper. Reilly pulled a stray piece of paper out, examining the scribbles for a moment, only to find they were what looked to be poetry, or song lyrics. She glanced at the overtly macho room around her and wondered if perhaps this was a note from a girl, or maybe a classmate's paper? As it didn't seem to fit with the profile she'd built up of this kid so far. But of course, as Reilly knew well, appearances had a habit of being deceiving.

As she riffled through some other papers in the drawer, she came across a box of what looked like prescription medication. She carefully pulled the box from the drawer for closer examination. The instructions on the outside were not written in English, but rather some form of Cyrillic script. Inside the box were two blister packs, one full, the other half-used.

Reilly placed the box into an evidence bag, trying to fathom why a teenager would be prescribed medication which didn't come with English instructions.

The other drawers featured the same messy configuration of chewed-on pens and crumpled papers. She visualized the kid swiping them off the desk and into the drawer, telling himself he would sort through everything when he got the time. She regarded the overall mess again with a hint of the feeling that had hit her when she saw his body the first time that morning.

Would her future son or daughter be this disorganized?

She shook her head in an attempt to clear the thoughts that had permeated her head since she had eventually acknowledged that this pregnancy was, in fact, real and happening. Soon she was going to have a baby that would turn into a toddler and eventually a kid, then a teenager, and there would be nothing she could do about any of it.

She was about to turn away when something on the floor next to the desk caught her attention. Reilly pulled the chair out and crouched down awkwardly. She still hadn't quite gotten her balance settled with the additional load she was carrying, and it took her a moment to maneuver so she could reach the object, glad she hadn't missed it.

An iPad was wedged between the leg of the desk and the wall, its screen completely shattered. But Reilly definitely didn't miss the blood that had seeped into the shattered portion of the screen as she slid it into an evidence bag.

"So much blood ..." Gary was saying, shaking his head. "Surely it shouldn't be that hard to track down someone from the party who went through a fight like this."

He was right; there was a considerable amount of cast-off spatter on the walls, typically occurring when an object swung in an arc flings blood onto a nearby surface. Secondary cast off spatter occurred when the assailant swings the bloodstained object back before inflicting another blow, and it was easy to tell the direction of the impacting object by the shape of the spatter. Counting the arcs also revealed the minimum number of blows delivered - in this case at least three.

Reilly placed the newly bagged and tagged iPad into an evidence bin. "There were more than a dozen guests apparently; with luck the detectives will be able to identify them quickly enough. For gatherings like this it's nigh on impossible to know who came and went in the relevant timeframe though."

"Yep. And add booze and whatever else to the mix and you've got one hell of a breadcrumb trail ..."

Reilly continued to walk the grid, her meticulous eyes moving over every inch. The spatter was clearly indicative of blood coming off the weapon as the attacker swung it. Based on the patterns, she suspected something long and thin, like a baseball bat.

"Look at this," she said then, indicating a piece of spatter on the wall just behind Gary. Unlike the others, this appeared smudged a little, as if something - or someone had been pressed up against it. "Someone involved in the attack hit the wall here - be it the victim or his attacker. When Dr. Thompson is done, check the marks against whatever the victim's wearing. And then make a note of the smudge and input it to iSPI," she said, all the while scanning the room for anything that could work as a potential murder weapon.

Gary raised an eyebrow at her, "Oh, so you're actually going to let me do it this time," he said looking pleased.

It was true that Reilly liked to handle as many of the tasks involved in cataloguing a scene that she could - including the GFU's virtual crime scene reconstruction program – but the main concern in the back of her mind just then, rapidly inching its way to being the most important, was her aching feet and the twinge in her side every time she twisted it just the wrong way.

As Gary placed markers and input measurements and photos into the iSPI app, Reilly moved back towards the corpse again, able to examine the blood on the carpet more closely now that the ME was done. It had pooled beneath the spot where Graham Hackett had eventually fallen and spread onto a blue blanket near the kid's head.

The fracture on the crown of his skull was stark and revolting; Reilly couldn't look at it for too long without feeling nauseous once again.

This was not a crime of precision, or of planning, she decided. Whomever had committed this crime had done it on impulse, without any plan or logic for disposing of the body or avoiding leaving evidence. The recklessness of the attack, coupled with the complete battering that Graham Hackett had taken, indicated that what had occurred was a crime of passion.

Whoever had murdered this kid was consumed by blind rage.

But this was a plus from a forensic point of view, because a crime of passion by its very nature meant that the attacker (or attackers) were likely not very precise or careful about concealing their presence. When they'd finished dusting the doorways and surfaces, they should be able to find some prints as well as shoe impressions, skin tissue etc. In a crime scene this bloody, there should be plenty of grist for the GFU mill.

Gathering the materials she needed to dust the frame of the doorway, she eyed to the younger investigator. "Any initial observations?" she asked.

When she'd first taken the GFU position over three years before, Reilly had launched straight into the role of coach, always pushing the bar higher and higher in terms of her expectations for the team. Her teaching moments were fewer and farther between now, but Gary recognized the question as one of those moments and took another glance around the room, trying to see things the way Reilly would.

"It looks to me as if the poor divil put up a pretty good fight. The attack looks to have started here ..." He gestured to the disturbed items on top of the drawer by the window, sounding like a nervous medical student presenting a case to their supervisor, then took a few steps across the room. "There was a struggle, the attacker got hold of some kind of weapon, and the victim and his attacker moved across the room, until one of them ended up pressed up against this wall. Based on the size and shape of the impression, we can only assume it was the victim or someone roughly the victim's size. His final position near the bed appears to be where he fell after multiple disabling blows from the weapon dropped him, as there are no tracks on the carpet to indicate that the body was dragged or moved.

And the final blow to the head definitely happened when he was down."

"And kept him down," Reilly said, swallowing afresh at the severity of the head contusion. There was no question the attacker had intended that final blow to inflict the worst damage possible, and send poor Graham Hackett to his death.

She nodded along with Gary's observations, having come to much the same conclusions. No obvious sign of a baseball bat or anything resembling a murder weapon in here though, so they could only assume the attacker took that with them when they left.

She finished dusting the doorway, finding numerous partials and a couple of solid prints as expected. Once they'd run the comparisons on the Hackett family fingerprints and shoe treads, hopefully something out of place would stand out.

But as always, Reilly knew from hard worn experience that things were never that easy.

CHAPTER FOUR

Michael Glynn glared down at the morning newspaper in disgust. The cover story featured a piece on one of his previous clients, and he knew for a fact he would soon be hearing something about it. There were days when he seriously questioned his decision to become a solicitor, especially when he had to consider the caliber of some of the people he had as clients. The more he thought about it, the more he managed to work himself into a rage.

He threw half of his toast down on the plate and muttered a curse under his breath, grasping the paper with both hands.

His wife, Susan was sitting across the table from him, gauging his mood. It wasn't uncommon for the stories in the paper to get on her husband's nerves, especially early in the morning. But Michael was particularly annoyed by the paper today, so she brought up the one topic that always seemed to pull him out of such funks.

"Have you seen the kids this morning?"

"Conor rushed out the door as I was getting up," her husband replied, his tone bubbling barely contained rage, as he glanced over at her, "Told me he'd be training all morning."

Susan sighed and scooped her porridge around in her bowl, intending to draw Michael's attention away a little more. "Won't he have time enough for that in Sydney? We hardly see him anymore. He'll burn himself out training so much with those boys."

"It seems to me that *Holly* is the one who is always out with boys," Michael folded the paper up and set it to the side. Gratified, Susan smiled as he continued on, taking the last bite of his toast, "Where is she anyway? I didn't hear her come home last night."

He frowned at the thought of his seventeen year old daughter staying out all night. He always worried about her, especially given the crowd she was hanging around with recently. As a solicitor, he knew how to pick out the good from the bad. Despite that distinct quality, he supposed he was like most fathers in the way that he didn't particularly like the idea of his daughter being out with *any* boy.

Susan checked the time 6:58 – two minutes before

her husband needed to be out the door for the morning commute.

She stood and started clearing the table, humming a tune as she went, "I'll go check on her in a minute, she was probably just careful not to wake us coming in last night."

Holly had just finished secondary school and spent the night before celebrating the end of the state exams with her friends, promising to be home by one AM at the latest.

Michael glanced at his watch and nodded. He walked over to his wife and wrapped his arms around her waist, placing a quick kiss on her cheek.

"I'll see you tonight, pet," he said, before grabbing his briefcase and making his way out. Susan caught him for another kiss and straightened his tie before he finally went out the door, right on time.

But if Susan had known what she would find when she went to look for her daughter, she might have hurried the post breakfast clear-up, or skipped it altogether. As it was, she finished tidying the kitchen at a leisurely pace, singing and opening the windows to let in the warmer late-June air before she finally went upstairs to rouse her daughter.

The family lived in a relatively quiet housing estate, and the Glynns liked to keep to their strict schedule. If they had been paying attention, the couple might have noticed the Garda cars gathered in the estate only a half mile down the road, or the collective hum of gossip that was spreading through the locality with news of what had befallen their neighbors.

Phones throughout the area were buzzing with the shocking story of what had happened to Graham Hackett as Susan made her way up the stairs to wake her daughter, completely oblivious.

Approaching Holly's room and opening the door slowly, she poked her head in, expecting to see her youngest sprawled out on the bed snoring against her bright blue bedspread.

Instead, Susan saw the bedroom left exactly the same way it had been the previous day, when she had gone in to tidy it up. The bed was still made, the curtains were pulled open.

Susan frowned. Maybe Holly *hadn't* come home the night before? But that was most unlike her.

She pulled her cellphone from her pocket and tried to remember how her daughter had shown her to get to the contacts. But before she could completely confuse herself, she caught the sound of the en-suite shower.

She snuck up outside the door and put her ear against the door, listening for Holly's usual singing, but there was nothing but the sound of running water. Then she knocked on the bathroom door. "Holly, honey? Are you in there?"

When no response came from inside, Susan feared her daughter might have just left the water running, or maybe even fell and hit her head while inside, so she pushed the door open slowly. The light in the window-less bathroom was off, so she fumbled for the light switch, eventually getting it on and flooding the room.

A whimper sounded at the sudden introduction of light, and it took Susan a moment to fully comprehend the scene before her.

Her seventeen year old daughter was in the shower, fully-clothed, crouching under the water, her eyes closed tightly. She was whimpering softly as the water beat against her back and ran down her clothes and body.

Susan took another step into the room, her shock dissipating as parental instinct took over. Holly's black dress was torn up the side, her legs and her chin bruised, casting a dark shadow over her pale skin, and creating a sickly effect. Her face was red and shiny, eyes red-rimmed from crying and her hair was tangled beyond belief, wet and matted against her head by the stream of water.

Susan's mouth went dry. She took another step forward, and when Holly saw her mother, she fell towards her, grasping at her mum's clean, dry blouse.

The tears on Holly's face mixed with the water streaming down her cheeks and into her mouth, masking the words that she was desperately trying to get out. Susan couldn't understand what her terrified daughter was trying to tell her, but she could guess, and she felt a fresh plume of fear rise in her chest.

Her arms went around Holly, and she held her little girl's cold, shivering body against her own, murmuring words of comfort, all while trying to stay calm herself.

Susan's mind and emotions were scrambled as she tried to keep her own tears at bay at the sight of her daughter in such a distressed state.

But she knew enough at that point to call an ambulance, and eventually her husband, who returned home only minutes after the paramedics' arrival, his face white with concern.

At the hospital, Susan remained at her daughter's bedside, holding Holly's hand.

While Michael paced the hallway outside the room, working the justice system and calling everyone he knew that might help him find the bastard who had done something unthinkable to his baby girl.

CHAPTER FIVE

Reilly was just finishing up at the Hackett house and talking through various scenarios with the GFU team when her phone rang. She excused herself from the bedroom and removed her gloves, walking out onto the landing. She just managed to answer the call before it went to voicemail.

"Steel," a deep voice came through the phone, and Reilly quickly identified it as belonging to Jack Gorman, her GFU counterpart. "Are you still working the Hackett residence?"

"Yes, we're here now. Shouldn't be much longer though - why?"

There was a short pause, almost like Jack had swallowed or cleared his throat, Reilly noted. Something he only did when he was uncomfortable. The older man finally continued. "Seems there was a second assault in that area last night."

Reilly's mind jumped with the possibilities – Jack hadn't said 'a second murder', which must mean the victim was still alive. But if the two victims were related by a common attacker, the live one might be someone who could tell them who the assailant was, or at least give them somewhere to start.

"Seventeen year old Holly Glynn is currently at A&E in St Vincent's Hospital with her parents. Seems she was sexually assaulted on her way home from a party at the Hackett house. She lives close by, the next estate over."

Reilly's heart stopped in much the same fashion it had that morning when she had seen Graham Hackett's body for the first time. She found her hand moving to her stomach almost subconsciously, in a purely emotional response, even as she spoke in a controlled and professional tone to her colleague. "Are we aware of any definite correlation between the two assaults?"

"No, but the girl's parents consented to an interview after they heard about Graham Hackett. The parents also have the clothes the girl was wearing last night, though apparently she wore them into the shower." Reilly's heart sank, realizing that any potentially helpful trace they could get from the clothes would be diluted and tainted, if not full-on obliterated. "Still, if there's a chance you can get something from her that helps find the boy's killer..."

Reilly was already gathering her things, "Which hospital did you say she was in?"

CHRIS LOOKED up as Reilly emerged from the house, walking with a purpose toward her car. He glanced at Kennedy who rolled his eyes, inclining his head in her direction as if to say 'so what else is new?'

Saying nothing more, Chris took off in a light jog across the grass to catch up with her. "Where are you heading to in such a rush?"

Reilly was looking for her car keys, her sleepless fingers fumbling through the contents of her handbag three times unsuccessfully.

Chris leaned down and gently took the keys from her other hand, the one she was using to hold her bag open. "This what you're looking for?" he asked, the hint of a smile on his lips.

With that, his phoned buzzed with a text message and he read it quickly, then nodded at her. "You're heading to see the girl who was assaulted?"

"Yes, the parents have her clothes at the hospital. We need to get them." She reached for the keys, but Chris pulled them away, "Why don't you let me drive you? I'm headed there now anyway, you're clearly tired, and this way we won't have another body to take care of before the day is done. I can drop you straight back here or the lab when you're finished."

In most circumstances, she would have argued with him and insisted it was her car, and those were her keys, but her eyes were blurring as she looked at him.

His logic wasn't exactly misplaced.

After a few seconds of tired, internal deliberation in which her prouder self quickly lost, Reilly nodded, making her way to the GFU van with Chris in tow.

He got in the driver seat and adjusted it so his knees weren't against the dash, chuckling at the considerable height difference between him and Reilly.

When he was ready to move off, he looked over at her to ask her something, but her eyes were heavy-lidded in the passenger seat.

Chris shook his head, worried a little, as he made his way through the streets of South Dublin almost effortlessly.

Tall brick facades flashed by the windows and he quietly took in the scenery, being careful not to turn too sharply, or hit his brakes too quickly, so Reilly could doze off for a bit and get what he guessed was some much needed shut-eye.

He didn't know all that much about pregnancy, but he figured with her insomnia, she must have gone much of the whole night before - if not all of it - without rest, and it couldn't have been a good thing. Did she need to sleep more, for the baby? Or was that only with food?

He didn't disturb her until he had parked in the subterranean car park beneath the hospital. She woke up immediately, and if she was embarrassed by her nap, she didn't show it. She snatched her kitbag up from the floor and was out of the van and walking toward the hospital before Chris had a chance to gather his thoughts, let alone get a leg out of the vehicle.

The hospital's tall-standing glass exterior loomed above them, exuding an air of modern development that contrasted with some of the much older Georgian buildings in the area. As they entered through the sliding glass doors and Chris approached the desk to ask about the whereabouts of the assault victim, whose name was Holly Glynn, Reilly took a moment to dispel her sudden nausea.

The smell of the hospital, one that she felt particularly more acutely than most others, was more debilitating than actual crime scenes sometimes. The antiseptic and cleaning products did nothing to mask the odor of the sick and dying, little scents that she could easily single out.

Her nausea wasn't just caused by the smell, however, as she was suddenly and painfully reminded of a previous admission she'd had in this very same building a few months back following an encounter with a killer called Tony Ellis.

When Chris returned with instructions on how to

get to the right room, they made quick work of finding Holly Glynn's location.

As the two approached the relevant hospital unit, they both exchanged a knowing glance at the sight of well-known Dublin solicitor Michael Glynn pacing outside the room.

"Glynn ... I was wondering why the surname rang a bell," Chris said. He exhaled. "Better watch our backs with this one."

Holly Glynn's father was not a tall man, in fact he was rather stout and round. And right then was on the phone with someone, nearly shouting, his face a full angry red. As Reilly and Chris got further down the hallway, they heard him in all his rage. "...don't care what McGowan says! You'll do what I bloody well tell you to!"

They paused as they came to a stop outside the room Chris had been given as the assault victim's location. As the two onlookers observed the father's anger with growing unease, a woman slipped from a door behind them.

"Are you the detectives?" she asked, in a voice that had seen too many tears recently.

"Good morning, Mrs. Glynn is it?" Chris said, his hands clasped respectfully in front of him. "I'm Detective Chris Delaney and this is my colleague, Reilly Steel from the GFU. We're here to talk to your daughter, and to pick up Holly's clothes for forensic analysis."

Reilly gave Mrs. Glynn what she hoped was a sympathetic smile, and the woman attempted to return the gesture, but fell just short.

"She's ... just in there," Susan Glynn said worriedly. "She says nothing happened ... that he just tried to hurt her. But still ..."

"I'm sure it's been a terrible morning for you, Mrs. Glynn," Chris said. "Why don't you pop down to the canteen and get you and your husband some coffee, maybe take a breather while we talk to Holly?"

"I don't know if ..." She looked dubiously at Chris then turned back to Reilly. "I think a woman might be better..."

Reilly shifted uncomfortably; she wasn't trained or indeed familiar with questioning sexual assault victims. Though by all accounts, she realized with some relief, recalling what the mother had just said, that this was an apparent attempt rather than outright sexual assault. Which would hopefully make things a lot easier on both her and the victim.

"I'm happy to talk to your daughter in lieu of the detective if you'd prefer." She looked sideways at Chris for his blessing and he nodded, confident of her ability to get the maximum information out of the girl. "In the meantime, if you wouldn't mind getting together her clothes ..." When Chris cleared his throat she added quickly, "after picking up a coffee of course."

"Well, if you're sure. I'll just let Holly know. Can I

get you anything?" she asked automatically, and Chris shook his head. Then, looking at Reilly she jumped, as though startled, "Oh, dear I didn't even notice, sorry. Of course you wouldn't want anything with caffeine," she said, her eyes flitting downwards at Reilly's midriff. For the first time, Mrs. Glynn managed what appeared to be a genuine smile. "When are you due?"

"On second thoughts," Chris said, like he had suddenly changed his mind, "I think I will have a coffee, black. Would that be okay?"

Mrs. Glynn smiled automatically at him. "Yes, of course. I won't be long."

Once she'd given her daughter the heads-up about the impending interview, Susan Glynn disappeared down the hall, and Reilly sent Chris a grateful glance before she stepped into the room, leaving her colleague with the victim's father who was still pacing the hallway, shouting at someone on the other end of the phone.

The lights were low in the hospital room, and a teenage girl who was obviously Holly Glynn was lying in the bed. Her honey-brown hair fell over her face as she faced the window, shifting with each breath she took. Reilly moved silently to the head of the bed and watched her for a moment.

Much like her teenage counterpart this morning, she looked so young and innocent, and the way the girl lay there almost managed to intensify that innocence.

Reilly felt that same punch in her gut, thinking about the tragedy that had befallen both teens.

"Holly?" She cleared her throat, introducing herself, "my name is Reilly Steel. I'm an investigator with the GFU. I hear you guys had a rough morning…"

The younger girl swallowed and looked away, nodding a little.

"Why don't you tell me what happened last night?" Reilly asked.

Holly closed her eyes and pushed her head into the pillow. "I was with Megan and Sarah … my best friends and some of my other classmates at Lisa's house. We were celebrating the end of our exams. One of the boys texted us, telling us about a free house and a party at Graham's, so we headed over there."

"By the time we got to the house, I was a bit … tipsy. I can only remember it in snatches really - the music was really loud, and the place was smoky, like I was walking through a haze or something. We stayed together for a little while, us girls, but then we started thinning out as usual. I remember being outside on the decking with Graham, we were just talking about stuff…"

Holly stopped for a moment, as if trying to remember their conversation. "I remember lots of older guys being there too, his brother's college friends. I saw Megan go off with one of them, headed down at the end of the garden towards the trees. Megan can be a bit ... careless, so I went after her, tried to stop her, but I couldn't catch up and then they disappeared."

Reilly remained silent, preferring just to let her talk.

"I remember deciding to go home after that, the party was breaking up anyway and a few people were heading into town to a club. But I was tired and I'd promised Mum I'd be home by one, so I headed off. After a few minutes, someone - this guy - came out of nowhere and started talking to me... The next thing I remember, I'm flat on my back on the ground. But I managed to get away before he ..." She winced. "All I remember after that is crying and stumbling through the dark, heading for home. I went in through the back door and straight up to my room."

"What time was this - when you got home?" Reilly asked.

"I really don't know - it felt like hours but I have no idea really... as I said it's all a blur."

"You said you got away before he did anything ... " she prompted gently.

Holly started to cry a little. "Yes. I managed to wriggle free when he was ... opening his jeans, and kneed him between his legs. And then I ran off."

Good girl...

Suddenly Holly asked her own question. "Is it a boy or a girl?"

The question took Reilly by surprise. "I don't know yet."

The teen gave her a weak smile, one that almost sent Reilly tumbling over the edge again. There was nothing more dismal than a victim's smile. She wrapped the hospital blanket around her fingers. "You want it to be a surprise?"

Reilly wanted to tell her that the pregnancy was already surprise enough, but she stopped herself. The girl was obviously taking comfort in the fact that her interviewer was about to be a mother, and she didn't want to dispel that, so she smiled instead and said, "Yeah. Something like that."

For some reason she noticed, people equated being pregnant with a sort of positive quality, as though the fact that Reilly was carrying a child changed who she was, essentially. The fact was that she was no more caring or maternal than she had been before she'd discovered the pregnancy, but people treated her as though she was.

The thought made her uneasy – she was determined not to let this baby change who she was, or indeed others' view of her.

She guided Holly through some routine forensic examination; held her hand as she took some finger nail scrapings and fingerprints. The teenager's hands were so soft; entirely absent of any defensive marks, and her elaborate gel nails remained intact, suggesting it was unlikely that she'd fought back too hard, or left much of a mark on her attacker. She was a lucky girl that she managed to get away.

Reilly's thoughts returned to Graham Hackett then. When she had initially learned about Holly's attack, she immediately wondered if the boy was involved and whether an ensuing struggle could have led to his own demise. But seeing Holly now - a wisp of a thing as Kennedy might say - she knew that this girl had not been the one to overpower someone as well-built as the Hackett boy, nor indeed wield a weapon with the type of force that would have caved in the teen's skull.

"OK, I think that's us about done for now," she said as she packed away the samples. "The detectives will want to interview you in more detail at a later date though - about your friend Graham and what went on at last night's party."

The girl looked terrified, but then smiled weakly and ran her hands over her hair in what appeared to be an attempt at straightening it out. Reilly wondered if Holly knew the full extent of the tragedy that had befallen her friend last night, but figured it wasn't her place to tell her.

She was trying to figure out the best way to announce that she had to leave, when Holly dropped her hands and looked down at the blanket. "You'd think I would remember more," she said, her voice just above a whisper, "you'd think every last detail of such a horrible thing would stick in your mind. Instead, I'm not even sure that it happened at all..."

Reilly nodded quietly, unsure what to say. If her maternal instincts were going to kick in at some point, right now would be awfully helpful.

"Is that normal do you think?"

Just then the door cracked open, and Susan Glynn poked her head in. "Everything all right?"

Holly's face brightened upon seeing her mother and Reilly automatically stepped back from the bed. She took it as her cue to slip away without answering Holly's question.

But as Reilly made her way out to rejoin Chris, she couldn't help but think about what she would say if her own offspring asked her something like that someday.

Would she again just slip out of the room, tight lipped, hoping someone else would materialize to help her child?

CHAPTER SIX

When Reilly had disappeared into the hospital room, Chris was left alone with Holly's father. Even with the formidable solicitor in his presence, he slipped right into detective mode.

"Good morning, Mr. Glynn, I'm Detective Chris Delaney," he began smoothly, but the man turned on him with a piercing glare so fierce it made him question his decision to issue a greeting at all.

"Is it?" Michael Glynn snapped, his cheeks flushed a fiery red, something made more apparent under the bright wash of the fluorescent lights, "is it really a good morning? Is it a good morning for you, Detective? A vicious attack on a young girl and the murder of a teenage boy are things that really make your mornings?"

He must've looked taken aback, so Mr. Glynn continued, "Of course I know about the Hackett boy.

I'm not some clueless member of the public, detective. It would do you well to remember that. And you're only here because I want you here."

Chris recovered quickly, having faced dozens of men like Michael Glynn throughout his career. Just as people grieved differently, people reacted to severe trauma differently too, and Glynn was obviously one of those men who reacted to situations outside of their control by doing everything in their power to control them, no matter how impossible that was.

Nothing Michael Glynn did now could change what had happened to his daughter, but he would try to compensate the best he could.

Chris leveled his gaze and said in an even voice, "I understand your frustration sir, and I'm going to do everything in my power to find the person that assaulted your daughter but if you do want me here, then I suggest you let me do my job."

Glynn took a moment to breathe, visualizing his beloved wife with her hand on his arm, advising him to remember the things that calmed him. Most people would think his quick-to-anger disposition would ruin him as a solicitor, but he was one of the few who had managed to harvest his passion and turn it into something productive and successful.

He had to remind himself, as Susan would, that the whole world was not a courtroom, and that he didn't actually have any beef with the detective that was now preparing to pocket his questions and leave, which wouldn't help his poor little Holly in the least.

"Okay," Michael Glynn said, crossing his arms over his chest and letting out a breath of resigned air. "Ask away."

"Thank you. About what time did Holly leave your house for the party last night?"

The anger Glynn had just about managed to dismiss, quickly bubbled to the surface again, "She didn't leave for the party - she left to meet up with some of her friends to celebrate the end of exams. How she ended up at that godforsaken house is lost on me."

Chris made a note of this and pushed forward, "Does your daughter attend gatherings like this one often?"

"I would like to say no, but after this, I'm not sure I know for sure where she's been or what she's been doing. I never would have allowed her stay out all night like that drinking and doing God knows what else with those Hackett boys."

"What was your daughter's relationship with Graham Hackett?"

Michael rolled his eyes. "Apparently they were ... friendly, a few months ago, but then it just seemed to die out. I don't know why, but I was glad when it happened. Holly needs to focus on her schooling, not some hotshot who thinks he's some kind of sports prodigy."

Chris made a note of the tone in Mr. Glynn's voice when he spoke of Graham Hackett. If Holly and Graham had once been an item, and the father assumed the kid was responsible for his daughter's attack...

"And about what time were you made aware of Holly's...misfortune, Mr. Glynn?"

"Not until this morning, not long after I left for work - so about seven thirty. Susan rang in a state, said she'd found Holly crying in the shower. Of course I guessed what had happened, what father wouldn't? But it seems, thanks be to God, that the worst didn't in fact happen. Some animal didn't ... have his way with my daughter."

"Where were you in the early hours of one and five AM this morning Mr. Glynn?" Mr. Glynn's perceptive eyes, honed by his years of arguing in the courtroom, zeroed in on Chris's train of thought. The solicitor huffed and crossed his arms again, reminding Chris of an angry dwarf. He added quickly, "I'm sure, Mr. Glynn - given the circumstances - you can appreciate why I need to ask that question."

The other man harrumphed. "I can and you're right to. Because believe me, if I thought for one second that that young upstart Hackett had laid a hand on my daughter ..." He seemed to think better of his utterance then, because he sighed heavily and said: "I was at home in bed with my wife. You can ask her. Either way, I grilled Holly about her attacker, and she's adamant that it wasn't him - she says it was a complete stranger. Someone pounced on her on her way home. I'm raging with her that she didn't phone one of us to pick her up even though the Hackett place is only half a mile down the road. But that's not the point. Clearly no young girl is safe out on her own at night - respectable area or not."

Chris figured that given the man's profession, Glynn should know better than to assume that just because he and his family lived in and frequented a middle class neighborhood that it should be somehow immune from criminal behavior.

From what Chris had seen, no such place existed.

The solicitor huffed and crossed his arms again. "I think that's enough questions for now," he said, his eyes narrowed. "Rest assured I'm not the Hackett boy's attacker as I'm sure your investigations will reveal pretty quickly. However, I'm counting on you to also find my daughter's. Chances are they are one and the same."

There wasn't yet enough information available about either situation to agree or disagree with him, but Chris concurred that the events were almost certainly related. Somehow. "I assure you, my colleagues and I will be working all angles, Mr. Glynn. And we will need to talk to your family again as the investigation progresses."

As Mr. Glynn turned on his heel and stomped down the hallway, Reilly exited Holly's hospital room. Chris caught the remnants of the same pained expression that had been on her face when she saw Graham Hackett for the first time that morning, and he was starting to think that her condition was making her more emotionally vulnerable.

She shook her head at him as they met up in the hallway and made their way back out of the hospital. Chris, having been around her long enough, caught the meaning of the gesture.

"What is it?" he asked, as they came to the top of the stairway. Even during her pregnancy, Reilly refused to take the elevator. She wasn't going to give up her fitness until she absolutely had to, though her bump was starting to grow rapidly, and it was a small struggle for her not to puff for breath as they made their way down the steps.

She looked up at him, mildly surprised that he had said something to her about it. What surprised her most though, was that she answered him truthfully.

In other situations, she wouldn't have been so quick to dump her issues on a colleague but Chris was a good friend and confidant.

And of course unlike Reilly, he understood children very well. His relationship with his goddaughter, Rachel was case in point. Not too long ago Chris had invited her to come along for supper at his good friend Matt and Kelly's home.

Whenever Reilly entered the family's quaint little

house in a well-heeled Dublin suburb not too unlike the Hackett's, one of the first things that struck her was the smell. Although the house was immaculately clean and tidy, a latent scent remained, hinting at the messes that had been made previously.

The second thing came almost immediately after: little Rachel's squealing trailing behind her as she raced for Chris's open arms. Reilly took a step back and watched as he scooped the four year old up, grinning ear to ear and planting a wet kiss on her temple.

"Hello there, Trouble. Where's Dad?"

Rachel had taken his hand then and led them to the kitchen, where Matt and his wife were having a discussion under their breaths, their smiles hinting at the content of the conversation.

Reilly noted the way Chris acted with the small girl, so easily, despite the lack of children of his own. They continued on like that throughout the night, Chris sporting and laughing with Rachel and she in turn gazing up at Chris like he was a knight.

Reilly's own pitiful attempts at interacting with the child had left the household in an awkward silence, just the scraping of forks at the dinner table as Rachel either shook her head or completely ignored Reilly. But she was a nice kid, and Reilly knew the problem didn't lie with her. She'd never been a kid person but perhaps she wasn't fit to be a mother if such a sweet four year old couldn't take to her?

She sighed. Holly Glynn had seemed to like her well enough just now, but of course that interaction was under entirely different circumstances. She suppressed a shudder at the thought of Kelly and Matt worrying about their girl the way Holly's parents were right now. How could any parent bear such strain?

Slowly, trying to contain the mess in her head, Reilly answered Chris's question.

"It's just... seeing these kids - the teenagers. The way life's treated them so far, and they're still only kids - or were in Graham Hackett's case," she added softly. "His parents and Holly's obviously love them and would do anything for them, and still — something terrible happened to them both. That makes you think there really is nothing a parent can do to keep their kids safe."

Chris regarded her for a moment. Rather than coming straight out and saying she was worried about her own mothering skills, she had slid it into an observation of others.

He sighed and contemplated the best way to answer her, to help quiet her fears.

"Of course nothing a parent does in this world can make sure nothing bad will *ever* happen to their child, but I believe that the best parents try their utmost to put their children in a position to take the world by the horns. Bad things happen to people, you and I both know that only too well. But that has nothing to do with parenting. You teach them what you can and prepare them the best you can. And for what it's worth," he added softly, "you'll do a great job."

She rolled her eyes at him, but hid her secret pleasure at the compliment. His confidence in her managed to quiet her troubled mind, at least for a little while.

Chris sighed as they headed back outside into the sunshine. "This case is going to be a tough one, isn't it?" he commented.

"Is it ever any other way?" Reilly answered wearily.

Already they had experienced multiple hostile and broken people, and it was only day one.

CHAPTER SEVEN

Later, Chris and Kennedy drove to interview the first of what would undoubtedly be a long line of witnesses; the kids in attendance at the Hackett party.

When they stepped out of the car, the two detectives took in the scene.

Chris took a deep breath of the heavier midsummer air and glanced down the street. The house they were standing outside now was much smaller than the Hackett's house a couple of streets over, but still looked expensive. The house was painted a pristine white, sported a recently mowed lawn, though a couple of rogue daisies poked up through the ground in a determined pattern by the door.

The crimes committed in the more salubrious parts of the city were less numerous or intense than those committed in the rougher side of town, but perhaps they were more impactful here because they were so unprecedented.

According to the information Simon had given them, this was the house of Tiernan Williams, Graham Hackett's best friend.

Kennedy knocked on the door and the two took a step back to wait.

It was a few moments before the door cracked open and a teenage boy looked out. His face went white when he saw the detectives standing on his porch. "My parents aren't here," he said, rubbing his eyes like he had just woken up. "They're at work."

Chris smiled at him, trying to appear friendly, "That's all right, Tiernan, we just want to ask you a few questions about last night. Nothing serious."

Tiernan seemed to deliberate for a moment, then he relented, opening the door for the detectives to come in. "Okay," he said, his voice tired and sleep-ridden.

The two men followed the teen to his living room, where he nervously sat down and gestured for them to take a seat on the couch.

Chris was in awe of the house – each room they passed through looked like it came straight from a magazine. There wasn't a surface in the house that went undusted, nor an object in a place it wasn't supposed to be.

Tiernan must have noticed the men's reaction,

because he cleared his throat and ran a hand through his red hair, "Yeah, my mum's a bit of a neat freak."

Kennedy pulled his trusty notepad out and flipped it open to the last page he'd used. "Alright, Tiernan, what can you tell us about your friend Graham and what might have happened last night?"

An intense look of sorrow passed over Tiernan's face, and Chris recognized he was trying his hardest not to cry. He took a moment to clear his throat again before answering. "Graham was one of my friends – *best* friends. We play - played hurling together - he was an amazing player, and we hung around together all the time. He liked playing video games too, listening to music, hanging out - all the normal stuff really."

Chris nodded while Kennedy scribbled down some notes. "Did Graham have any enemies Tiernan? Did he ever do anything to give anyone a reason to attack him?"

Tiernan swallowed and shook his head, "No, I don't think so. Though, a lot of opposition players really hated him, you know, because he was so good. But that's just match rivalry, I don't think any of the lads would do anything to Graham personally. Not like ... that." When the detectives stared blankly at him, the teen explained further. "Well it's just...when you're on the pitch, you've got to hate the guy who's marking you, don't you? He's got to be your number one enemy for the thirty-five minutes of each half. But when you step off the pitch, all that goes away. Well, for most people anyway."

"Can you give us the names of any specific people who might have had such 'match rivalry' with Graham?"

Tiernan tentatively rattled off a few names, evidently feeling torn with guilt as he did so, terrified he'd get somebody innocent in trouble.

"Okay, can you walk us through everything that happened last night, start to finish?" Chris asked, eyeing the boy. It was understandable that the kid would be upset and nervous in their presence given what had befallen his best friend, but Tiernan seemed a little bit *too* nervous, and he wanted to keep a close eye on him for any signs of deception. Though when dealing with teenagers could it ever be any other way?

Still Chris knew the giveaways all too well – eyes glancing away, biting the lip, rubbing palms on clothing to be rid of nervous sweat.

"Well, we were on the way to Graham's gaff when he sent the word out about the free house. We had just finished practice, and stopped at the chippers to get something to eat."

"Who's we?" Kennedy asked. "Give us some names, son."

"Sure. Just a few of the other lads on the team." He listed off the names of his companions as the detectives made note of the particulars to compare against the list of attendees they'd already compiled. "We all went back to Graham's then and had a few scoops while waiting for people to arrive."

"Where did you get the alcohol from?"

Tiernan swallowed hard and a warning light went off in Chris's head. "It was already there," he protested, rather unconvincingly. "it was Graham's parents' stash I think. Then more showed up as more people came, and his brother's mates brought some too but I don't know where they got it."

"Right..." Kennedy said, his tone overly sarcastic.

"So when was the last time you saw Graham last night?" Chris asked, referring to the rough timeline they'd established so far. Simon had reported seeing his brother last sometime between twelve and one AM, before he left for the club, and according to his phone already in evidence, Graham had sent out his last WhatsApp message – ever – just after midnight.

"I don't know to be honest," Tiernan said, pulling at his trousers, "I don't usually watch the clock when I'm on a night out. It was probably around half twelve, maybe? He was out on the deck with Holly, then she went upstairs with him so I thought maybe they'd be getting back together."

She went upstairs with him ... Could Holly Glynn have been in the bedroom when Graham was attacked? And was her attacker one and the same? According to Reilly, the girl insisted she didn't know the guy, and that the attack was just some random stranger pouncing on her on her way home.

But what if she was lying?

"What about Simon?" Kennedy asked then. "What was Graham's relationship with his brother like?"

Tiernan shrugged. "I don't know, decent enough I suppose. We all used to play club hurling together before Simon went off to uni. They're like ... normal brothers I suppose, except..." He grew very quiet for a moment, as though realizing something.

"What were you going to say?" Chris asked, wanting to get it out of the kid before he thought about it too much.

"Yeah," Tiernan said, "last night ... Simon and Graham got into a fight out in the garden, or an argument at least. I don't even know what it was about. They were yelling and arguing anyway and I think Graham threw something at him - a bottle maybe? I remember something shattering anyway."

"How was the fight resolved? Or was it?" Chris asked, eager to follow this line of questioning. Simon certainly hadn't mentioned anything about an argument this morning.

"They both stomped off after a couple of us got between them. That was when Holly and Graham disappeared upstairs."

"So no resolution? The two brothers were still angry at one another for the rest of the night?"

"I think so but ..." He ran his hand through his hair. "Christ man, you don't think that Simon ... surely he wouldn't ... I mean they're brothers!"

"Relax, we're not suggesting anything, Tiernan. Just trying to establish what might have happened at the party. Everyone seemed drunk so reports are sketchy. You know that Holly was attacked too, don't you?"

His face drained of color. "What? Attacked, like Graham you mean? Is she okay? Christ I had no idea."

"No, not like that. She was set upon by someone on her way home to her house. We're not sure if it's related. She's still pretty shaken up but okay."

"Christ. No, I had no idea. Like I said we were all pretty drunk..."

"Okay. One last question before we go," Chris said, gathering his things, "where were you between one and five AM this morning Tiernan?"

The teen's face whitened again. "Jesus, I had nothing to do with that! I went home after Graham and Simon got in that fight, and like I said Holly was still there at that stage. A lot of us left around then actually. It was kind of a downer."

"Did anyone see you leave?"

"Well, the other lads - and then - yes, when I came home my mom was here, waiting for me. That was around oneish," Tiernan perked up a little then, at the thought of a trusty alibi. "I wasn't supposed to be out late, cos even though the others' exams are finished, I still have a Construction Studies one left, and she caught me as soon as I tried to sneak in. It was just after one - definitely. You can check with her if you like, she'll confirm the time."

Kennedy threw in his own final question. "Forensics found some pills in Graham's bedroom, Tiernan. Know anything about those?"

The kid's face went white and he bit his lip, as though trying to decide what to say at this juncture.

"It's in your best interest to just tell us son," the detective said, his eyes narrowing.

"Graham was... juicing," Tiernan admitted, the words spilling from his lips, "some of the other lads on the team do it too but not me I swear..."

"Relax," Chris said, "we're not drug enforcement. We're just trying to figure out what happened to Graham. Do you know where he might have gotten those pills?"

Tiernan licked his lips and shook his head, "Um..."

Chris raised his eyebrows, "Like I said, Tiernan, we're not drug enforcement but if you aren't willing to help us out, we'll have no problem going to them. I have a good mate in that department."

"Dean," Tiernan blurted, immediately looking guilty, "one of the lads, Dean Cooper. He sells them to the team. I don't know where he gets them, though. I just know that's where the others get their stuff."

"OK, thanks for that - you've been very helpful,"

Kennedy said, wrapping up. "And you're right to stay clean too. Hurling should be all about the game, not about winning at all costs."

Chris raised his eyebrows at this unexpected nugget of sporting wisdom from his decidedly non-sporty partner.

The big man never failed to surprise him.

"Cheers," Kennedy said afterwards, as a steaming shepherd's pie was slid onto his place mat. "Lovely stuff."

Chris looked down at the wholegrain spinach and grilled chicken pita he had ordered from the barfood menu of a nearby pub, and tried to tell himself it was just as good as the shepherd's pie.

"So this Tiernan kid," Kennedy asked, "what did you make of him?"

Chris shrugged. "He's a teenager. Not as innocent as he makes out to be."

"Just polite because he's talking to authority," Kennedy agreed, "Christ, I really hated those assholes when I was in school. The ones that were total dickheads when they were around you, then butter wouldn't melt as soon as the teacher walked in. At least the other dickheads were dickheads all the time, and not just when it suited them."

The thought of Kennedy in school made Chris chuckle. Him sitting there, pimply faced and concentrating on what the teacher was saying, taking detailed notes while others around him goofed off. For all his bluster, Kennedy was definitely a nerd in school, he decided.

"Do you think he's our man?"

"No," Chris said, "I mean, while everyone has to be a potential suspect at the moment, I don't think Tiernan is tall or strong enough to be our man for a start. The likes of Hackett would eat a dweeb like him for breakfast. And he was a bit too forthcoming with information. Our man would have been a little more nervous than Tiernan. And, although he may well be a different kid behind the scenes, I think he was genuinely too affected by his friend's death to be his killer. To say nothing of the fact that he has an alibi. Yet to be confirmed mind you, but my gut tells me he's okay."

Unfortunately, Chris thought, knowing Tiernan wasn't the killer did not bring them much closer to figuring out who was.

CHAPTER EIGHT

CMc2020: *What the actual f**k!! Just heard about G......can't believe this! Was coming on here to say what a great night it was. RIP HackR, hope they catch the bastard responsible before I do. This shit is F****D UP!*

KrustyClown: *Can't believe it either - what the f**k happened......didn't notice a bit of aggro last night, everybody was havin the craic afaik. Don't know what to say... #RIPHackR.*

Missislippy: *OMG! So sorry to hear about Graham. Thought it was pretty chilled out last night when I left. Then I hear about this and that poor Holly was put in hospital as well - I will never be allowed leave the house again!*

CMc2020: *Seriously, Sarah? That's your take from all this s**t? One of your friends is dead and your best mate was attacked, but all you can think about is the negative effect on your social life... #stayclassy*

PuckingNinja: *I actually just found out about Holly from the cops when they called to my house earlier. She was attacked as well... f**k, can't believe this.*

KrustyClown: *Hey T, what else have you heard? Cops tell you anything?*

Missislippy: *F**k you @ CMc2020 - that was a joke, you insensitive prat!!! Of course, I'm devastated about what happened last night. We don't all go around swearing vengeance macho man-style. @ PuckingNinja So sorry about Graham, Tiernan. I heard Holly's ma found her in an awful state this morning, she's in the hospital now. Lisa's mum is besties with Mrs. Murray, and she heard it's pretty serious. Apparently, Holly's in an induced coma!*

PuckingNinja: *S**t, this feels like a nightmare. Wish I could have told the cops something more useful. Tbh, I don't remember much after all that cider...*

MuddyPaws: *Guys, not wanting to point the finger, but can we please post only what we know to be fact. Holly is not in an induced coma Sarah, that's bulls**t. I texted her brother this morning, the whole family is going apes**t. She was badly shaken up after some weirdo tried to attack her on the way home. I don't want to say anything else until I speak to her myself, but everyone better have a long hard think about what happened last night. The cops are supposed to be coming to see me too, so I'd say they're working their way through everybody. I haven't a clue what happened to either of them but poor G.*

Missislippy: *Sorry Megan - I was just repeating what I heard, glad Hol's okay - tell her we're all asking for her okay?*

CoolChulainn: *Same as. Well, I've had no contact from the cops yet about G or Hols. But I've a couple of things I'd like to tell them...*

CHAPTER NINE

When much later that evening, Reilly unlocked the door to her flat and walked in, the sun's strength had dissipated and even though it was supposed to be the height of summer, it was cold.

She turned the heating on and made her way to the kitchen to make something to eat, but her stomach told her that she couldn't eat, even if she needed to.

Reilly brought some current case files with her into bed, sorely missing her usual glass of red wine, and looked over the various associated lab reports with excruciating concentration, until her back started to hurt.

She tried to reposition her pillow, but found that she couldn't reach it without causing an awful pain in her side.

After squirming in an attempt to make herself

comfortable, she eventually put the files away and tried to sleep. Then as she lay in her bed, a pang of hunger shot through her stomach.

Typical...

Instead of getting up and making herself a bite, she dropped her head into a pillow, thoroughly annoyed. Though there were many downsides to having a room-mate, times like this having someone in the flat with her would be nice.

Someone to help her with things, someone to talk to. Although she did enjoy the peace and quiet of her Ranelagh flat most days, there were times when she felt the undeniable loneliness that came with living alone.

Yes, at times she wholeheartedly preferred the life she had – living by herself (besides Glubs the goldfish) eating by herself most nights, and handling all of her personal affairs as she saw fit. However, she would be lying if she said she never felt like human contact occasionally.

Which reminded her. Todd Forrest, her baby's father was coming for a visit from the US next week. They hadn't yet finalized the final details, but she was certain he expected to stay at her place while he was here, rather than spring for a hotel.

And she wasn't sure how she felt about that.

Obviously they needed to talk about the baby and what would happen - if anything - when it arrived. Todd was adamant he wanted to help out as much as he could, but he lived in Florida, an ocean away, so realistically how could he help?

And Reilly wasn't sure she wanted to have the conversation with him anyway. It was embarrassing enough that she and Todd had ended up in this situation, following a glorified one night stand while she was in Florida on what was supposed to be a sabbatical. Fat lot of good that had done her.

Her stomach growled again and she grabbed one of the pillows to her left, pushing it over her face and sighing into the pillowcase.

Despite a tiring day, Reilly knew another sleepless night was on the cards. And no doubt, many more thereafter.

THE FOLLOWING DAY, she was awake with the sun and the chirping birds. The early morning sunshine streamed optimistically through the open window and warmed her bare skin. Her back still ached and her head was pounding, but she got out of bed anyway, pulling on her clothes and grabbing her gym bag.

When she had first been officially confirmed pregnant by her GP, the doc had told her she could keep running throughout her pregnancy. What the woman hadn't predicted however, was that Reilly was expecting to keep up her morning runs right until the baby actually made an appearance - and with luck, pretty soon thereafter.

But at a recent appointment when Reilly was complaining of shin splints, the doc suggested that she partake in yoga, instead. So now every morning before work, she grabbed her stretchy pants and marched to the yoga studio, much to the enjoyment of the other women in the class.

If middle-aged women had a tendency to fawn and coo at babies, the only other thing that even matched that level of strange dedication, was a middle-aged women's reaction to a pregnant one.

They doted on Reilly and asked her all sorts of odd questions about what she was eating and where/how she planned to have the birth, all the while congratulating her on keeping her figure while at the same time carrying a hefty bump. This special treatment even extended to some of the poses; Reilly struggled to remain zen when the rather hippy dippy instructor called Tina continually singled her out in an irritating way.

'Maybe Momma and babs should skip this pose,' and 'If Momma and babs want to lie on the back rather than the stomach...'

Reilly knew the woman was just being kind by adapting the routine to suit pregnancy, but the constant reminder of her burgeoning size grated like hell.

Not all of the women in the class were so supportive

however, and Reilly was pretty sure some of them had a betting pool on how long she would go before quitting. She hoped at least one of them had bet right until the end, because they would be winning a lot of money. She planned to go to the class while actually in labor if she could.

After her yoga class, she was the first one to arrive at the GFU lab. She immediately began processing evidence collected from the crime scene and the assault victim the day before, and as she prepared swabs and trace for analysis, dozens of questions kept racing through her mind.

Were the murder and attempted sexual assault connected? Was there something Holly Glynn wasn't telling them? And what about Graham's brother, Simon? Chris seemed certain the older Hackett kid knew a lot more about what had happened than he was willing to reveal.

Now was the time to start connecting some of the puzzle pieces.

She was hard at work when Lucy and Gary strolled in, laughing happily together. Reilly turned a wary eye on them as they approached their workstations and the two lovebirds, having not expected anyone else to be in the lab before them, stopped their giggling immediately.

They'd recently started a relationship and while they were usually very good about not letting this affect their professionalism, the knowledge of it tugged at the part of Reilly's brain that was willing to at least partially admit to her loneliness.

She continued working, extracting the nail scrapings taken from Holly Glynn as well as any remaining trace from the girl's shower-soaked clothes to prepare for comparison with any evidence taken from the Hackett crime scene.

A few hours later she stretched, deciding it was time for a pick me up. Before making her way downstairs to the vending machines, she stopped by Lucy's workstation. "How are we doing?"

"Well, obviously lots to get through considering how many people were in that house - it's a mess of treads, fingerprints and whatnot," the younger girl said. "Nothing yielding much so far. Most of the blood in the bedroom came from the victim obviously, but I think I've also isolated some skin tissue from the room which Julius thinks might be useful for epithelial DNA. We can only hope it belongs to his attacker."

"Sounds promising..."

"I've also since cleaned up the iPad and sent it down to Tech," Gary told her. "Not a lot to go on from that trace-wise, but quite a bit found on our victim. The usual hair and skin, as well as some interesting chemical components that require further analysis." He shrugged. "But early days, you know yourself."

Reilly nodded, satisfied as much as she could be with their progress thus far.

After that, she made her way to Julius's workstation. The older tech looked up at her as she approached, already knowing what she was going to ask.

"Yep Lucy's right, I've extracted some epithelial DNA from organic tissue found in the victim's bedroom. What's interesting is I've also matched some of that with the female assault victim, taken from what you brought back yesterday," he added, confusing Reilly.

"What's the source?"

According to Holly Glynn, there had been no sexual contact between her and Graham on the night of the party, but of course that didn't mean there was no contact at all. Holly and Graham were friends, and had even been a couple at one point, so she may well have been in Graham's room that night, or sometime before.

"Just skin tissue, nothing sinister," he said, quieting her concerns somewhat.

But was Holly's presence in the bedroom significant in any way? And had she lied about her interactions with Graham on the night of his murder, or lack thereof? Reilly didn't think so, but who knew with teenagers - scared ones especially?

"Anything else?" she asked Julius then.

"Eliminated most of the surface prints in the

bedroom as the victim's as expected, but there are dozens of unidentified partials in there too - including the older brother's. Would be good to get those comparatives for all family members when we can - the parents especially."

Reilly nodded - she knew the detectives would aim for prints from the parents once they had the opportunity to see them upon their return from Spain.

She grabbed a coffee and a muffin from the vending machines, and then headed over to the GFU's newly created Cyber Unit, which sounded snazzy, but was basically just Rory and a bunch of computers. It was also typically where they set up the iSPI virtual crime scene simulations.

The computer whizz looked right at home. "You got the iPad from the Hackett house?" Reilly asked him.

He rolled his chair out from his desk, can of Red Bull in hand, took a sip and nodded toward his workstation. "Just came down this morning. I'm running a diagnostic on it now."

"If you can, try to get a solid handle on the social media and electronic correspondence for the kids at that party. Would be good to set up some kind of timeline for the night so we can narrow a few things down. As well as figure out who knows who and how."

"You got it, boss," Rory saluted her as she turned to leave.

CHAPTER TEN

A couple of hours later, she was on her way out of her office when Kennedy and Chris intercepted her.

"Good timing," she groaned with heavy irony. "I was just headed out for lunch."

"Could do with a bite ourselves anyway," Chris shrugged. He looked washed out in the florescent lights of the GFU offices, his skin pale.

Another area in which Todd Forrest and Chris Delaney were almost directly opposite, Reilly thought. So rarely exposed to the sun, Chris shared the same pasty color she herself sported now, while Todd was lucky enough to be exposed to the sun all year round in Florida, so his skin held a permanent golden hue.

She sighed wistfully then, thinking of white sand and palm-fringed beaches.

Chris looked speculatively at her. "You do sound hungry. Let's head out and we can catch up over a bite."

They glanced at Kennedy, who was just then desperately trying to wrench his ringing phone out of his pocket. When the older man caught her and Chris looking at him, he waved them away.

"Go on ahead without me," the big man said, still trying to wiggle his phone free from its tight hold in his pocket, "I'll catch up."

The two made their way downstairs and out of the GFU building to one of their regular haunts down the street - a gastropub that was usually heaving with workers from the surrounding businesses in the industrial estate.

Inside, several people were gathered for lunch and some early-bird drinkers had already taken up posts at the bar as Chris and Reilly slid into opposite facing seats in a booth.

They were silent as they viewed the menu – even though they knew the offerings almost by heart. Kennedy could get his fill of greasy, fried food, while Chris and Reilly could order salads or wraps without feeling too guilty about it.

But today, Reilly did not order her usual.

"A burger *and* a milkshake?" Chris queried, genuinely surprised at this out of the blue request. In all the years he had known her, he couldn't say that he had ever seen her order junk food.

She shrugged and shook around the ice in a glass of water while they waited for Kennedy. "It sounded good," she shrugged. She wanted to add that a lot of things in her life just now didn't sound so good, so one freakin' burger couldn't be that bad.

Milkshakes reminded Reilly of childhood hot summer nights in California with her sister Jess. They would haul out their blender and drop vanilla ice cream and chocolate syrup in until they both had freezing shakes to take the edge off of the summer heat. Of course, they would leave the mess out on the counter for their mum to clean up the next morning.

Happier times ...

Yup, a milkshake sounded good.

Chris nodded once, unsure how to continue the conversation. Even after brushing away all of the bias and obvious assumptions about how this pregnancy wouldn't affect her, he was left with the resounding knowledge that she *had* changed - a lot.

Though chances were Reilly's current behavior wasn't due just to her pregnancy, but also the ever-growing discomfort between them. No matter how often they tried to talk about the personal boundary they'd overstepped a few months back, or overcome the gulf that remained as a result, they still couldn't quite manage to get truly back to normal.

The two sat in silence for a moment, both searching for something to say, until the food came.

Reilly's resistance to chat fell away as the waitress slid a towering burger surrounded by deliciously thick fries under her nose, then a cool milkshake just in front of the plate.

Chris munched on his salad in silence, almost wishing he had followed her lead and indulged a little. When they had cleared the bulk of their food, he brought up the one thing that always got Reilly talking.

"So any preliminary results from the Hackett scene yet?"

Reilly shook her head, her mouth full of fries. She waited a moment, then said, "Too much to sift through before anything jumps out, though we did a lot of the prep work yesterday afternoon, and Gary is isolating potentially helpful trace evidence from the bedroom. The rest of the house is a mess though; so many people at that party." She paused for a moment to take a drink of her milkshake and offered Chris a fry, which he took willingly. "Any handle on a suspect so far?"

He finished his salad and began wiping his hands off in the meticulous way he did, one finger at a time with extreme detail-orientation. He really would make a good criminal, she thought idly.

"Talked to the neighbors who previously reported noise disturbance from some of the get-togethers the Hackett brothers had been throwing when their folks are away." He shrugged. "Potentially grounds for motive: annoying kids play their music far too loud too often and the long-suffering neighbor gets a little too worked-up, marches over to the house, they argue and he grabs the nearest weapon. Then, when we get the call for the Holly Glynn thing, you'd have to assume the obvious, but having spoken to the father and based on what you got from the girl, I'm thinking sheer coincidence."

"You don't think that maybe the father rushed over to the Hackett house to defend his little girl's honor?" That was certainly Reilly's first thought, though they had yet to assess whether the timelines added up.

Chris nodded. "It's the obvious one, but it's too easy. For one thing, I don't think the father - a solicitor remember - would've been that keen to have the authorities involved so quickly in what was an attempted - rather than all-out assault." He shook his head. "Nah, I'm not feeling the revenge thing, Reilly. In any case, the girl seems adamant that it was a stranger who pounced on her and why would she lie?

Why indeed? Reilly thought. But as always, there was still a hell of a lot about this picture that they weren't seeing. Hopefully that would change soon.

"Have you talked to the parents yet?"

"They flew home from Spain late last night and are holed up in a hotel somewhere while the house is still off limits. Heading there today once we get the details."

"Could be a while yet before we release the crime scene," Reilly told him. "We're only getting started."

With that, Kennedy arrived, took one look at Reilly's burger and promptly ordered the same - minus the milkshake.

"That was O'Brien on the phone," he told Chris, referring to their immediate superior. "He says Michael Glynn is throwing shapes already, trying to make sure we don't prioritize the Hackett thing over his little princess."

"I hope the Chief reminded him that unlike the Hacketts he still *has* his little princess," Chris said, unimpressed. But he supposed he shouldn't be too surprised - parents only wanted the best for their kids, and Holly Glynn's father obviously wanted to ensure no stone remained unturned in finding his daughter's attacker.

"So, besides a ginormous feck-off burger," his partner said, licking his lips and stealing one of Reilly's fries. "What have I missed?"

Chris and Reilly brought him up to speed on what they'd discussed so far.

"Tech's working on the retrieved iPad, focusing on the victim's social media posts, photos etc to help pin down a timeline on the night, as well as a list of those in attendance." Reilly popped another fry into her mouth "I'm hopeful that will throw something up. Luckily for us, kids these days actually do leave a virtual bread-crumb trail. I'll have Rory email you anything of interest - particularly in relation to key witnesses, and we'll obviously keep you guys updated on any lab findings if and when they turn up. Autopsy's happening Monday, Karen says, and she's ordered toxicology reports based on the pills found in the kid's room."

"Ah yes, one of the victim's friends has already confirmed our boy's impressive physique was bought and paid for,' Kennedy told her and when Reilly looked blankly at him, Chris translated further.

"Seems Graham Hackett was using steroids to help his game. You saw the room; the guy's an out and out sports freak. Seems he wasn't the only one on the team using either."

"Well, that's interesting," she mused, kicking herself for not immediately recognizing the pills as illegal medication. Hence the foreign language instructions. "So we could be talking a deal gone bad, or maybe an unpaid debt; something like that?"

With drugs involved, all bets were off.

But she felt a bit sad that the dead boy had already gone down that road at such a young age. Kids experimented, certainly, but it sounded like Graham Hackett was doing more than that if he was actively seeking out performance enhancing drugs to boost his physique and thus his game performance.

"Who knows?" Kennedy said wiping his mouth, as he read a text message on his phone. "In the meantime, we'd better love ya and leave ya Blondie - just got word about the Hackett's location." He nodded at Chris. "Time to talk to Mum and Dad."

CHAPTER ELEVEN

Chris looked at their surroundings as he and Kennedy entered the lobby of the hotel in which the Hackett family were staying while their house remained cordoned off as a crime scene.

Fountains sparkled and real plants grew from every turn of the room. A large chandelier hung over the center of the reception area, the natural glow from the skylight shining through each crystal.

They approached the desk, where an older, smiling attendant was speaking with a hotel guest. Other people bustled through the lobby, dressed up in business clothes or elegant and expensive outfits – the cost of which Chris didn't even want to hazard a guess at.

"We're here to see Mr. and Mrs. Hackett," he announced, approaching the counter and offering his credentials. "They're expecting us."

"Ah, yes, good morning, detectives," the man said, typing something into his computer. "They are in suite 3B."

Kennedy shook his head as he and Chris moved to the elevators – where inside a concierge pressed the button for them. "You'd think being well off meant you couldn't do anything for yourself," he muttered under his breath.

"Well, if you've got enough money to pay someone to push your buttons, why shouldn't you?"

When they reached the Hackett's hotel room, they were answered by Jim Hackett, Graham's father, and his wife Tara. The man appeared to be in the state anyone would expect from a father who had just lost his son in such a violent and unexpected way.

Despite the extravagance of the hotel, Jim looked the worse for wear. His clothes – a gray shirt and checked pajama pants – were rumpled and worn. His chin and cheeks were speckled with a salt and pepper beard that hadn't been shaved in days, and his eyes were baggy and red-rimmed.

"Detectives," he said, his voice tired and rough, "come in."

Tara Hackett seemed to be doing mildly better than her husband, as she had managed to get dressed for the day, but her advancement stopped at the jeans and blouse she sported. Her hair was at a point just before being wild, and her face lacked even a dash of mascara or lip-gloss. Her eyes matched and surpassed the redness of her husband's, and both detectives knew that she had been crying, perhaps non-stop since learning of her youngest son's demise.

"Our sincerest condolences for your loss," Chris began, knowing the words passed right by the bereaved parents. He glanced around, but didn't see anything to alert them to the presence of Simon.

The hotel suite was just as elaborate as the lobby had been. The carpets were plush and immaculate, the adjoining bedroom looked bigger than Chris's own apartment, and he could see the corner of a claw-footed bath from where he was standing in the sitting area. He hadn't ever been in a hotel room that had its own sitting area. This was a place where people usually came to luxuriate and treat themselves, but the bereaved parents in front of him were immune to the niceties.

"We'll try to make this as brief as possible, Mr. and Mrs. Hackett. We just have a few questions we'd like to ask to aid us in our search for your son's attacker." Kennedy said, his voice in the same placating mode.

"Is your other son - Simon - here?" Chris asked, his eyes zeroing on another door of the suite.

Mrs. Hackett shook her head and brought a hand-kerchief to her nose, daintily blowing it before answering fully, "He left a while ago, for a walk to clear his head."

Chris didn't buy this, but he did his best to hide his

suspicion. The poor parents had just lost a son; they didn't need to know that the detectives on his case considered their remaining child a person of interest.

"I'm sorry, here, please, take a seat," Mr. Hackett said then, gesturing to the sitting area where his wife already sat.

The detectives sat down opposite them, and Mr. Hackett sat next to his wife on the chaise longue, finding her hand and holding it gently.

"Let's start with Graham's school life. Were things going well?"

Mrs. Hackett sniffled, "Oh, yes. Graham was very good in school and was planning on going to UCD in the autumn. He was very active, really sociable and had so many friends. He's always been a ... spirited boy but he was very respectful and well behaved. I still can't believe he's .... This would have never happened if we hadn't -"

Her sentence broke and Mr. Hackett wrapped his arm around her in a comforting gesture. Chris felt for the poor woman, but at the same time, he agreed with her.

He figured that no matter what a parent did, their child could never be perfectly safe, but something like this wasn't likely to happen if the boys hadn't been home alone and unsupervised.

He couldn't imagine Kennedy leaving his daughters by themselves during something as stressful as exams –

in fact, he couldn't imagine the big man leaving them home alone, full stop.

"Graham was a good boy," Mr. Hackett stated, like it was something that needed to be reinforced.

"What was your relationship like with your son?"

Mr. Hackett's eyes narrowed suspiciously. "We love both of our boys," he said, "our children mean the world to us. There's nothing else that matters more."

Besides a trip to Spain, Chris thought rather uncharitably.

"Can you tell us anything about Graham's relationship with Holly Glynn?" Kennedy asked then, to assess if their story matched up with what they'd heard from Holly herself.

Mr. Hackett looked confused, but Mrs. Hackett waved her hand through the air, her handkerchief trailing behind as she spoke, "Oh, the Glynn girl and Graham went out for a little while a few months back, I think. It wasn't anything serious, and it didn't last that long either. I don't know if they're still friends, now, even. With teenagers you can never tell. But she's a nice girl and a good influence, I thought."

When the detectives didn't reply, Mrs. Hackett gasped, as if realizing something, "You don't think it was the Glynn girl who did this, do you?"

Kennedy shook his head. "No, Mrs. Hackett. The person who attacked your son was strong, considerably stronger than a female and likely taller than Graham too. We're asking about his relationships simply to get a feel of what his life was like. It might help us figure out where to go next. In any case Holly Glynn was also the victim of an attack that night, and we're still trying to establish if both incidents are related."

"I see...I didn't know. Is she okay?"

"A bit shaken, but she's fine." Chris continued on with the questioning, "And what about your other son? What was Graham and Simon's relationship like?" He watched the expressions on the parents' faces, not wanting to miss any sensitive first reactions to what (to him at least) was a loaded question.

"Oh the boys are very close," Mrs. Hackett was quick to say, "Were close, I mean. They grew up playing Gaelic games together you know, and of course sport brings boys together. Graham always looked up to Simon, and Simon always protected his little brother. I remember once there was a boy in primary school who was bullying Graham for some time, and Simon just went for him, and the boy stopped."

"And now?" Chris asked, scribbling down a note, "The two of them still that close these days? There was some talk of an argument on the night in question."

Mrs. Hackett glanced at her husband, "Well, we were in Spain, so we really don't know ..." she trailed off, as though unsure what to say. She seemed to sense the thoughts running through the detective's heads though, because she was quick to add, "Our boys loved each other, that I know for sure. Even if they might have had a strange way of showing it."

KENNEDY POLITELY DUCKED out of the interview as his phone continuously buzzed against his leg. It was Inspector O'Brien demanding an update, and he was just finishing up when the elevator opened and Simon Hackett stepped into the hallway, a distracted look on his face.

When the older teen saw the detective he cursed under his breath, but continued on to the suite he and his parents were sharing.

Kennedy hung up quickly, intercepting the boy before he could get to the door. "Just the man I've been looking for," he said pleasantly, "mind if I ask you a few questions?"

Simon raised an unimpressed eyebrow, "Didn't you already do that yesterday? I feel like I should have a solicitor or something ..."

Kennedy raised an equally unimpressed brow in return. "Not if you have nothing to hide."

He rolled his eyes. "You think I don't know what you lot are about? You want to twist my words and make it seem like I did something I didn't do. Instead of asking me the same questions over and over - why not try and find out who killed my brother?"

Simon moved to the door and Kennedy, in one last

attempt to get the kid to talk honestly said, "Your parents are in there right now talking to my partner, without a solicitor."

At the mention of his parents, Simon's hand stopped an inch from the doorknob and he turned to Kennedy. "Okay," he demurred, "there's a coffee dock downstairs. We can talk there."

Kennedy nodded his consent, and the two of them rode the elevator down to the lobby area. He expected the kid to order some fancy milk and sugar concoction, but to his surprise, Simon ordered his decaf coffee black, just like his.

After they'd brought their drinks to the small, secluded booth in the corner, Kennedy opened up his notebook and took a sip of his coffee, reveling in the sharp, bitter taste.

Simon did so too, readying himself for another barrage of questions.

"Did Graham have any enemies?" Kennedy asked, "Anyone who had something against him?"

Simon snorted and put his coffee down. "Yeah, probably. For one thing, my brother didn't seem to know when to keep it in his pants. He had all sorts of lads pissed off at him after he hooked up with their girl-friends, or whatever. Some of 'em probably jealous of his talent on the pitch too," he added.

Kennedy almost chuckled at that – from what Graham's best friend had told them, a large part of

Graham's 'talent' had come from little white pills in his underwear drawer. Nevertheless, he took a note of Simon's insights. "We found some drugs in Graham's room. Know anything about that?"

Simon's eyebrows knitted together. "What do you mean? What kind of drugs?"

Determining that the kid really didn't seem to know what he was talking about, Kennedy continued. "Steroids, Simon. Do you have any idea where Graham might have gotten the stuff?"

Simon's expression turned angry and he shook his head, "Jesus. I warned him about that shite and he swore he - " He paused, vehemently shaking his head. "The game; it's about doing the best you can, working every day to get better. It's not about pumping your system full of fucking chemicals to get one up on the other guy. There's no honor in it. That's not what the game - our game - is about."

"And what is your game Simon?"

"Hurling of course." Simon seemed to realize he was ranting a little, so he stopped and cleared his throat. "Sorry. It's just, I told Graham that drugs were never the way to go. Ever. No matter what. You'd think he'd listen to me about some things, but as usual, Graham thought he knew better."

"As usual?" Interesting that the brothers had disagreed about the doping - could that be the cause of the argument Tiernan Williams had referred to? Maybe

Simon had, in fact, found out that Graham was juicing and became enraged, confronting him about it?

"Yes. My brother liked to go his own way. He might be younger than me, but he was no kid."

"How about you walk me through everything that happened that night as you remember it," Kennedy asked, pen poised. "But this time, go back a few days to before your folks left for Spain."

Simon sighed and took a long drink of his now cooler coffee. "Graham hadn't studied much for the exams, so was staying up late cramming a couple of nights in the run up to them. I helped him out with it, I remember what it was like." Here Simon's gaze grew annoyed. "The little prick could be so ungrateful at times. He thought I was being too hard on him. He never thought about schoolwork in the same way as sport – you have to work your ass off in both to get anywhere, but Graham didn't think so. After all, shit came easy to him.

"So on the night the exams finished, he posted some crap on Snapchat about our house being free for the night. Then, he sends out an invite to all his WhatsApp mates too. By the time he got back to the house after practice, he had nearly half the school promising to turn up for a session. At first I was pissed off – obviously the folks would hit the roof if they knew we were having a party, but what could I do only go along with it? A couple of my mates came over too, so at least I wouldn't be completely surrounded by kids the whole night.

"So I stayed around and kept a watch over the whole thing until roughly twelve, when me and my mates headed into town. I didn't see Graham or anyone else when I got back to the house sometime after three. And then when I woke up the next morning, that's when I found him."

It seemed like he was finished, so Kennedy started to reply, but then Simon gripped his coffee and continued.

"I was going to his room to tell him he had to help clean up the mess. I was pissed off that we'd have to spend the time before we left for Spain cleaning up the bloody house, and packing too, so I steamrolled to his room. I threw the door open and saw Graham there ... like that and ... I don't know, it took a couple seconds for it to sink in. That my brother was dead. I mean, it was obvious; he was staring right at me and half of his fucking head was missing, but still it didn't twig with me. And there was so much fucking blood and I remember thinking, *fuck, now we gotta clean this mess up, too?* I actually told him to get up, twice. That's when things actually sunk in and I understood that my brother wasn't going to be getting up. Ever."

Kennedy watched Simon closely, gauging his state of mind. The kid might have appeared unaffected when he and Chris had questioned him at the scene yesterday, but now he was showing very obvious signs of emotion, like clearing his throat and scrubbing at his face, not to mention real tears brimming in his eyes.

He knew then that their initial suspicions of this kid were off. Simon had a chip on his shoulder - that much was for sure - but now Kennedy could sense true grief beneath the kid's apparently emotionless façade.

"Okay," he said, after asking a few more questions, "I think that's all I need from you. For the moment at least."

"Fan-fucking-tastic," Simon replied, his tone once again sarcastic but Kennedy sensed his relief at the same time, "think everyone can leave me alone now?"

CHAPTER TWELVE

Reilly read through the social media correspondence Rory was beginning to collate from the teens in attendance at the Hackett party, trying to ascertain a clear timeline for the night, as well as exactly who was at the house and when.

A tricky task given nobody used their real names online, preferring self-aggrandizing screen monikers.

(HackR 7:18 pm) *End of Exam session at my house 2nite!*

Having been initially puzzled by some of the Irish lingo on her arrival from the States, Reilly had long since figured out that a 'session' in Ireland was short-hand for a booze-filled get-together.

Graham's initial share about the 'session' in his house had managed to acquire multiple reactions from others, 'liking' the post, confirming that they would be there, or asking if they could bring others along.

"This guy posted an Instagram picture of him, Graham Hackett, Holly Glynn and another girl at the house just after ten thirty that night," Rory said, pulling the photo up along with the associated timestamp.

Reilly leaned forward to look at the teens grinning faces. At that point, Holly's dress was still intact and her innocence unsullied, and Graham's face was smiling and unbruised.

"Yes. Holly did say that she and her friends arrived at the party shortly after ten ..." she mused, but Rory cut her off by bringing up another response to Graham's missive.

(**Cat Woman** 9:59 pm) *We're here to wreck the gaff...*

Reilly thought back to the wreckage in the Hackett 'gaff' and judging by the state of the house the following morning, most of the kids that had been to the party had done just that. Looking at the social media interaction, and taken with early witness reports, the estimate of teens at the house that night now stood at around twelve people at peak.

The investigators had to face the sobering fact that with so many people in the house at the time, it would be very difficult to determine exactly who (if any) had killed Graham Hackett, and whether that same person - or any other partygoer - had been involved in Holly Glynn's assault.

"Any interaction from Simon Hackett on the social media?" Reilly asked, conscious of Chris's initial suspicions about the older brother.

Rory shook his head and took a sip of his energy drink. "Nope. I compiled a list of all the replies to the post, as well as screen names of anyone who posted anything with the hashtag - #HackRhouseparty."

Reilly shook her head in bewilderment at how kids were communicating these days – she didn't consider herself to be *that* old or out of touch, and she did have a (mostly dormant) Facebook page so she could keep in touch with some of her old work buddies back home, but a lot of the things happening on the internet now didn't make sense to her.

Everything was so fast and instant, giving people less time to react and formulate responses. Some of the stuff Rory was talking about and the terms he used were apparently common parlance amongst Millennials, but double dutch to her.

She didn't partake in any of the image-based social media like Instagram and Snapchat, but knew enough about the world and the things that happened in it to know that posting information about yourself where anyone could see it was a very bad idea.

A case she had been involved with not too long ago - the one in which she herself had fallen victim - centered around a serial killer who poisoned his victims. The last girl the guy targeted before he was caught had been contacted via social media. Without such interaction, it would have taken him much longer to get to her, or he might not have been able to at all.

It struck her suddenly, that members of her own team might well have profiles on all sorts of social media sites. They were all considerably younger than she, enough to make a difference. She turned to Rory. "Do you have a Snapchat account?" she asked him, already knowing the answer by the incredulous look on his face.

He grinned sheepishly, having sensed the reason for her question. "Social media isn't dangerous if you know how to use it boss," he defended. "Anyway, what I do on my own time is none of your business."

Reilly looked back at the screen and muttered under her breath. "It does if the next case we work is yours."

Laughing, Rory ignored the comment, instead pushing back from his desk and wheeling his chair to the other side of the room, where Graham Hackett's broken iPad was situated. He scrolled through some of the apps listed on the homepage, showing them to Reilly. "Some of these are harder to get into. The kid was pretty savvy, as far as teenagers go, and he has much of his personal information mildly protected. It'll just take me a little longer to access."

She watched as Rory went through some of the victim's correspondence with his friends and some girls via private message. "Still, you can see a few interactions here between Hackett and Holly Glynn, which might be of interest. These are from a couple of months ago, and indicate that the two were romantically involved at that time. Then the messages are few and far between until they stop completely. There isn't any direct communication at all between them before or during the party other than being tagged together in photos."

Rory scrolled back through some of the other messages. "When you read these, it's clear most of these guys were at the party. I checked out their profiles: they all go to the same school and most were on the club Gaelic team with the victim. I managed to work back from the screen names and interactions and figured out most of their real names as well as home address."

Reilly nodded. "It's a good start, thanks. I'll pass the info onto the detectives."

"*This* girl though ..." Rory said, opening some correspondence between Graham and a girl using the relatively run of the mill screen name *Becks*, "is the person our victim contacted the most in the run up to that night. And they're best friends on Snapchat."

Reilly ignored his last comment, not entirely sure what it meant, and looked through some of the messages. Most were harmless flirting, just two teenagers going back and forth, but something about the more earnest tone of the conversation sent her on alert.

"Find out who this girl is," she said to Rory, hoping whomever *Becks* was might be able to give them some clue as to which way to head next in their investigation, "and see if you can get a look at Holly Glynn's social media too. Find out who she was talking to, especially that night."

CHAPTER THIRTEEN

Mc2020: *C'mon spill @CoolChulainn. What did you see?*

CoolChulainn*: We all saw the aggro that night with G and Big Bro. Remember the way he tore into him over D-Man or Biception or whatever name that gym rat uses to big himself up. Not cool to be raining his shit around at someone's house....*

PuckingNinja: *Don't be talking out your a**e, sure that was only pure banter between bros. And Biception wasn't dishing out gym candy last night afaik.*

Biception: *Hey @CoolChulainn, you're a brave man behind the keyboard. If u have something to say, maybe try saying it to my face?*

CoolChulainn *@Biception I'm on my phone not a keyboard. Anyway, I've no probs saying it to your face. It's time you were called out: what good are you to the team standing* *around taking selfies of your pecs for Insta? Plenty of cops around now to take an interest in your not-so-secret sideline ...*

Missislippy: *Guys, this isn't helpful. @CoolChulainn if you do remember something helpful about that night, you should contact the police. Slagging off D-Man doesn't help ...*

Biception: *@CoolChulainn, start throwing accusations like that around and you'd better be able to back them up. Much as I'd love to knock you out, I'll make it official and have my 'oul fella haul you to court for slander.*

CoolChulainn: *@Biception... threatening me with your big-shot solicitor dad? Bahahaha....priceless. I don't need proof; one of my best friend's is dead.*

PuckingNinja: *Chill the f**k out people. Everybody is going through a s**t storm right now, no need to turn on each other. There has to be a reason for what happened, I knew everybody there that night and we know it wasn't one of us.*

Missislippy: *Then who was it?*

CMc2020: *It's all a bit of a blur to me TBH. There were a couple of dudes I didn't recognize, like that gobshite friend of Simon's who thought it would be a good idea to slide down the stairs on a freakin' DOOR? How the f**k did he even get it off its hinges?*

PuckingNinja: *Yeah, that guy was pretty wasted all right. I heard Si telling him to f**k off home after that stunt, the dumb d***head...*

Missislippy: *Tool. Thought he was God's gift too, tried it on with me a couple of times. Does anybody know if the house* was maybe burgled or anything? Maybe G stumbled across somebody trying to break in?

Biception: Or maybe there's a connection between our two 'victims'...

Missislippy: What the hell does that mean Gym Rat? Are you suggesting Holly had something to do with what happened to HackR? You really are a piece of s**t!

Biception: I'm just saying anything is possible...

CoolChulainn: Well, thank f**k you're not the one running the investigation if you think Holly is capable of anything like that....

CHAPTER FOURTEEN

Next, the detectives paid a visit to the other family affected by the fateful events of Wednesday night.

The Glynn house looked almost identical to the Hackett residence about half a mile over in a similar estate. A prim front lawn, colorful flowers lining the windows in the front, and a bright red door that stood out in contrast to the white pebble-dash wall out front. By looking at the cheery exterior of both houses, you would never guess the tragedies that had recently befallen their younger inhabitants.

Chris knocked on the door and the pretty middle-aged woman he'd met briefly at the hospital answered. Susan Glynn was today dressed in a simple blue blouse, white pants and ballet flats, her hair pulled away from her face with a headband.

"Good morning," she said, her tone automatically polite but with an underlying gravity.

"Good morning, Mrs. Glynn. We spoke on the phone earlier - Detective Delaney from the hospital the other day. This is my partner, Detective Kennedy, and as mentioned, we'd like to ask you a few more questions about Holly's attack."

The woman glanced back into the house, then licked her lips nervously and regarded the two men, "Yes, I think that should be all right, but Holly's upstairs, and she is trying to get some much-needed rest."

"We'll try not to take up too much of your time, Mrs. Glynn," Kennedy said sympathetically, "our condolences for your daughter's recent trouble. I have two girls of my own and ..."

Mrs. Glynn nodded quickly then, as though that was all he needed to say. She opened the door wider and led the two men into the living room and showed them where to sit, before rushing off to the kitchen to bring them some refreshments to enjoy over their conversation like any decent Irish host.

Tea served, Susan Glynn looked nervously between the two of them. At first, she had been unsure about answering questions without her husband present. Holly's attack had sent Michael on a crazed man-hunt, and Susan was aware that he had spent most of his time since he first got the call trying to gather answers, and pressing the police to work harder to find their daughter's attacker.

But she knew it wouldn't hurt to talk to the detectives - she felt terrible for the Hackett family and she didn't have anything to hide. If any insight she could offer might help the police find the person who'd hurt her Holly or Graham Hackett, it might well help both families.

She was nervous and sat on the edge of her seat, her hands clasped tightly together. A plate of Rich Tea biscuits sat untouched on the coffee table between them. "Okay," she managed to say, though her word came out in one choppy syllable, forced from her lungs in one desperate gasp.

"Mrs. Glynn," Chris said gently, opening his notebook. "Let's start first with your daughter. We know Holly attended the get-together at the Hackett residence. Did she often attend parties like this one?"

Susan shook her head and bit her lip, her nervousness apparent in her posture. The poor woman looked on the edge of tears, or a nervous breakdown and Chris took note of this as she attempted to answer. "I..." she started, before trailing off and looking to the floor.

"Mrs. Glynn," Kennedy put in, "my partner and I are here to help you. We need to put together a timeline and establish a roll call for those present at the house that night - just a few simple questions to help us establish the facts."

Susan nodded and sat back in her chair, and Chris could tell that she was doing her best to try and relax. Her neatly styled bob was pushed back away from her face and her blouse and jeans were impeccable.

"Holly didn't attend student parties often, the focus has been on study for so long now, there hadn't been much time for parties," she managed to say, finally. "Only when there was something to celebrate, or when her friends were getting together. And she always asked permission."

Kennedy rolled his eyes at that. *Yeah, right.*

Raising two teenage daughters of his own, he knew for a fact that they didn't always ask for permission. He loved his two more than anything on earth and would fight to the death for them – but that didn't mean he thought they were perfect, or that they never made mistakes. "Okay, and who are Holly's friends - can you give us some names?"

The woman's lips tightened a bit more, and she glanced down at her hands in a sign of clear discontent. "They're mostly nice girls..." she started, with an air that told Chris and Kennedy that she was just saving face. "It's some of them are... involved with some things I don't necessarily want Holly associated with, you know. Behaviors with boys and whatnot."

Kennedy nodded earnestly, and Chris could tell by the look in his partner's eyes that he understood such fears.

While Susan Glynn listed off the names of the girls she wasn't all that sure about, Chris's eyes wandered. He noticed a cage in the corner of the living room, big enough for a small dog, but different in design. Perhaps the Glynns had a budgie, or a rabbit or some such.

"And what about Holly's relationship with Graham Hackett?" Kennedy was asking, "They were going out together apparently?"

Mrs. Glynn shook her head, "In so much as teenagers go out together these days. Of course I don't think they even call it 'going out' anymore. Whatever it was, it was nothing serious, and I don't think they broke up on bad terms, or anything. I wasn't too disappointed when she told me she and the Hackett boy were no longer an item, as she didn't need the distraction with exams coming up. He did call here to pick her up once or twice, and from what I could tell he was a nice boy, respectful and well-mannered. He was on Conor's team too, I think."

"Conor?" Chris queried.

"Holly's older brother. He plays - played - hurling with Graham Hackett too. By all accounts Graham was very talented."

"Was Conor at the house party that night?" Chris glanced up and over Susan's head, examining the photos on the mantle. His gaze settled on one of Holly and a boy, evidently the brother. Though Mrs. Glynn had said

Conor was older, it looked like there was no more than a year or so between them.

"No, he and Holly..." Susan's eyes drifted to the opposite wall and she chewed on her bottom lip, "they were really close when they were younger. Twins," she added, surprising Chris. "Holly and Conor are twins, but he's older by ten minutes. We used to do the matching outfit thing as much as we could with boys and girls clothes, you know, because who couldn't resist such cuteness? But I suppose they got tired of being a twosome and towards the end of primary school they grew apart. They hardly spend any time together now, except for family occasions, or when they're forced into the same room. Typical teenagers."

"But he and Graham Hackett were team-mates you said?"

"Yes, they play - played - both football and hurling together as far as I know. Conor was lucky enough to get a football scholarship to play Aussie Rules in Sydney after the summer break."

"Nice one," Kennedy said enviously, obviously thinking about the sunny, outdoor Aussie lifestyle. Not to mention the famed barbecues.

"I'm sure you'll miss him," Chris supplied, knowing by the look on Susan Glynn's face that she was torn by pride for her son's achievements, and the fact that those same achievements would be taking him away from her.

Just then, they all heard the sound of footsteps making their way along the landing on the floor above them.

"Sounds like Holly's awake," Kennedy said pointedly. "Do you think we might be able to speak with her now?"

Mrs. Glynn looked pained, but acquiesced. "I'll check, but please be patient with her detectives. She's been through a torrid time and has been very withdrawn since she came home from the hospital."

"Of course," Chris told her. "The victim liaison officer will be in touch soon to offer counselling if she hasn't already. I would highly recommend availing of their services Mrs. Glynn, they are highly trained and very good at their jobs." As Susan stood up to fetch her daughter, he put a comforting hand on her arm. "Any information Holly gives us could potentially help find not only her attacker but also the person responsible for the death of her friend. If she and Graham were close, like you said, then I'm sure she'll want to help."

Susan nodded. "Okay. Wait here and I'll get her. But I've asked ... and she really doesn't remember much about what happened."

Chris and Kennedy exchanged knowing looks as they both reflected on the sensitivity of the situation. Usually, it was Special Victims Officers or female detectives who questioned victims of sexual assault. What made this case different was the fact that there was a victim of another sort now lying in the morgue.

Muffled voices came from overhead, followed by movement on the landing and then footsteps drew closer heralded by creaking floorboards.

Mrs. Glynn re-entered the room, followed by her daughter, who was wrapped in a bright pick dressing gown and wearing flowery pajama bottoms and novelty slippers featuring smiling cartoon characters. Holly walked behind her mother with her head bowed slightly, her hair tied back in a ponytail and looking infinitely younger than the social media profile image the investigators had seen in the meantime.

For his part, Kennedy felt his chest tighten. Seeing this poor kid, so young and lost reminded him of his own girls. The thought of them being in Holly's position was enough to make even a hardened detective like him swallow with a mixture of pity and discomfort.

Both men stood to their feet as the mother and daughter sat closely on the two-seater couch opposite. Instead of offering a handshake, the detectives simply waited for Holly and her mother to get settled before retaking their own seats.

"Holly, my name is Chris and this is Pete. We won't keep you long; there's just a couple of simple questions we need to ask about the other night."

He looked across at Kennedy then to allow him take the lead, aware that his position as a father of two teenage girls probably gave him an advantage in making a connection.

His partner took the cue. "Pet, before we start I'd just like to say we are very sorry for what happened to you, and want to reassure you we will not rest until the person responsible is brought to justice," Kennedy said in a tone that Chris rarely heard from his partner. Even though the big man was a true professional, he had no doubt the nature of this investigation would strike a personal chord.

"If you're finding any questions too difficult, let us know. This is just a quick chat to see are there any stand-out details that can assist us get a handle on your attack or indeed the attack on Graham," Chris added, wanting to also let her know that there would be some questioning in relation to the murder of her friend.

Holly nodded in a weak fashion.

"The most important thing we need to establish is whether you can give us a description of the person who attacked you - do you think you could do that sweet-heart?" Kennedy soothed.

"I don't know...the whole thing is such a blur..." Holly trailed off looking sideways toward her mother who wore a pained expression as she tried to exude a reassuring warmth to ease her daughter's discomfort.

"It's okay, take your time," Chris offered. "I know you mentioned in your initial statement to my colleague at the hospital that you didn't recognize the person who attacked you. Is that still the case?" he pressed.

"No.... I mean yes, I don't remember seeing his face...it was dark and I was...." The girl trailed off again, gazing down at an invisible object on the coffee table. "I mean, it was late, I was tired and I'd had a good few drinks - well not that many really but I just felt....you know, desperate for sleep," Holly said, as she retracted her hands further up her sleeves avoiding eye contact and evidently embarrassed that she had put herself in a vulnerable position.

"That's okay, Holly. Sometimes people in these situations think they don't remember anything at all, but the tiniest of details might be useful to us - like say the color of hair or clothing?" Kennedy encouraged.

"It was dark...his clothes were dark, at least I don't remember anything specific ..." Holly shuffled in her seat uneasily, as she forced herself to think back to a moment she would have gladly wiped from her memory forever given the chance.

"Okay, dark clothes, good, what about hair color?" Chris pressed, trying to harvest as much information from her mental journey back to the scene of the crime.

Holly shook her head without lifting it. "Sorry, no."

"That's good Holly, you're doing great. So let's go back to the house party for a second - what do you remember from that?" Kennedy changed tack slightly to try to ascertain what she did remember.

"It was a good night, everybody was buzzing...we just felt....I don't know, free I suppose, after the exams?"

"Was there any trouble at the party?" Kennedy asked. "Any messing around amongst the lads maybe?"

"No, it was all good-natured. Graham and Simon were buzzing off each other a bit, but that was nothing new," Holly told them.

"Buzzing off each other?" Chris prompted. "Was it a serious argument?"

"No, like I said they always buzzed off each other. Simon was a bit grumpy because Graham was drunk and too many people kept showing up."

"When was the last time you spoke to Graham that night?" Kennedy asked gently.

She looked sideways at her mother and Chris knew she was obviously reluctant to say anything about being in Graham's bedroom as reported by Tiernan. "I'm not sure ... we'd all done some shots in the kitchen and then outside on the decking I started to feel a bit woozy, so Graham showed me where the bathroom was upstairs..."

I wonder, Chris thought, keeping an open mind on that one.

Then a bit after that, Megan hooked up with some fella I didn't recognize, one of Simon's friends. I went after Megan and followed them down the back of the garden but didn't know which way they went after that.

Graham was back inside the house at this stage, I think....

Anyway, as I said, I felt a bit sick after the shots; the lemon slices we'd taken with them turned my stomach. And by then it was late, so I decided to just head home. That's when things got blurry ..."

Holly was in obvious discomfort recounting her underage drunken exploits to not only two detectives, but also her mother.

"Do you know what time that was?" Chris asked. "When you headed for home?"

"I'm not really sure ... I tried to ring Megan but it went straight to message minder. I checked my phone and it says that was around one forty," Holly supplied. "So it would have been a little after that when I left."

That was good and easily verifiable information, Chris thought satisfied. If nothing else, it gave them a firmer timeline between Holly leaving the house, and Graham Hackett's time of death.

"Is there any other activity on your phone that might be useful?" Kennedy asked. "We'll need to take it to the lab for analysis."

Holly looked horrified at the idea, but at the same time realized she had little choice. "I don't think so, we took a good few snaps at the house earlier in the night and posted some stuff on Insta too. But mostly just texts between me and my friends...Do you really need to take my phone?"

"Sweetheart, some of the information on it may well be important ..."

"Your mother is correct, Holly. Some of the info on there, photographs etc might prove very useful to help figure out what happened to you - and Graham. Don't worry - our tech team will not under any circumstances invade your privacy. Our investigators are simply trying to collate images and correspondence from various people on the night to help establish a full list of attendees, things like that."

"Well I have no objections per se, but I'd rather discuss that with my husband before agreeing to release the phone if you don't mind," Mrs. Glynn put in then, knowing that her solicitor husband would want to be kept in the loop. He was already annoyed not to be here for this. But he was in court this morning and couldn't get out of it.

"Of course that's fine, we can discuss it with your husband and I can arrange for someone from the GFU to collect the device at a later time," Chris said knowing from experience how difficult Mrs. Glynn's husband could be.

Yet at the same time, wasn't the man already banging the table with Inspector O'Brien, insisting that they find his daughter's attacker? He could hardly then refuse to hand over a piece of evidence that could well be crucial in doing just that.

Chris smiled inwardly, realizing that Reilly and the

gang would probably be getting that phone a lot faster than they'd thought.

"OK Holly, that's about it for now - you've been very helpful. Is there anything else you think might be helpful to us? It doesn't matter how random you think it might be," he asked, as a visible wave of relief crossed the young girl's face at the mention of the word 'finished'.

Holly looked up and gently shook her head. Chris and Kennedy stood to their feet, a little disappointed that they'd been able to get so little from her.

"Thank you for your time ladies, we appreciate it. Holly, here is my number if any other details happen to come back to you over the next few days," Kennedy said smiling at her.

He and Chris stood up and were making their way round the coffee table toward the hallway when Holly spoke up again.

"Cigarettes..." she announced, as if answering a direct question. "His breath ...it stank of cigarettes."

Chris wasn't entirely sure if this piece of information could possibly help, but it was better than nothing. From what he could tell about Holly's friends and classmates so far - particularly the Gaelic players - the boys were more interested in building muscle via chemical means than sullying their lungs with cigarettes.

But if nothing else, it gave them something to look out for once they did manage to put together a better picture of the people in attendance at the Hackett house that night - despite Holly's insistence that she didn't know her attacker.

The true question was: would any information they gleaned from Holly Glynn - today or in the future via her cellphone - help find Graham Hackett's killer?

CHAPTER FIFTEEN

"What are you guys doing?" Lucy asked as she entered the Cyber Unit.

Gary and Reilly were standing in front of a PC screen display Rory had projected on a blank wall to enable them read through the information on his computer.

"Correspondence found on Graham Hackett's iPad," Reilly told her.

Her curiosity piqued, Lucy looked up as Rory scrolled down through some of the messages he had extracted from the iMessage app.

(GH, 10:44 pm) *Hey, I saw that you liked my picture*

(BS, 10:46 pm) *What's not to like? ;)*

(GH, 10:47 pm) *If you liked that pic, I've got another one you might like more...*

(BS, 10:48 pm) *I'll be the judge of that...*

"Holy hell..." Lucy let out a shriek of revulsion as a 'prominent' picture of Graham Hackett's anatomy unexpectedly followed.

Gary tittered at his girlfriend's discomfort, while Rory scrolled quickly back to the top of the message feed.

"Lots of similar stuff, all with different girls," Rory was telling them. "Some older than him judging by their profiles, and even some younger, flirting and freely sharing explicit pictures like this one. Hackett maintained lots of these kind of conversations, some of them concurrently."

"For feck's sake..." Lucy gasped, "Who *are* these girls? And why are they sending around pictures of themselves like this?"

Reilly recalled that Lucy had grown up in a small suburban part of Dublin, her life hugely sheltered once her sister Grace, had gone missing. For her part however, she remembered what it was like to be amongst boys like these growing up, boys good at sport and admired and adored for it - you felt special just to talk to them.

She could recall easily the girls in miniskirts at her old high school back home, flooding around the boys after their big Friday night football games. Hanging off their arms as they all left to celebrate the latest win.

The drama that rang out through the hallways during school hours was nauseating though. There were many times one girl had stolen another girl's guy and fights would break out, hair pulling, scratching, even clothes ripped off in revealing places. Reilly could still hear the insults the girls hurled at each other as these fights sprouted up spontaneously. What she always found sad was that these girls blamed the other girl for stealing their man but they were never upset with their man for cheating.

Boys in the US were getting football scholarships all the time. And once they were in college, there was almost always the chance that they would be drafted into the professional leagues. If a girl managed to hang on to him for that long, she would definitely get a piece of that money. So overlooking a bit of cheating on the side was not too high of a price to pay. She figured it was the same in Gaelic games, though from what she'd learned, the domestic game was not a professional sport, so nothing in it for those players except pride and plaudits.

Rory took a sip of his Red Bull. "You aren't even seeing the half of it, Luce. Imagine if this was your job, going through kids' saucy pictures to try to find a murderer amongst them."

"That isn't your job though," Gary pointed out, "you get to go through adults' saucy pictures, as well."

Rory rolled his eyes at him and reached for the can, which he put back down when he discovered it to be empty. He picked up the phone, buzzing for one of the interns in the lab to get him a new one, and Reilly crossed her arms, glaring disapprovingly.

"What?" he said, throwing his hands up. "Isn't that what interns are for."

"Those pills found in Graham Hackett's drawer," Lucy said then, catching Reilly as she headed out, "turn out to be performance enhancing drugs, anabolic steroids to be precise."

So Graham Hackett was definitely a substance abuser. Reilly used the information to update her mental profile of the victim's personality. He was a talented athlete, and very popular with the other kids at school - especially the girls. He came from a solidly middle class family, yet was clearly engaging in illegal activity in the form of performance-enhancing drugs. Where'd a kid that age get the drugs from? That aspect alone might give someone a reason to come after Graham Hackett – maybe he didn't pay his debts, or shot his mouth off about something he shouldn't have ...

Heading back to her office, she fished her phone

from her pocket and called Chris, but it was Kennedy who answered. "What is it?" he said gruffly.

"Hello to you, too," she said, raising an eyebrow.

"Chris is driving. We've just finished interviewing the Glynn girl and her mother," he told her. "She seemed pretty shaken up 'bout the whole thing. According to the mother, Hackett and the girl went out for a while and he also knew the other Glynn kid, Conor. The brother wasn't at the party that night, but was on the gah team with Hackett."

"Gah team?" she repeated frowning.

"GAA team. It's how the culchies say it."

"Okay." Reilly already knew that 'culchies' was slang for country people, and from her limited research, she knew that Gaelic games originated from more rural areas of the country. She sighed, realizing she'd never fully get the hang of the multi-faceted and often down-right bewildering Irish lingo.

Gah.

"Spoke to the parents yesterday, and got a bit more out of the older Hackett kid but he's not off the hook just yet."

"You know, it might do some good for you to refer to people by their names now and again," Reilly said, holding back a chuckle. Whether intentional or not, Kennedy always managed to lift her spirits.

"Been doin' it this way for fifteen years Blondie, and it's worked Okay so far."

"If you say so," she laughed, then added, "Well, the reason I called was the pills in Graham Hackett's room have indeed been confirmed as steroids - which I'm assuming will also come back in the tox-screen. Ask around about that, whomever he got his 'roids from will surely be of interest."

"Rightio," Kennedy replied. "We'll keep an eye out."

CHAPTER SIXTEEN

A little while later, Reilly gathered her things and loaded the preliminary case files into her bag, ready to go over them at her kitchen table during the weekend.

She sighed. While she always enjoyed her work, today she wanted nothing more than to go home to her bed where her mind had been going all day long.

If such horrible things could happen to kids - Graham Hackett in his own home and Holly only minutes from hers - both kids with loving parents and promising futures - just how helpless would Reilly be to protect her child?

Despite herself, she was suddenly reliving a moment during a previous case when the serial killer dubbed The Chef was stabbing her with a syringe filled with poison.

She had managed to save another girl from certain death at the time, but when Reilly was falling to the floor and there was nobody to help her, she was aware she had made a very bad decision.

For her baby as well as herself.

If Reilly couldn't keep herself safe, how could she be trusted to keep her future son or daughter safe? Wasn't her own job already a major source of danger? But what were her options, giving up the thing she loved, or risking danger for her child?

Her mind readily supplied her with a vision of Holly Glynn in the hospital post-attack – shaking, scared, and emotionally scarred – and she tried to suppress her shudder.

What did the world hold for girls? Constant danger, constant threat, to one like Holly, who had just been attending a party with her fellow students, to celebrate their long-awaited graduation.

Reilly recalled the countless times her gender had been shoved in her way on the path to a successful and carefree life. In her line of work, it was always a hindrance, something that her colleagues took extra care to notice. They ranged in their actions anywhere from trying to protect her, to openly harassing her.

The thought had been stewing in her head since she'd interviewed Holly the other day, and though she had tried to ignore it, now it was being broadcast in her mind as something of utmost importance.

A boy would have a better chance in the world.

All of the evils Reilly had seen, every dark act she had observed in all her years of service, from the darkest alleys in San Francisco to the most elegant households in Dublin, the blood stained the same. Men and women bled the same, but the thought still wouldn't quit.

If her baby was a boy, it wouldn't have to suffer the sexist comments she'd so often received every time an ignorant male was threatened by her position of power.

If her baby was a boy, at least he wouldn't have to fear for his safety every time he made his way down the street.

Graham Hackett's twisted form shoved its way back to the front of her mind and she tried to shake it.

Maybe it didn't matter what gender her baby was.

As if thinking about her future as a stressed new mom wasn't enough to distract her from her work, the prospect of Todd's imminent arrival was weighing her down too.

What would his take be on all of this? What would he expect from her or vice versa? Their fling in Florida had primarily been based on passion and the intensity of the case they were working together. Beyond that they didn't really know one another - certainly not long enough to be bringing a child into the world together.

Whereas she and Chris had been working side by side since she moved to Dublin – and for a very brief moment they had crossed a boundary between colleagues, between friends. More than once she had leaned on him for emotional and mental support, and they had confided in each other. Reilly wanted nothing more than to confide in him her thoughts and worries about Todd.

But her instincts told her that bringing up Todd to Chris at this point would be a mistake, regardless of how comforting he could be. Now was not the time for her to be giving in to the kind of feelings Chris elicited.

Instead they needed to return to their usual rhythm, colleagues and friends, nothing more.

Later, she stood in her small kitchen, making what she hoped was a nutritious supper. The smell of spinach and chicken wafted around her but it did nothing to spike her appetite. She had all sorts of nutritional pill bottles lined up on the counter that she was supposed to take every morning, and some at night, but she still felt pressed to eat well.

As she turned to plate her food, she caught a glimpse of her couch, stagnant in the small sitting room. That was where Todd would be sleeping next week, and thinking about it made her glance at her food with distaste.

Although the time she had spent with him in Florida was amazing, Reilly had never expected or wanted anything lasting. Neither, she suspected, did Todd.

Still, once she'd finally told him about the unexpected result of their brief liaison, he had immediately stepped up, offering to help in any way he could. Hence the upcoming visit to 'talk through their options.'

Reilly sighed and looked down at the food she had prepared, no longer feeling hungry enough to eat it. But she knew that it was essential for Bumpasaurus, so she braved it and picked up her fork.

CHAPTER SEVENTEEN

"Steel," a voice called out, as Reilly was approaching her office on Monday morning. It was none other than Inspector O'Brien, the police chief and Reilly's boss.

The sun was streaming through the windows of the GFU building – a rare sight – and the air was poignantly strong with the heady smell of coffee.

Although Reilly had been tossing and turning all weekend with the uncomfortable aches in her back and the disturbing thoughts in her head, the lab had been the first place she wanted to go when she awoke at the sound of her alarm.

Now being here, everything was right with the world again – except for the eternally disgruntled O'Brien currently headed her way. "What news have you on the Hackett situation?" he asked without preamble.

Reilly took a deep breath and regarded her superior with a calm look, recalling how it was O'Brien who had insisted on the enforced leave period that set her on course to the sojourn in Florida, which had resulted in her pregnancy.

She still hadn't quite forgiven him.

As always O'Brien's bluster seemed to calm a little when faced with Reilly's imposing form. Normally she was a force to be reckoned with anyway, but her pregnancy had lent her a whole new air of intimidation that hadn't gone unnoticed.

"I just got here, Chief," she said, aching to make it to her office and find a seat. She had taken the stairs instead of the lift again, though for maybe the last time until all of this was over. Her feet were swollen and tired, and her back begged her to rest it against the soft leather of the chair behind her desk. "However, while we don't yet have a murder weapon, we do have lots of trace and a strong social media trail to follow."

The chief had since taken a step back and was eyeing her ruefully, as if he too was becoming aware of just how far along her pregnancy now was.

"Good," he said, in a tone uncharacteristically meek for him, "And just to let to know the father of the Glynn girl called my office, *my office*, twice on Friday and again this morning to make sure we're 'doing our jobs'. I did my best to ensure Mr. Glynn - in so many words -

that my finest investigators are working tirelessly to find out who attacked his daughter, while also trying to ascertain Master Hackett's killer ..." Here he donned his disgruntled face again. "But he informed me that if we don't turn up some relevant information soon, he's going to the press - or worse."

Reilly recalled Michael Glynn pacing outside his daughter's hospital room the other day, as well as the look of frantic fury on his face.

"Normally - as you know - I wouldn't pay any attention to such threats," O'Brien continued without a trace of irony, "but the man is well known in the High Court for being...well you know, and I have no doubt he's got a few tricks up his sleeve. Men like that are used to having things their own way."

"We're doing what we can with the limited information his daughter's given us," Reilly assured him, mindful that if she didn't sit down soon, she would seriously injure someone on her way to the nearest chair. "But rest assured we'll find something soon."

"Good." The chief nodded gruffly again, and she turned to make her way to her office with a relieved sigh.

She'd barely made it a step further down the hallway before someone rounded the corner and nearly ran her over, stopping just in time to grab her by the arms and avert his body weight. Which was considerable.

Kennedy looked like he'd just rolled out of bed, and

was chomping on a huge baguette filled with sausages, eggs, rashers and goodness knows what else.

"You know," Reilly said, "I don't think Josie would be happy about what you're eating for breakfast..."

He looked back at her, his eyes sleep-ridden, his jaw unshaven, "Breakfast? I've been up so long this is practically lunch. And what my lovely wife doesn't know won't hurt her." The big man grinned at her and took the last bite. When he had finished licking his lips he said, "Just stopped by to see if you wanted a lift over to the morgue?"

Damn. Reilly had forgotten that Karen Thompson had scheduled Graham Hackett's autopsy briefing for this morning.

She looked longingly at the door to her office, only a few feet away. She could imagine the expensive leather chair she'd purchased herself, and how relieving it would be to sit down, just for a moment. But she looked back at Kennedy and sighed. "That'd be great, thanks." She hefted the files in her arms to her other side. "Just let me set these on my desk, and I'll meet you downstairs."

She unlocked the door to her office, balancing her files and bag precariously on one arm. When she got the door open she took one step in and flipped on the light, reveling wistfully in the space she was able to call her own.

The room wasn't scented – there were no candles or perfumes anywhere around. While her overly sensitive nose could be a blessing at crime scenes, it was torture for her to be around candles or diffusers - like someone had stuffed a piece of lemon or lavender right up her nose.

She set the files down on her heavy wooden desk and slid her handbag from her shoulder, placing it in her chair so she wouldn't be tempted to sit. As nice as five minutes off her feet sounded, she knew that if she did sit down she wouldn't be getting back up.

As she passed back through the glass door she caught a glimpse of her reflection. Despite the growing heft to her stomach, she still looked the same as she did every day at the office. A professional outfit, usually gray or navy, and a business-like ponytail pulling her blond hair away from her face.

Reilly lifted her chin and walked back through the door.

Tired or not, you got this.

CHAPTER EIGHTEEN

"Would you like a chair, Reilly?"

Although she could detect no hint of condescension in Karen Thompson's motherly tone, Reilly still resented the idea that anyone - least of all the ME - thought she needed special treatment.

She shifted her weight to distribute it more evenly on her feet and said through slightly gritted teeth. "I'm fine standing thanks."

The city mortuary was a stark contrast to the GFU lab. The walls were painted white, the ground a stark white tile, and the examination table a cool steel gray. The only speck of color in the room was Dr. Thompson's blue scrub outfit.

The ME shrugged, though Reilly saw something flare in her eyes, and she got the feeling that if she could do so without damaging Reilly's pride, her colleague would insist that she take a seat during the briefing.

As it was, Thompson glanced at each of Reilly's detective counterparts before commencing a report on her findings. She cleared her throat and donned her gloves, before pulling back the sheet to reveal the top portion of Graham Hackett's naked body.

Chris, Kennedy, and Reilly, all had nose plugs and face masks, but Thompson was much more comfortable around the pale body, and she stood over the corpse free of facial garments.

"Just to start off with the usual observations. Based upon lividity and rigor present upon preliminary examination of the victim, he was deceased no more than four to five hours. I would also speculate, again based on blood lividity, that the body was not moved post mortem. There is no indication of sexual activity in the hours leading up to death, but swabs have been taken for analysis to be certain. The victim's stomach contained little by way of food: some semi digested peanuts, likely consumed three to four hours before death, although it's harder to accurately give timings due to the large amount of alcohol consumed."

Made sense, Reilly thought, nodding.

"I can now make the victim's only item of clothing - a pair of boxer shorts - available to the lab, also fingernail scrapings and hair samples for analysis." Doctor Thompson moved towards the body. Pale and covered in black bruises, it was clear that the wounds on the victim's head, shoulders and hands were random and indiscriminate. Whereas the damage inflicted by Karen Thompson was far more deliberate and methodical.

Freshly-stitched post mortem wounds extended from both shoulders to below the sternum, with a third incision tracing from the pubis across the abdomen to join the other two incisions.

Seeing what had only days before been the toned, athletic body of a young man, who obviously cared deeply about his physical appearance, now lying violated, triggered a mixture of sadness and pity.

"As you can see, the attack was concentrated on the head and upper body. The majority of the contusions to the head, bruises and lacerations to the shoulders are consistent with that of a blunt weapon wielded with excessive force." Dr. Thompson pointed to the discolored portions of the boy's skin.

"Based on the bruises and the direction of the breaks in the skin here, these injuries were most likely caused by a right-handed attacker and a weapon wielded in such a manner ...." She brought her hands up above her head like she was chopping wood, then brought it down towards the lifeless body. "That's why we only see such injuries here – this kind of swing would have trouble landing anywhere else on a standing person. I have counted thirteen blows in total, though two appear to have been aimed at the head and rebounded onto the shoulder."

So whoever attacked Graham Hackett had to be at least his height or taller, Reilly thought, in order to be capable of landing such blows. And right-handed.

"The left collar bone has also been fractured, along with the left eye socket," Dr. Thompson pointed out the injuries with her little finger, the rest of her fingers curled towards her.

"The victim's hands took quite a bit of punishment too," She continued to move their attention along Graham Hackett's muscular arms, to his hand where his fingers pointed in several unnatural directions.

"Ring, middle and index fingers on the right hand were all fractured, as well as open fractures to the middle and index fingers on the left. If we look closer at the left hand it appears the skin has been split from the metacarpals all the way down to the capitate."

At this point, Reilly found herself looking away from the gruesome image of a skilled young athlete's hand that had been all but split in half.

"But the blow that I speculate ended the attack, as well as the victim's life, is indicated here." Karen Thompson gestured to the partly caved-in part of Graham Hackett's skull, "and I can only speculate, based on the condition of the injury and the fissures in the skull, that this was the same weapon used to distribute the bruises. Although coming from a slightly different direction - diagonally, right to left - again indicating a predominately right handed attacker. The width of the impacted area is roughly ten centimeters by twelve centimeters in an oval shape. The bruising of the outer skin also has some unusual impression markings ..." The pathologist indicated the impacted area. "The damaged area is bisected by this impression here, which may well be easier to make out from the original crime scene photos."

At this, Thompson snapped off her gloves and retrieved some photographs from a folder on a workbench nearby. "You can clearly see the variances in discoloration of the skin. And the victim's shorter haircut means this rather distinctive impression marking, almost certainly resulting from the murder weapon, is clearly visible."

The others took turns looking through the gruesome photographs.

"Any thoughts as to what kind of weapon would have caused such impression markings?" Reilly asked, studying the photo.

"Not particularly, though it does seem to suggest the weapon could consist of two different materials. If you also look along the length of that rather defined rectangular shape, there are also what appear to be small round indentations." Thompson pointed out the very faint markings on the photo with the pen. "All laceration wounds are relatively clean, but we did isolate a fibrous material found in one of the deeper wounds to the victim's shoulder. Perhaps you can cross reference this with any other trace found at the primary scene. Given the material's location inside the wound, I would surmise it was either on or part of the murder weapon," the doctor concluded, as she placed the photos back in their folder.

"I think I know what it is..." Chris said suddenly, studying the photos again. "The rectangular impression gives it away."

"What?" Kennedy asked. "The murder weapon you mean?"

He nodded. "Remember all those trophies in Hackett's room?"

Kennedy seemed to think for a second, but Reilly didn't have to. "The hockey stick?" she supplied. Although in truth, the sports implement depicted on the trophies was flatter and much longer than that. But yes, such an object could definitely inflict the kind of damage poor Graham Hackett had suffered.

"Not a hockey stick, a hurley stick. They're made from wood - ash to be specific - but some of them also have steel bands across the curved part. Gary will know what I'm talking about."

"Jesus ..." Kennedy shuddered, obviously visualizing the attack playing out in a whole new way.

But as always, Dr. Thompson was unmoved. "Sounds about right. I've ordered the usual bloodwork as always," she told them, "but we won't have the results for a few days at least. Otherwise, that's all I've got at present."

The four stood silently in front of the body, then, almost as though they were giving Graham Hackett a final moment of silence he could no longer appreciate.

Soon the doctor spoke again. "I must admit these are some of the hardest," she said quietly.

Surprised, the other three looked in unison away from the corpse and up at Karen Thompson. She was famously stoic, worked with dead bodies every day, and it was easy to assume that to a certain extent, these things no longer bothered her.

"Such a young kid, his life so cruelly ended," she said, glancing down at the body, "just as it was truly about to begin."

The others seemed to understand exactly the kind of feeling she was expressing, and they stood solemnly in the room for a moment more, before eventually leaving Thompson to her work.

CHAPTER NINETEEN

Kennedy straightened up when they were out of the ring of despair that seemed to hang over the mortuary building. He pulled his thumbs through the belt loops of his pants and hiked them back up, muttering under his breath. "Walloped in the head with a hurl ..." He ran a hand over his head. "This whole case is depressing, honestly."

Chris seemed to nod his agreement, but distractedly so.

For Reilly's part, seeing the kid's body again like that under the artificial lights, triggered unwelcome emotions in her chest yet again. It was as though the new part of her, the budding life inside her, was now reacting to the evil and wrongdoing that she had been exposed to for much of her adult life.

Normally she let nothing get to her, and when something *did* get to her, she kept it far from her workplace. Certainly, none of her coworkers needed to know about such concerns.

"Reilly."

Chris said her name like he had uttered it a few times before, yet failed to garner her attention. She looked up at him, and satisfied she was listening this time, he looked at her closely and said, "We should head back for a quick debrief, and cross-reference any preliminary findings with the investigation so far."

"Of course," she said, a slight blush coming to her cheeks at the obvious signs of her distraction.

The three made their way back to the GFU in Chris's Ford, lightly discussing between them what they'd established from witnesses so far.

"The girl is still insistent that her attack and Graham Hackett's murder is just coincidence and completely unrelated," said Chris. "But you know what they say about coincidence..."

"Dunno, for what it's worth I think the whole Holly Glynn thing is a bit ... off," Kennedy proffered.

"How so?" Reilly asked from the back seat.

"Well, I would like to think my two would keep their wits about them for starters...it's a big deal to be set upon and attacked by a complete stranger like that, and yet have no recollection of any of it."

"Well, alcohol would have been a factor..."

"Yes, but surely it's the kind of thing that would

sober you up quick-smart? All we got from the young one is dark clothes and the smell of fags off him - I mean, it's next to nothing."

"So what are you thinking? That she's holding back? Or could be that there was something stronger than alcohol at play?" Reilly mused. She'd wondered about this now given the drugs element to the boy's attack.

"Rohypnol?" Chris suggested.

"Perhaps. She could well be holding out either."

"All I'm saying is we still don't know for sure that she didn't know the guy. Best to keep an open mind. And speaking of which," Kennedy added, rolling his eyes as he angled his head towards Chris. "Yer man here has a real hard-on for Simon Hackett."

Chris was quick to explain. "I don't know ... the kid's had a bad attitude from the get-go. His reaction to his brother's death was plain ... weird. He was completely unaffected."

"Everybody is different though. I've seen people totally withdraw when something like this happens. Circumstantial denial: some people, especially younger ones are unable to process what is happening around them."

"Reilly, this guy is no kid - he's nineteen years of age. That term you use so much springs to mind - Okom something." Chris searched for the phrase.

"Occam's Razor?"

"Yep that's the one; sometimes the simplest explanation is the correct explanation. There's a drunken party, two brothers fight, everybody leaves and one brother is dead the next morning...Occam's Razor." Chris insisted as they pulled into the GFU car park. "Multiple witnesses have confirmed aggro between the brothers that night. Simon says he went to a nightclub, but we haven't yet been able to confirm that and even if he did, he still had plenty of time to attack and kill his brother after he got home, if say, the argument started up again. I just think Simon Hackett needs to remain a strong suspect, if not our most likely one at this point."

"I hear you, but it's still early days," Reilly demurred.

When they reached the building, Kennedy made a quick pit-stop, while she and Chris proceeded back to her office.

"You seem preoccupied lately..." he commented idly. "Try not to let this case get to you. I know it's not easy with the victim being so young, but..."

Reilly squared her shoulders and braced herself, keen to change the subject. "It's not just that. There's something else on my mind actually."

She looked up into his soft brown eyes then, realizing that they held a spark of uncharacteristic hope. She then wished her admission could have been uttered slightly differently so Chris knew for sure that the news he was about to receive was not something he would be happy to hear.

"Todd ... he's coming to Dublin," she blurted, unsure

why she was telling him this. "Arriving next week. He'll be staying with me." She also couldn't figure out, for the life of her why she had added that last part. Sure, she ·felt like she needed to tell Chris, but now it just felt like she was pushing it too far, rubbing it in, even.

He stared at her for a moment, and Reilly saw that brief optimistic flare quickly disappear. She felt a growing sense of dread as the look was replaced with something akin to disdain.

Chris blinked, then said in an indifferent tone, "That's great news - I'm very happy for you. But do you think we could go through those reports now - particularly the ones from Tech? We've got a lot to get through."

"WHAT'S UP YOUR HOLE?" Kennedy had managed to completely sidestep manners and come out with it in the brashest way possible, as usual.

He and Chris were grabbing a bite before heading out to question some of the other kids in attendance at the Hackett party.

At the GFU, Rory had provided them with a comprehensive list he'd collated of teens in attendance - as well as their full names and addresses based on his analysis of Graham Hackett's iPad and social media correspondence, giving them a good idea as to who they should talk to next.

The cafe they had chosen for lunch was out of the way, small and local. It was hardly ever busy and that helped them to get in and out fast. Plus, the food was decent.

The mid-afternoon sun was barely peeking through the clouds that spread over the sky like slush on concrete, and a gray glow from that pushed through the blinds to the right of their table, casting Kennedy in an artificial light.

The big man took a bite from his chicken burger shortly after asking the harsh question, and as Chris stabbed a piece of his own salad he watched as grease dripped from his partner's chin and back onto the plate.

It was fortunate the menus of their favorite cafe for lunch were so varied in their options, or the two might have never eaten together. The staff always managed to get a laugh out of the detectives' very differing orders, no matter where they went.

Salad is for rabbits, Chris could hear Kennedy saying, and often did on countless occasions. He watched as his colleague took another huge bite of his burger, and this time a glob of mayonnaise fell from the bun and hit the plate like a bomb. If Josie knew about the poison her husband consumed for lunch (or indeed breakfast) on a daily basis, she would probably kill him. Or Chris, for letting it happen.

"I'm fine, thanks for the concern," he responded gruffly, stuffing another bite of greens in his mouth.

Irrespective that he'd never met the guy, he couldn't get the visual of Reilly and Todd Forrest together under the same roof out of his mind.

Alone, together, cooing over their impending new arrival. Her admission earlier had knocked him for six and while he did his best to conceal his surprise not to mention annoyance, he wasn't so good at concealing his resultant mood.

Kennedy muttered something under his breath and Chris ignored it, certain it was better for the both of them if he didn't hear what he had said. He was always muttering something or other under his breath, and Chris never knew whether or not he was meant to hear it.

He had to wonder again what exactly Todd's relationship with Reilly was. He knew of course that they'd had a torrid affair during her time in Florida, but was she in love with the guy? Did she potentially want to spend the rest of her life with the father of her child, raising it together?

And likely in the US.

It made sense, if Chris thought about it objectively. Reilly was American, her baby's father was too, so it was only logical that their child should grow up in the States, with his or her two all-American parents with their perfect white teeth and bright smiles...

Would Forrest's visit herald the start of that process?

"You've hardly touched your rabbit food," Kennedy said, wiping his face with a napkin, then balling it up and tossing it on his now-empty plate. The older man wasn't stupid – he had an idea why Chris was off-form, "so either tell me what's up, or suck it up so we can get the job done."

Chris looked up at him, grateful for his partner's intervention into his quickly deteriorating thoughts. He pushed his salad away, his appetite as absent as it had been when they walked in, and slid out from under the table.

"You're right," he said, standing up, "let's just get this job done."

CHAPTER TWENTY

"So we've now definitively ruled out any recent sexual contact between Graham Hackett and Holly Glynn, but there is ... " Lucy had been speaking when she entered Reilly's office, and when the younger tech finally looked up from the lab reports she was holding, she saw her boss and mentor sitting behind her desk, her head in her hands.

The gray from outside was pushing its way into Reilly's office too, and it only managed to wash her out in a light of sadness. Lucy tried to decide whether she should go to her and comfort her, or if she should just leave. They were close but their relationship had always been one-sided - Reilly the one helping her.

She finally concluded that perhaps Reilly would prefer if she didn't see her in such a vulnerable state, so she turned to the door to make her silent exit.

Reilly snapped her head up before she could leave, however. She inclined her head toward the report, with only a hint of a wobble in her voice, "There is what?"

Lucy swallowed and stepped back inside, quietly closing the door behind her, before looking back down at the report in her hand. "There is definitely matching trace evidence from both scenes. Julius extracted epithelial DNA as you know, we've run the comparisons and he's now confirmed it as definitely being from Holly Glynn."

Reilly ran her ponytail through her hand thoughtfully, before continuing on as though Lucy hadn't just walked in on her in a vulnerable state. "Any luck in narrowing down any of the other trace?"

Lucy tried her utmost not to look at Reilly's face and glanced back down at her notes, "We've isolated many different components rolled from the victim's body, but have yet to identify some of them. Gary has been focusing on one substance in particular, and though he doesn't have all of the chemicals figured out yet, he thinks it might be some kind of undiluted soap or shampoo or something. There's also some interesting organic trace that might be ..."

Reilly nodded and cleared her throat, "Okay. Why don't you head back to the Hackett house before it's released, and take samples of all the shampoos and body wash you can find. Then if we can narrow it down to one of those, we can rule it out as being significant."

"Of course." Lucy nodded again, tucking her papers under her arm in her haste to leave the room. Despite herself, her eyes darted from Reilly's face to her ever-expanding girth and Reilly knew what she had concluded.

Once everyone at the lab found out about her pregnancy, all of them had been treating her differently. As well they should when these days she was liable to fall to pieces at the slightest provocation.

It looked as though Lucy was going to leave, so Reilly gratefully sunk back into her chair, but then the door was opening again.

"Do you want to talk about it?" Lucy asked, her expression showing obvious concern. She closed the door behind her to give the two of them privacy.

Reilly shook her head, knowing that the younger tech just wanted to comfort her, but wanting to scream at her to leave. Most of her emotions were intensified from the pregnancy, and she knew that she really wasn't mad at Lucy, just frustrated in general.

"I'm fine," she insisted, trying to regain her authority. But the ball of emotion in her throat was still there, and it came through in the slight wobble and distinctly higher pitch of her voice. She cleared her throat again and said, "Go get those samples."

For the first time in her career, Lucy ignored a direct order from her superior and did her best to don a logical tone, one she knew Reilly would respond to.

"Cut the crap," she said, throwing her notes on one of the other chairs and taking a few more steps up to the desk. "I just came in here and saw you upset. The evidence clearly shows that you are *not* fine, and now I am gathering more information to try and determine what I can do to alleviate your distress."

Reilly ran her hand over the smooth leather of her chair, feeling a flutter of humor rise up in her throat. "Lucy, I'm fine honestly. While I appreciate your power of deduction, I'd rather you focused it on the current case, and not on my emotional ... " With that, her voice broke off as her mind wandered through her spiel to Lucy, and brought her back to the reasons she was upset in the first place, sending a fresh wave of emotion through her. Defiant tears brimmed in her eyes.

Lucy rushed over to her, attempting to comfort her but Reilly held her hands up, attempting to ward her off, but still she moved around and put a reassuring hand on her arm. "When Grace disappeared all those years ago," she said, "my parents were there to comfort me and help me get through it."

She felt a few moments pass as Reilly said nothing, then Lucy continued, "When last year - thanks to you - we finally found out the truth, my folks and friends were there to comfort me too. And you helped give us the closure we needed. Just like with a physical injury, you're never going to heal if you don't let someone take care of you. You can't walk around on a broken leg and expect it just to heal. You have to let someone help you."

Reilly took a few seconds to calm herself, then turned to Lucy. "Thank you, but honestly I'm fine - just tired," she said sincerely, though deep down knew that the younger woman was right. She needed to purge.

Maybe when Todd arrived she could discuss all of this with him - outline all her fears and worries - irrational or otherwise. He worked in the same field so would surely understand.

He'd also promised on multiple occasions that he'd be there to help her every step of the way.

But try as she might, Reilly couldn't imagine Todd Forrest being able to comfort or reassure her in the way that Chris had done the last time she'd fallen victim to overwhelming emotion.

And she wondered if it was this realization that made everything feel so hopeless.

CHAPTER TWENTY-ONE

"Next up.... Megan Wright - friend of the Glynn girl apparently," Kennedy said, checking the name against another partygoer the GFU had provided. The report was a comprehensive biography that included the girl's name, address, age, height, even her weight... as well as her most recent Instagram post: a picture of a coffee cup and a biscuit.

Kennedy shook his head; that kid who sat in the GFU computer room all day staring at screens had really outdone himself. For the life of him, he could never remember the guy's name but what did it matter. Techies ... they were all the same.

He and Chris made their way to the door. Seventeen year old Megan was obviously expecting them, and she opened the door before they even knocked. Her bright green eyes shone out from under a pair of thick rimmed black glasses, and her dark brown hair was pulled up into a high bun on top of her head.

She was dressed in lounge clothes; a pair of yoga pants and an oversized sweater. It was apparent by her wide eyes and fidgety manner that the girl had never been involved with the police before, and she seemed incredibly nervous, if not resigned to the fact that they were bound to show up at her door.

"How are you doing, Megan?" Chris began kindly, once they were seated in the house, wanting to warm her up before they got to the actual line of questioning. "I know Graham was your friend. Holly too."

"Well ..." she said, swallowing and licking her lips, "I mean, not so great really. Graham is dead and my best friend was practically raped. And I..." she trailed off as she started to tear up.

"Why don't you just walk us through the details; everything that happened the night of the party," he urged gently.

"Well," she began again, "Holly, Sarah, Lisa and I were all at Lisa's house when Graham Whatsapped us about a party he was having that night. His parents were away and he had a free house. So we decided we might pop over there later. We were in good form and in the mood to celebrate, with the exams being over and everything. Lisa's parents are pretty cool so they let us have a few drinks there, and Sarah brought along a bottle of vodka. Though Lisa's folks didn't know about that - we drank it in her room. You won't tell anyone? She would get in serious trouble."

Chris assured her through gritted teeth that her secret was safe, but he wondered why the parents had been so lax about seventeen year olds getting hammered under their own roof. Then again, would they really have been able to stop it? If the kids didn't drink at the house, they'd do so elsewhere.

"By the time we got to Graham's house, we were all fairly... well on." Here Megan gave the detectives a guilty look. Evidently a euphemism for 'blind drunk', Chris figured. "I don't really remember what we did there other than dance a bit and have the craic, but I do remember there was this one lad, and he was hot, or at least I thought so at the time. He looked to be older, college guy. I think he was one of Simon's mates."

Chris nodded, satisfied that this so far checked out with Holly Glynn's account of events that night.

"So ... we got chatting, flirted a little and eventually he asked if I wanted to go somewhere a little quieter. We walked down to the trees behind the house, and I thought he was fun, he seemed really nice ..." At this point in the story, Megan started sobbing again.

"On our way out," she said through her sniffles, "we saw a few others on the back deck - Graham was there I think, and definitely Holly. When Holly saw me with Simon's friend she came after us." Megan rolled her eyes a little. "She's always acting like a kind of mother to the rest of us, holding us back and stopping us from hooking up with just anyone ... you know." At this, she reddened massively and Chris had to try to remind himself that this was a seventeen year old girl talking about 'hooking up' with complete strangers.

He worried for little Rachel his god-daughter, and what she would have to face by the time she reached Megan's age.

"So me and the guy ... Peter his name was ... we ducked and dived a bit until we lost her." Megan was really crying now, her tears rolling out in thick sobs. "We thought it was funny."

Kennedy found a box of tissues on the table next to her and handed her one so she could collect herself.

"I didn't see her again for the rest of the night. Simon's mate and I ... hooked up in a field behind the house. Afterwards, I went back inside, and when I couldn't find Holly, and as most of the others had gone home, I assumed she'd gone too."

"Peter...do you happen to remember his surname?"

"I didn't ask," she said guiltily. "It was my fault wasn't it? What happened to Holly. I went off with some guy and left her, which meant she had to walk home on her own and was attacked ..."

"We're not sure what or why it happened," Chris said, hoping to move her off the subject of Holly a little. It was an important aspect of their investigation yes, but the whys and wheretofores of Graham Hackett's murder was more central.

"What can you tell us about Graham? You two were friends?"

"Yes, I didn't know him very well though - he and Holly were closer. I still can't believe he's dead... who would want to - "

"That's what we're trying to figure out. You said that you noticed Graham and Holly together out on the decking that night. Can you remember who else was in that group?"

"Well, his brother, a couple of other guys from the team - the usual crowd. I don't know; I really didn't take much notice."

"What about your...friend, Peter - did he also go back to the house after your ... encounter?"

She reddened again. "Yeah, I think so. We walked back together but I went upstairs to look for my friends and I don't know where he went after, sorry. But you couldn't think - he's a nice guy - he wouldn't..."

"Again, we're just trying to piece together events on the night Megan, we're not suggesting anything. You're sure you don't know Peter's surname? But you said he was a friend of Simon's."

"I think so because he was older, but I can't say for sure. He could just as easily have been one of Dean's mates."

"Dean?" That was the second time the guy's name

had come up in the student interviews - Tiernan had pegged him as Graham Hackett's steroid provider - but there was no mention of him on the GFU info as yet.

"Yes, he hangs around with the team mostly. I've spoken to him a couple of times but I don't really know him, or anything." Now Megan looked guilty afresh, as she obviously wondered whether or not the detectives were aware of the guy's illegal activities.

He hangs around with the team...

"What's Dean's surname, Megan?"

"I'm not sure to be honest - he doesn't go the same school as us. Goes to Andrew's."

Private school, Chris realized, surprised and cursed himself for his innate bias. He'd been imagining some scumbag dealer from a shady part of town, but it sounded like this particular dealer's family was minted.

Clearly they needed to find this Dean and have a word.

"I'VE BEEN DIGGING a little deeper into the older brother," Rory told Reilly, just as she was about to head for home.

It was after seven PM but he was pretty much working round the clock on the online aspect of the Hackett investigation. "Seems there's a little more to Simon that meets the eye."

"How so?" she asked, again mindful of Chris's adamant suspicion of the brother.

The computer tech pushed his chair over to an adjoining terminal and woke the screen from its sleep. "I've been backtracking, and a couple of Facebook memories on Graham's profile from five or six years back - as far as Simon's secondary school days - reveal that big bro was quite the Gaelic star - even better than his brother."

"Facebook memories?" Reilly wrinkled her nose. "Those annoying little reminders of old posts or pictures that appear out of nowhere now and again?"

"Not out of nowhere; - they're set up to appear automatically on the corresponding day you shared the info or photo. It's supposed to incite nostalgia - like an anniversary of sorts."

"Wonderful. So what kind of nostalgic moments did Graham post featuring Simon?" She leaned forward to look at the pictures Rory indicated of the older Hackett brother hurling on the pitch, and some of him with fellow team members. She shuddered a little, reminded of the damage the sports implement they were so innocently using could do to a human body.

Hurling: a cross between hockey and murder ...

"That's not all," Rory said, clicking through more posts, "seems Simon played Gaelic games throughout secondary school, and even in uni for a bit. But once his studies started becoming too overwhelming I suppose, he gave up sport and started to focus on exams and whatnot."

"Okay, but..."

"I also looked through some of the posts other people were making about Simon quitting. His team-mates were upset for starters – seems big bro was pretty good. No one seemed happy with his decision, least of all his brother. Look at this one from Graham, posted just a couple of days after Simon announces he's packing it in..."

Some people just don't take the game seriously... smh.

"SMH?" Reilly asked, figuring it was Simon's initials. They'd have to find out his middle initial to be sure. When she said as much to Rory he started laughing, nearly doubling over in his chair and Reilly watched him, bewildered.

When the lab tech had recovered a little, he wiped his eyes and said, "SMH means *shaking my head*, Reilly."

"Oh. Okay." She rolled her eyes, feeling older and more out of touch than ever.

"So given that the brothers had some big argument the night of the murder, I wondered if this might be related. With tensions already high after Graham's big brother gave up Gaelic, and by all accounts everyone seemed disappointed in the decision, maybe something Graham said about that might have sent Simon over the edge?"

Reilly nodded. "I'll flag it up with the detectives."

She thought about Graham Hackett's body, senselessly beaten to death with a hurl on the floor of his own bedroom.

Something had certainly sent someone over the edge that night.

CHAPTER TWENTY-TWO

The following morning, Chris and Kennedy walked into a lively youth hangout cafe, both men uneasy and out of place.

Teens were scattered throughout, lounging in comfortable, weird shaped chairs, sitting at tables with their ears plugged up by music.

"Kids these days ..." Kennedy remarked, shaking his head as the two detectives made their way to the counter.

Chris could only imagine how Reilly would feel in a place like this. His nose was hardly half as sensitive as hers and he could smell all sorts of stuff. First, the coffee was incredibly strong, then burnt milk, cooking smells, and the stench coming from the guy sitting in the corner, watching them closely.

Who knew being a part of the cool crowd meant

you wouldn't shower - ever? Chris glanced back at the guy, then turned around when it was apparent he had no intention of lessening his gaze. Deodorant must have been off limits, too.

Neither of the detectives particularly liked tracking people down at their place of work, especially in dives like this. The person of interest they were looking to talk to, Rebecca Davies aka *Becks* - flagged as important by Rory's analysis of Graham Hackett's social media - had listed this place as her job on her own social media profile.

A boy aged around nineteen or twenty was busy working the counter, filling cups with coffee and low-fat vegan mocha lattes. His jet black hair was freshly washed and brushed up on top of his head in a common metrosexual style. He was thin and reedy, a pair of thick-rimmed glasses perched on his nose. The kid was what Chris would have called a 'Norman' when he was in school, but these types were the new cool, apparently. He thought of the slogan on Rory's T-shirt back at the GFU: *'Nerds rule the world.'*

Kennedy wrinkled his nose as the boy poured something made of soy into a cup and served it up to a young girl. What had happened to good old coffee?

"Excuse me," Chris said, approaching the kid from the side of the queue. "Is Rebecca here?"

The boy narrowed his eyes, looking immediately

suspicious, "Who's asking?" he muttered in an insolent tone.

Chris matched the kid's flippant attitude by pulling out his credentials. "We need to talk to her," he stated in his most authoritative tone. The kid's eyes widened and he glanced over his shoulder before looking back at the detectives.

"She's out back," he said quickly, his loyalties to Rebecca stretching only so far, apparently. Then he stepped to the side and unlatched a small door that would allow them through to the kitchen area. "She's on a fag break," the kid added.

"Cheers mate," Kennedy said, as the two walked around him and through the door.

Outside the dimly lit cafe, the sky mirrored the cement's depressed gray color, and heavy clouds threatened rain. It had been drizzling earlier when Kennedy and Chris set out and their clothes were still damp.

Summer in Dublin.

A girl was sitting on a concrete step, her legs bent at a right angle in front of her. She was clad in a casual uniform similar to the one the kid inside the shop wore, minus the black apron. Her long brown hair was streaked with multiple colors and tied up on top of her head. She brought a cigarette to her lips as the men approached her.

"Rebecca Davies?" Kennedy asked, horrified by the sight of someone so young poisoning her lungs like that.

A heavy smoker himself, he'd always told his own two that hell would descend on them if he ever caught them smoking anything.

She looked up at them, her gaze almost bored. Her face was small and young, though her eyes were hardened with experience which made her look older than a teenager. Her lips were painted pink and she had heavy eyeliner around her eyes, shadowing her face.

She looked away as she blew the smoke between her lips and into the heavy city air. When she turned back, she threw the butt on the cement, snubbing it out with her trainer, and said, "I suppose you're here because of Graham?"

Kennedy and Chris looked at each other. So she knew the grim fate of the boy with whom she had been flirting online. "Yes, we are," Kennedy said, "you're a person Graham was in touch with most in the lead up to his demise, so we'd like to ask you a few questions."

The cigarette butt she had thrown on the cement was already long dead, but she kept turning it over and over with the bottom of her worn footwear. "Well, it doesn't sound to me like I've much of a choice," she said coolly, picking up the mostly demolished cigarette and tossing it in a nearby skip.

"Did you attend the party at the Hackett residence last Wednesday night?" Chris asked. He'd never understood smoking - there were much better ways to stimulate the dopamine in your brain.

"Nope," she said, "I was here, working until closing at 11. You can ask Jonathan in there, or any one of the regulars. Security camera in there, too, but doubt it works."

Kennedy nodded and made a note to get a copy of the footage as soon as they were finished. Likely just hours and hours of those weirdo kids in there with their strange hippy music, but they'd have to cover all the bases.

"What about after 11?"

She shrugged. "I just went home - you can check with my roommate. Teenage parties aren't really my thing."

"Tell us about your relationship with Graham Hackett? You two were....close?"

The girl regarded them indifferently for a moment, then she sighed and said, "Listen, I know why you're here, so I might as well just tell you the whole story so we can get this over with. I don't know anything about Graham's murder, other than the fact that it happened. And to be honest, I wasn't that shocked to hear about it. For someone who was so fucking obsessed with popularity, Graham wasn't that popular. He loved the rush he got from people being impressed by his GAA shit. I think maybe that's why he was interested in me in the beginning, because I didn't pay him any attention."

She stopped and picked at her shoes for a moment, taking a deep breath as if gathering her thoughts.

"Okay. So how did you two meet then? He seems a little ... out of your circle."

"You mean younger than me?" She snorted. "I went out with his brother for a while. Over that time, I got to meet Graham a bit, but I didn't really know him - Simon used to just parade me around the house just to annoy his folks - like he was the cat and I was a dirty mouse he'd dragged in. That's part of the reason I broke up with the wanker — he was just using me to get back at his parents for something. Who knows what? But it worked; they were terrified their golden university kid was going to stick with someone like me," she let out a snort and started digging around in her pockets, probably for another cigarette.

"Someone like you?"

"Yeah. Let's be honest detectives, I'm not exactly the kind of girl you bring home. The Hacketts didn't want their high-achieving son getting involved with a no-hoper dropout."

"And what about Graham? He obviously didn't feel that way."

Her face changed a little then. "Graham came in here one day a while back to get out of the rain. When he saw that I was working here, he started hanging around a bit more. We talked a bit, and I realized he was actually okay - a lot sounder and more down to earth than his brother. Then after a while he took it a bit further, asked me for my number.   Started texting me and the like. Looking back, maybe I shouldn't have encouraged him but Graham was Okay. Everyone had him pegged as this brainless jock type but he had a smarter side, too. He listened to music ... and poetry," she jerked her thumb toward the brick hall behind them, "like it was more than background noise. I liked that about him. It was a shame he had to keep all that flare inside him a secret from his other friends. A pain to have to pretend to be something you're not but I guess we can all be like that." When she found the cigarette she was looking for, she lit it. "Like I said, what Graham cared about the most was what people thought of him. How many points he could score, how many *girls* he could score."

"And did he score - with you?"

She shook her head defiantly. "When I started thinking about Graham as more than just Simon's little brother, I ended things with Simon. He didn't know anything at all about us being friends unless Graham told him since." Her composed face was falling away as she desperately puffed on her nicotine, "But I guess I'll never have the chance to ask him, will I?"

"When exactly did you break up with Simon?" Chris asked, the wheels turning in his head.

Rebecca looked down and sighed. "Last week - the day before that stupid party."

Bingo...

Chris's senses were immediately on high alert. Was *this* the cause of the argument between the brothers that night? Perhaps Simon found out that his brother was sniffing around his girlfriend, and the two had come to blows? Which might explain why Simon seemed so unmoved - self-righteous almost - when they interviewed him the following morning.

But was Graham - apparently a known player with the ladies - moving in on his girlfriend, motive enough to make Simon his little brother's killer?

"I know what you're thinking. You're wondering if Simon knocked off his brother because Graham was interested in me. But that's not the way Simon works. He likes to act like he's all tough and apathetic and all that bullshit, but when it comes down to it, he wouldn't do anything to hurt Graham. I know he sat up late with him the whole week of his final exams to help him study and in fairness, he's the one who helped make Graham the player he is." Rebecca shook her head, "Graham never even gave him credit for that. He never did realize what he had in Simon. He might have been a wanker to everyone else but I know he really cared about his brother. Some of us get useless waster siblings who never help us with a thing in our lives, but Graham got Simon."

"The grass is always greener and all that..." Kennedy quipped.

"Nope," Rebecca said, getting to her feet, "you pull the grass up, and the other side is usually made of muck. Are we done here?"

As the detectives made their way back through the hangout and out to the car, they were silent as they climbed in.

A couple of minutes passed before Kennedy startled Chris by voicing his thoughts rather suddenly.

"Do you think the kid was in love with that girl - the Hackett kid, I mean?" he asked.

Chris looked at him from the passenger seat — neither of them was keen about sharing their feelings. He considered the question and realized that he didn't know. It was hard to tell with other people, hell, it was nearly impossible to tell for yourself. Those two kids hadn't even known each other that long, and they were so young. Didn't it take a certain amount of maturity to be in love? Didn't it take a certain amount of time, of seeing them every day, spending moments together, until you knew for certain?

Then again, a person was a person, and love was love. Chris could recall one time in particular he had been so taken with a woman he hadn't even stopped to think. Just because the love wasn't convenient or logical didn't mean it didn't count.

"I don't know," Chris shrugged, after a long pause, "Maybe he was."

Kennedy shook his head, and Chris was surprised by how interested his partner was in all this. "So he loved her and didn't get a chance to tell her, didn't get a chance to see where it would go, where it would take them. Now he's dead, and she can move on and tell all the people she wants to tell, but it'll never be the right person."

When Kennedy caught the confused look Chris was giving him, he said, "I met Josie when we were around that age. What would it have been like to never tell her I loved her? Or got married and lived this long together? When you find your person, you find your person, Chris," his partner said.

Kennedy's words stirred something in Chris's gut, made him almost nauseous. Before he had a chance to try and figure it out, his partner went on. "When you find your person, you find your person. And if you decide to put off telling 'em they're your person, then you risk losing everything. They could be taken, or gone or even dead the next time you see 'em. So what I suppose I'm trying to say is, don't risk it, mate." He looked sideways at Chris, who by then truly didn't know what to say. "Don't risk your person."

CHAPTER TWENTY-THREE

MuddyPaws: *Hey S, have you spoken to Holly yet? How is she. Messaged her and her phone is still off.*

Missislippy: *Yeah called around earlier. She's still a bit shook up.*

MuddyPaws: *Oh no, it's sooo awful. Think I'll go see her later, I can't sleep thinking about it. If only I hadn't gone off with yer man...*

Missislippy: *She doesn't blame you Megan, she's just torn up because she can't remember what happened. Said it was so embarrassing telling the cops she was too drunk to know exactly what happened......and in front of her mam too!*

MuddyPaws: *Was she badly hurt? Hearing all sorts of rumors but don't know for sure, did someone try to ... you know?*

Missislippy: *He tried, but no, TG. She has some bruising* *and scratches, but she got away from him. She's more a mess mentally, coz she can't remember what happened.*

MuddyPaws: *Gosh, I know we all had a good bit to drink but I didn't think any of us had enough to black out!? You don't think maybe someone slipped something into her drink or something...?*

Missislippy: *I've thought about that myself, espec when she's always such a mother hen making sure the rest of us don't go mad. I told the cops that I didn't think she had too much to drink, but I could see them kinda just rolling their eyes.*

MuddyPaws: *Were you talking to them for long? They seemed to be here for hours, asking all these questions basically about what everybody has been up to since Junior Cert? I mean, you think it's more in their line to be out there trying to find out who attacked Holly and poor Graham. Made my blood boil!*

Missislippy: *They were here a little while I suppose, but they asked for my phone to see any photos taken from the party or earlier in the night. I was morto tbh - the state of us.*

MuddyPaws: *Yeah same here, don't think a load of grinning eejits will tell them much. When they asked me about my photos my heart dropped...*

Missislippy: *S**t - I never even thought of that. Did you tell them anything? About the photos - the other ones, I mean?*

MuddyPaws: *Feck no! That's ancient history as far as I'm concerned and I didn't want them to think I was annoyed* *at G for anything. Before you know it they'll haul me down the police station thinking maybe I did it or something.*

Missislippy: *You're probably right. But what if it comes out? If they asked for our phones they're probably going through G's too.*

MuddyPaws: *Well, fingers crossed they don't find anything and he deleted everything since. Last thing I need...*

CHAPTER TWENTY-FOUR

The sun shone down on Lucy Gorman's blond bob as she parked in the street and gazed up at the Hackett house again.

It looked so much like the others in the estate, the kind of normal unassuming home where the visit of evil feels alien and misplaced.

Gary got out of the car and stood next to her.

They walked up to the house. Despite the horror that had happened inside only days earlier, the exterior looked prim and neat, and the lawn was only barely grown up over the line of the concrete pavement.

The interior of the house was still trashed from the party that had inevitably been Graham Hackett's downfall. Empty beer cans were littered across the impeccable carpet and cups had tipped over on the tables. The refrigerator door was still hanging open, though someone had unplugged it, and the pile of vomit from the misfortunate first responder, still lay at the foot of the stairs.

Because of the astringent-related trace found on the victim's body, they were here to assess all bathroom products the Hackett family used to ascertain if there was anything they could rule out. If not, then they had to conclude that the trace had come from the killer and was worth pursuing further.

The small bathroom downstairs truly was also in a wretched state – it appeared that the pile at the bottom of the stairs had come from the same person who hadn't made it to the bathroom, because the remainder of the vomit was in the small, well decorated room.

The glass-fronted shower was elegant and the surround decorated with slate limestone up to the ceiling. A shining chrome shower-head arched from the wall at the height of the surround. The shower tray appeared to be clean, thankfully none of the partygoers had thought to take care of their business behind the sliding glass door.

Lucy carefully gathered samples from all the soaps and shampoos on the shelf inside, taking care to mark each with the specific brand and amount used.

Gary did the same in the bathroom upstairs, then poked through the bedrooms, though avoiding going into the victim's room, where the blood was still spattered on the walls in the same pattern now preserved forever on iSPI. Once they released the house, a team of professional cleaners would show up to take care of the gore.

He started to descend the steps back down, but stopped when something caught his eye.

A picture was hanging on the wall next to the multitude of photos of Graham Hackett and his teammates, but this one was of him and his brother Simon, clad in full GAA team gear and grinning at the camera, a hurley resting against their thighs.

A few generic family pictures were in the hallway too, but the majority of the photos proudly focused on the Hackett boys sporting achievements.

Ironic that the sport the brothers loved so much had ultimately proved to be Graham Hackett's endgame.

"Gary?" Lucy calling his name made him jump a little. She appeared at the bottom of the stairs, the samples tucked away inside her kit bag. "Come on,' she said, shuddering a little. "I'm ready to get out of here."

"Edward Lyons?" The late evening sun beat down on the backs of Chris and Kennedy as they approached two teenagers facing off in a hurling knockaround.

The training pitch Graham Hackett frequented was full of lads practicing and running laps, and the air smelled of freshly cut grass and sweat.

The two players stopped tussling, and one caught the *sliotar* under his foot. "That's me," Edward said, stepping forward. His teammate slunk back toward the goal, knocking the ball around and occasionally hurling it into the net.

"We have a few questions to ask you in relation to the incident at Graham Hackett's house," Kennedy began, taking out his notebook. He rattled off the relevant date, "You're Graham Hackett's former teammate, yes? And you attended the party at the Hackett residence on Wednesday night?"

"Yeah, I was at that party and Graham's my mate," Edward said warily, reaching down and grabbing a sweatshirt. He snatched a water bottle from the ground and took a long drink before pulling his shirt on.

"Can you just run us through everything that occurred as you recall it?" Chris put in, watching the boy's reaction carefully.

"Yeah. Well, we were down here training for a bit, then afterwards we went for something to eat and then over to Graham's - at around ten o'clock I'd say. We hadn't really planned on staying at his house that long, we just wanted to finish up the booze Simon scored for us, then maybe head into town -"

"Hold on," Kennedy said, his eyes narrowing, "are you saying Simon Hackett bought alcohol for you? What age are you?"

Edward shrugged as if it was no big deal. Which in

reality it wasn't. Underage drinking was par for the course in Ireland and Chris wasn't sure if he was impressed or horrified that the kid didn't even bother to hide it. "I'm seventeen and yeah when we got there Simon was heading out to the off license so we asked him to get us a few flagons."

"Cider?"

Edward nodded. "As more people showed up at the house more alcohol showed up too - beer, whiskey, tequila too, I think. I don't know if Simon bought it all, or it was just in the house or whatever, but it was there."

"Okay," Kennedy said. "So there was no shortage of alcohol at the house that night. Tell us what else you remember."

"Some of the girls showed up, so we stayed around a bit longer having the craic with them. Then, just as me and a few of the others were about to head away, Simon and Graham got into a spat over some stuff."

"What kind of stuff?" Chris asked.

"I'm not really sure. Graham said something smart about Simon's hurling, and I know that must have hit a sore spot."

"I see," Kennedy said, "what about you and Graham Hackett? How was your relationship?"

Edward shrugged, "Dunno really. We were team-mates, not like best friends or anything, but he was good craic. We hung out a bit now and then, but not usually just the two of us or anything. He was sound though - didn't deserve what happened to him."

"Do you know if anyone else might have had anything against Graham though?" Kennedy continued. "Anyone that was jealous of him - who might want to hurt him?"

"No," Edward said, appearing to think for a moment, "I don't think anyone really had a problem with Graham. Other than some of the teachers, just for not getting his homework done, or whatever. But not enough to... you know..."

Chris was watching the other kid on the pitch puck the ball into the net again and again, each one aimed with more intensity. He drove the *sliotar* with a precise skill that must have been honed by hours upon hours of practice. "Who's your friend?"

Edward glanced over his shoulder as if he didn't remember who he'd been practicing with. "Conor - our best player." Now he was blushing furiously, his cheeks burning a brighter red than they had been when he was training. "He's the best football player in the school too, leaving for Australia soon to go play Aussie rules in Sydney. We'll miss him though ... I mean, I'll miss training alongside him. I reckon I can learn a bit from him, wouldn't mind a shot at Down Under myself, but I'm not so great with the bigger ball..."

Kennedy seemed to have skipped over Edward's rambling while focusing on the other kid's talent, but

Chris had paid close attention to the boy's curious emotional reaction to the question. "Conor ... Glynn?" he asked, recognizing the name.

Edward swallowed, hard, and Chris watched his Adam's apple bob in his neck. The kid's cheeks reached a new level of maroon as he said, "Yeah. He's Holly's brother."

"And was Conor at the party that night?"

Edward shook his head and glanced back over his shoulder at the other boy, "No," he said, his voice holding more than a hint of discomfort, "he doesn't really hang around in our crowd."

Chris gave Edward a reassuring pat on the shoulder, understanding his situation to some extent. It was a certain kind of hell to be interested in a teammate - especially for a traditionally macho sport like Gaelic games.

Poor divil.

"And does Conor have a girlfriend or ...anything?" he asked pointedly, and Kennedy whipped back round, suddenly interested in the odd direction the interview had taken.

Edward met his gaze, confirming Chris's unspoken question. No, the object of his affection did not know the extent of Edward's feelings, nor his sexuality. "Not that I know of - but I don't really know him well outside of training."

"One last thing," Kennedy asked then, "what can you tell us about Dean Cooper? He a friend of yours?"

Edward rolled his lips into his teeth. "Dean? He's all right, I suppose. Used to play with the club at one stage, but he put out his shoulder a few seasons back, didn't bother coming back after. He's more of a gym bunny these days."

"We found some pills in Graham's room, Edward. Know anything about that?"

The teenager looked away and reddened afresh. "No, but it doesn't surprise me one bit. A lot of the lads on the team use stuff now. That's why some of them have it even more in for the likes of me and Conor – he doesn't do any of that shit, and he's still the best on the team."

Chris raised his eyebrows, "And yourself?"

"I couldn't afford it even if I wanted to."

"You have the right idea - only talentless gobshites do that stuff," Kennedy reassured Edward, as they finished up their questioning.

"Did you see the Glynn kid out there?" he said to Chris as they left the pitch. "Some technique. He'll be playing for the Dubs before I hit forty."

Chris looked sideways at him, and chuckled. "Well if he's off to Oz soon, he'll hardly be playing on the Dublin team. And aren't you fifty-two?"

Still chuckling, he reached into his pocket to take a call from base. Then he looked back at this partner.

"Nice one. For once a public appeal paid off. One of the neighbors in the Hackett housing estate just found something interesting in their recycling bin." He threw a glance back at the training pitch. "We might have our murder weapon."

CHAPTER TWENTY-FIVE

All heads turned when later that evening, Gary carried a long, plastic-clad piece of wood into the GFU lab, having safely retrieved it from the family who'd found it in their recycling bin not far from the Hackett house.

"Well?" Reilly asked, with raised eyebrows. "What have we got?"

"Looks to be the weapon all right." Gary was breathing heavily with the excitement of a potential breakthrough, coupled with his purposeful trot with the new evidence from the van to the lab. "Whoever put it there certainly wasn't trying to cover his tracks too hard. There's blood on the end - the *bas* - and lots of prints on the handle. I've dusted the recycling bin too, so here's hoping ..."

"Okay, let's take a look." Reilly took the lead,

removing the hurley stick from the large evidence bag. Putting the bag to one side, she carefully placed the slender wooden implement - about eighty centimeters in length - down on the examination table's recently sterilized surface.

This was Reilly's first look at a hurley up close, and it struck her how much craft had gone into shaping the stick from what was apparently a single piece of timber.

Her eyes scanned the flattened bottom, the now dried-in blood was indeed covering a large portion of the curved '*bas*' as Gary had referred to it. There were small clumps of bloodied skin tissue and even some hair protruding from beneath a thin metal band nailed around the curved and flattened base.

She immediately recalled the impression marks on Graham Hackett's autopsy photos, now realizing they made sense. "Julius, get ready to run analysis on the blood to confirm it belongs to our victim, and more importantly, if any of it belongs to our doer. Lucy, you do the prints."

"I thought this was interesting ..." Gary pointed with a pen towards the edge of the bas. "I'd say this has seen plenty of action, there's a few small chips out of this end, so much so that the edges are starting to flake off."

"What are you thinking?"

"Those small flecks of organic fiber the ME talked

about - inside some of the victim's wounds? Could be wood chips from there?"

Reilly nodded in agreement as she leaned in for a closer look, studying the banding. "Anyone know what this actually does?" she asked indicating the metal strip. "I would have thought it would be a dangerous addition to what already looks like a pretty lethal piece of sports equipment ..."

"It's added to give strength; stops the wood breaking in challenges," Gary told her. "Ever hear the expression; Clash of the Ash?" When she looked blank, he shrugged and continued. "Ash is a strong wood, and it needs to be to withstand the punishment these get in a game. Hurleys are typically made from the denser timber found in the lower sections near the root of the tree, but the metal is still added at the business end, for even more strength."

"I'd imagine it helps to puck the ball even further too," Julius commented.

"It's not allowed in *camogie* though, is it?" Lucy mused. "The banding I mean."

Reilly was baffled. "*Camogie?*"

"Women's hurling," Gary told her.

"Then why the hell isn't it just called women's hurling?" She shook her head bewildered by such intricacies. "Gary, process any trace and prints you took from the bin, and cross reference with the Hackett crime scene. Lucy you do the same with the stick, and with luck we'll soon be able to confirm we do indeed have our weapon."

Despite the gruesome circumstances, she felt a familiar, almost instinctive thrill when a breakthrough, a real breakthrough presented itself.

Finally, they were getting somewhere.

CHAPTER TWENTY-SIX

Biception: *Hey G, saw that pic of you lifting the Inter-schools trophy - nice one. Pecs looking ripped; that don't come free, you know.*

HackR: *Listen man, I've said you'll get your money. Lay off with the smart comments on my page, I saw what you wrote.*

Biception: *Well then, pay up and maybe I'll shut up. It's nearly 3 weeks since that last batch, you'll owe me a tonne at this stage.*

HackR: *I said I'd sort you out FFS.*

Biception: *Fair enough, those candies are the good stuff though, so don't go thinking of getting cheap imitations some-where else. They might make your c**k fall off...*

HackR: *Actually, there's a couple of other lads on the team that might be looking for 'improvement' - maybe cut me a deal if I introduce you?*

Biception*: Absolutely bro, as long as they aren't like that other snowflake p***k.*

HackR: *Don't mind him, he'll be out of our hair soon.*

Biception: *The sister is a different story tho, think you could hook me up - you've hit that up before, haven't you? Might be able to write off that last batch you owe me for...*

HackR: *Don't think a classy chick like H would be interested in a gym rat like you tbh. You'd be too busy making love to yourself to pay her any attention...*

Biception: *We'll see - I don't usually have any complaints in that department. Anyway, don't forget me bro, I have overheads to pay. If you're looking for anything coming into the summer hols let me know and I can get you stacked.*

HackR: *You're unreal D-man, coming on here to shake me down, and then end up trying to sell me Skittles too! Good luck with that.*

REILLY READ through the printout Rory had left on her desk of Graham Hackett's (who they'd since established used the screen name HackR) recent online correspondence. She was guessing from the topic of conversation that 'Biception' was the screen moniker of Graham's friendly steroid dealer, identified by some witnesses as Dean Cooper. Despite the detectives' - and indeed Rory's - best efforts, they hadn't yet been able to locate Cooper.

Notwithstanding the fact that Graham was clearly

falling behind on his payments - an obvious motive - it also seemed that the two were discussing Holly Glynn, albeit in a harmless generic manner.

It seemed to her that Cooper was a decent possibility as a suspect; perhaps on the night of the party he and Graham Hackett had an argument over this unpaid debt, resulting in a struggle that resulted in Cooper beating the former with a hurley stick? Cooper certainly knew how to use the thing - according to what Rory could ascertain, the teen had once been a member of the same club Graham played for, before apparently picking up a shoulder injury.

Still injury aside, the kid would have been well capable of wielding the weapon with enough force to cave in his former teammate's skull.

But would an unpaid debt have provoked such rage?

Just then, Reilly's phone rang interrupting her thoughts, and she picked it up, immediately feeling a rush of mixed emotion when she saw Todd's name on the caller ID.

As soon as she answered, his voice was coming through the speaker in a steady stream.

"Hey!" Todd greeted. "Good morning."

"Well, it's afternoon here but good morning to you," she said.

"So my flight's due in at threeon Thursday. Still all good for you to come pick me up - or should I just get a cab to your place?"

Reilly bit her lip. Picking him up might work, but what she wasn't sure was if this whole *visit* was all good.

She had no idea what would happen once she and Todd came face to face and they had to confront the uncomfortable situation they were in. Not to mention, try to figure out how to work it from here on out.

"It's fine - I'll pick you up," she finally replied.

She could hear the smile in Todd's voice as he said, "Great, see you then."

She hung up the phone and leaned back heavily in her chair.

For some reason, despite herself, Reilly's thoughts turned to Chris - something that happened a lot these days when she spoke to Todd. The kiss they'd shared before she'd discovered her pregnancy, the many times he'd consoled her with his arms, relaxed her with his words, saved her from the worst.

Every so often she was reminded of the feel of his hands in her hair and his inimitable musky scent. She determinedly shook the thought away as following a soft knock on the door, she came face to face with the man himself.

Think of the devil...

"Hey, good stuff about the hurl, "Chris stepped into her office.

She nodded. "It is. We're still waiting on analysis, but we're pretty sure it's the weapon used on Hackett. Nice catch at the autopsy about that band."

He shrugged modestly. "Kennedy's just in with tech, hoping Rory can help us track down that Cooper kid." Chris then quickly outlined the progress or more to the point lack thereof, he and Kennedy had made in finding Graham Hackett's drug dealer. "Seems kids are getting into this stuff younger and younger," he went on, shaking his head. "Idiots. You can only imagine the amount of damage it does. I see it all the time with some of the lads at the gym too."

Reilly tried her utmost to keep from her mind the image of Chris pumping iron at the gym, but it was difficult. "You haven't been tempted to buff up too?"

"What - you don't think I'm buff enough?" he quipped, a twinkle in his eye and she was glad that after the other day's wobble, they seemed more at ease with each other once again.

"True. Maybe it's Kennedy who needs help that way," she chuckled, thinking of the other detective's increasingly rotund form, despite his wife's best efforts.

"I wouldn't chance saying that to his face if I were you," Chris warned. "Poor divil would have a stroke at the notion of performance enhancement of any kind. Though" he added wickedly, "I'd be interested to know what Josie has to say."

She suppressed a laugh as Lucy appeared at the doorway. "We're all set up with iSPI whenever you're ready," the younger woman told them.

"Thanks. We'll be right there," Reilly stood up, and Chris followed her out towards the Tech room.

Murder weapon aside, the investigative team hadn't had much luck with either the evidence or the interviews for the Hackett investigation so far.

Hopefully, the virtual reality program would give them another perspective.

"So you're pretty sure most of Graham's teammates and friends from the party are too short to be his murderer ..." Reilly mused to the detectives, her hand on her chin as she paced back and forth in front of iSPI's virtual reenactment of the crime scene using the data Gary had input from the various scene markers and spatter analysis at the Hackett house.

The dark figure depicting the killer projected onscreen was about half a foot taller than Graham, but about the same build. Predominantly right-handed, they gripped the weapon - a composite rendering of the recently-found hurley stick - with both hands as they advanced.

As the footage played through, the virtual assailant stalked forward while the victim lay on the floor, bloody and beaten, but not yet dead, before setting up the weapon for the final blow that would end his life.

"Holy feck," Gary whispered. Watching this on iSPI

he knew it would be a long time before he sat down to watch a hurling match with his mates again - if ever.

Chris and Kennedy were standing in front of the projection, both going through the notes they had gathered from their interviews.

"Certainly none of the girls at the party would have been strong enough to inflict this kind of damage," Chris pointed out. "And not just that, but all of the attendees have solid alibis - Simon Hackett excepted."

"I dunno, I still think the brother's all talk," Kennedy said, insistent - for reasons unknown to everyone but himself, Reilly thought - that Graham's older sibling was completely innocent.

Yet to Chris, perhaps even more since the discovery of the bloodied hurley, and recent revelations about the brothers' sporting and romantic history, Simon Hackett remained the most likely suspect.

"The best fit for this dark silhouette is pretty obvious," he insisted again. "Simon Hackett got into an argument with his brother the night of the murder. He had both motive and opportunity; easy access to the room, and reason to be upset about the fact that Graham was making moves on a girl who had just dumped him. And Simon's own sports prowess indicates not only an easy familiarity with the murder weapon, but also represents an interesting choice for same. Graham taunts his brother about being a failed hurler, so perhaps Simon feels inclined to remind his little brother about his proficiency?"

It all sounded incriminating for Simon but Reilly wasn't quite persuaded. "Problem is we don't have any forensic evidence suggesting Simon," she said. "His prints weren't on the murder weapon, and there's nothing putting him in the bedroom that night either."

Chris threw his hands up in frustration. "Well, what the hell *do* we have then?"

Reilly bit her lip. Unfortunately, still not a whole lot.

CHAPTER TWENTY-SEVEN

The next morning, Lucy leaned over her computer, trying desperately to identify another piece of organic trace they had discovered on the victim's body - this one with petroleum components. Once they were able to figure out what it actually was, it might well lead them a step closer to finding the person that killed Graham Hackett.

She glanced up for a moment at Gary, who was working just as diligently, running comparisons for the substance they had found with that strawberry scented astringent. Although they had hoped the chemical make-up would match up nicely to some kind of soap, or shampoo, they'd been disappointed when they couldn't immediately identify a corresponding soap or shower gel from the Hackett house, and now Gary was doubly determined to find out what the substance could be.

"Stare much?" Gary asked, when he glanced up to find Lucy gazing at him, a thoughtful look on her face.

Though they had been officially going out for a couple of months, she still blushed when he caught her staring at him, which made him smile and briefly tear himself away from his work.

"What are you thinking about?" he asked, walking over to her workstation and leaning on the counter.

She glanced back at the microscope, trying to decide if it was okay to tell him what - besides lab work - was on her mind. In truth, she couldn't get Reilly's emotional state from the other day out of her mind. Though Lucy was certain the turmoil her boss was experiencing was not affecting her job performance, it didn't stop her worrying for her.

Reilly had relentlessly pursued the dormant case of Lucy's missing sister, and eventually figured out what had happened to Grace. Lucy would never be able to thank her enough for that, and since then she had considered the older woman a friend.

Lucy looked into Gary's concerned face and had to smile softly at him, for he had worked tirelessly to help Reilly with that too. "It's nothing," she finally said, deciding to protect her boss's privacy rather than appease her own worries. She grinned. "I just like looking at your ugly mug."

"Would you two stop goofing off?" Reilly said then, startling the two of them as she walked through the lab, her flats making no noise on the linoleum floor. Gary whirled around to look at her, his eyes skipping, as they always seemed to lately, down to her protruding middle before settling on her face.

"Gary," she said, gaze narrowing, "do we have an update on any more of the Hackett trace, yet? Anything useful from the murder weapon?"

He shook his head sheepishly and glanced back at Lucy, giving her his own discrete wink. "No, ma'am," he intoned in his best American twang, "but you can bet your bottom dollar that we're working on it as hard as we can."

"We're still going over the chemical makeup of that astringent-like substance," Lucy piped up. "It doesn't match any of the soaps or shampoos we took from the house yesterday. Nothing jumps out, but we have managed to discern that the substance is scented with synthetic strawberry."

"Okay," Reilly said, pondering what this could possibly mean - particularly if it related to Graham Hackett's attacker. Strawberry scented trace seemed overtly ... feminine.

They'd already established that Holly Glynn, or indeed any of the girls at the party could surely be ruled out – none of them possessed anywhere near the minimum height and strength projected by both iSPI and the autopsy findings, to have beaten him to death like that.

Curiouser and curiouser...

"Julius," she asked, moving across to the older lab tech's desk, "how's it going with the prints? Have you worked up any comparisons?"

He looked up from his computer, "I have and fat lot of good it did me. None of those prints on the weapon or the house were in the system, but as the majority of the latter belong to the Hackett family – with the exception of a couple of partials, there's really no reason for them to be."

Another dead end...

Next, she checked in with Rory.

"I've continued digging back through the various social media streams, which paint a pretty decent picture of what Hackett and his mates got up to in the run up to that night," he told her. "We already know that Graham Hackett and his closest mates are these big superstars of the school Gaelic hurling team. Which means they've almost always got girls throwing themselves at them. But looks like Graham isn't the only one on the team juicing. His mates do it too, as well as a handful of others who seem to be on the fringes. Holly Glynn's brother shows up in a couple of interactions in the team WhatsApp, but from what I can tell, Hackett and his mates don't think much of him."

Reilly leaned over his shoulder and read through

some of the interactions he'd highlighted. "Any idea why?"

Rory shrugged and spun around in his chair to face her, leaning back and taking a long drink of his favorite poison. "Probably because Conor Glynn is far and away the star of the team, despite the fact that he doesn't seem to use. Or maybe it's just that the whole team partakes in this PED crap thanks to Dean Cooper, but Glynn doesn't. That sets him apart, paints him to be this snowflake type - exactly as Hackett and Cooper described him in their interaction - like he thinks he's better than them or something? Judging from his own social media I don't think that's too far from the truth. He seems a bit of a self-righteous dick. Not to mention the fact that he's got a scholarship for Aussie rules, worth hating for that alone. Lucky bastard."

"Okay." Reilly figured most of her lab colleagues could really use a holiday. The Irish seemed unhealthily obsessed with sunshine, though hardly surprising when they got so little of it.

"Anyway, I'm still working on trying to find Cooper ...and I think I might have cracked it. This is very old - back as far as Cooper's playing days." Rory clicked around on his computer a bit, bringing up another set of interactions on Snapchat, this time between someone whose screen name was 'D-Man' and a girl using her own name and who Reilly recognized as being one of Holly Glynn's friends.

She leaned forward to read the feed, her eyes taking a moment to adjust to the screen.

D-Man: *Hey*

Sarah: *Hey*

D-Man: *What are you up to?*

Sarah: *Just watching TV - what are you doing?*

D-Man: *Just back from training. Thought of you in the shower ;)*

Sarah: *Of course you did. So how was training? Do you think ye'll win at the weekend?*

D-Man: *I don't know, maybe we will if you suck my...*

Reilly's eyes widened, reminding herself that these kids were what...barely seventeen? Possibly even sixteen if this particular discussion was from some time ago.

"So I'm thinking D-Man could well be an alias for Dean. I'm going to keep digging, see if I can get a full name and contact details. Or at least a work address or something."

"Good work. Sarah's a friend of Holly Glynn's isn't she?" Reilly asked. "Anything like this between Holly and the boys?"

She hoped not. The girl she'd met at the hospital seemed so innocent - a million miles from this sordid interaction. And she really hoped crap like this wasn't seen as a carte-blanche invitation from the guy's point of view. Never in a million years would Reilly suggest that a girl's own actions triggered a sexual attack, but surely this kind of stuff was playing with fire?

Rory shook his head. "Not that I've found anyway. Holly seems to pretty much keep to herself, except for a bit of harmless flirting here and there. Nothing too hair-raising."

Reilly hoped not. But still she worried what this kind of blatantly sexual interaction was doing to teenagers who couldn't possibly have the maturity to handle them, let alone the consequences.

Those were hard enough to handle for fully grown adults.

CHAPTER TWENTY-EIGHT

Chris drove around the perimeter of the Guinness Brewery on the city quays, a distinctive aroma of roasted barley wafting through the air vent of the car; the mere scent of Dublin's most famous export no doubt triggering Kennedy's taste buds.

For once the obligatory media public appeal had paid off.

The day before, a taxi driver had called the Garda hotline about a fare he'd dropped off in the very area Holly Glynn had said she was attacked. The driver had noticed a girl walking by, but didn't think anything of it. Now he did, and the detectives were wasting no time in going to talk to him.

Chris maneuvered around the parked open top tourist buses lined up outside Kilmainham Jail.

Further down the road he glanced at the piece of paper upon which he'd taken down the address, and slowed to check the name of the group of townhouses on the left hand side. Confirming he had the right place, he indicated and pulled into the nearest available space.

"Must be where all the taxi drivers live,' Kennedy quipped, as he unfastened his seat belt and opened the passenger door simultaneously. Parked in the residents' area were no less than three taxi cabs.

Chris scanned the house numbers on the brick clad homes which seemed to be uneven numbers on the bottom and even on top, all accessed by granite paved steps. They walked up the steps and pressed the door-bell of number twenty.

After a few seconds they saw through the frosted glass panel a shadow moving towards the door.

"Howyiz," a slightly balding middle-aged man greeted them.

"Andy Cummins?" Chris asked.

"Yep, that's me."

"I'm Detective Delaney this is my partner, Detective Kennedy - we spoke on the phone earlier...." Chris trailed off, allowing time for the man to join the dots.

"Ah sorry pal, I was in a world of me own there - come on in," Andy said pulling the door open fully.

"Cheers, we won't take up much of your time,"

Kennedy told him as they walked down the hallway in the direction the taxi driver ushered them.

"Ah, no worries, I'm not heading out till this evening. I was at the airport rank early this morning, and am not long home for some kip and a bitta grub. Here have a seat, do ye want a cuppa?" Andy asked, as he picked up the kettle and started to fill it at the sink in front of a window which looked out across industrial units alongside a network of railway tracks and idle train carriages.

"Tea would be great thanks," Chris said as he looked out across the yard through the sliding door beside a small table. The door opened out onto a tiny patio area railed off with a grimy glass-paneled balustrade. The patio/balcony seemed to be primarily used for drying clothes and storing bins as opposed to the alfresco enjoyment the architect had intended.

But this was Dublin, not Paris.

"What's all that over there?" Kennedy asked, following Chris's gaze.

"The old rail works," Andy told them, placing the kettle back in its dock and pressing the on switch. "Used to be the big employer around here, had hundreds of workers back in the day. Me old man worked there. Pretty dead down there now though. Some people think its ugly, but I like it. It reminds me of being a kid; I got to go down the country with the 'oul fella when he was sent out on maintenance trips."

"You from around here then Andy?"

"Yep, born and bred. Place has totally changed over the years though, you'd hardly recognize it now," he said in a wistful tone, as he continued his tea-making ritual.

"You been in the taxi game long?" Kennedy asked, continuing the small talk until Andy was finished.

"Yeah, pretty much all me life. Took over me uncle's plate before they deregulated the taxi game. Cost me a fortune. Had to take out a mortgage for the plate, then eight years later any Tom, Dick or Harry could roll up with a banger and get one for nothing," Andy said with some bitterness. "Ah well sure, them's the breaks. I'm still able to make a crust, and that's the main thing." He placed the cups on the table before fetching the milk and sugar. "There's another driver who lives a few doors down, they have two young kids; don't know how they manage with the rents around here."

"Yeah, I noticed there was a few cabs parked up," Kennedy remarked as he stirred his cup. "So I believe you had a lift out to Churchtown on the 18th?" he said, getting down to business.

"Yep, I remember seeing the news the next day and thinking I'd just been out there. I recognized the road straight away."

"You mentioned to the tipline operator that you let a fare out on Taney Road?" Chris continued, reading from his notes and trying to direct Andy - who they'd already established had a tendency to ramble – to the information that interested them most.

"Yeah, it was a really busy night. Lots of kids out after the exams finished, and plenty of tourists around too. I got back into town at around twoish from a drop off in Bray and joined the ranks on Dame Street. Young lad comes up heading for Churchtown."

"Do you remember the specific address he wanted?" Kennedy asked.

"He just said Taney Road. I asked him where abouts exactly, because it's a long road and it's often the ones who give you a non-specific address that end up doing a runner," Andy said nursing the tea cup in both hands on the table. "Though yer man didn't look like a runner to be fair. He was a well spoken young fella, and didn't seem too drunk either."

"So you dropped him to Taney Road and ...?" Chris prompted.

"Well, that's the thing that bothered me," Andy said shifting in his chair. "We passed a young one near the Luas bridge walking a bit wobbly. I remember her because it was quiet enough around at that stage – the pubs were all closed. I hate seeing girls out alone like that, especially with a few scoops on them," the older man said and Chris was pleased with this level of recollection. Dublin taxi drivers missed nothing, that was for sure.

"Anyway, my fare had been quiet enough all the way

out, but as soon as we passed the girl, he pipes up and says he'd get out on the side of the road. I look in the mirror and see his head swiveling looking back down the way and I just assumed he knew the young one," Andy said looking pained. "It was only the weekend when I heard the appeal about the beating over the road and an attack on a girl that I got a sick feeling in my stomach." He looked horrified by the notion that his actions in dropping off his fare might have played a role in the incident.

But Chris was heartened by this information. If that girl was Holly, it meant that she'd been telling the truth all along that her attacker had come out of nowhere. And more importantly, it suggested that the incident was thus likely unrelated to what had occurred at Graham Hackett's house.

"Can you give us a description of the guy you let out?" Kennedy inquired.

"He was young, late teens if not early twenties I'd say. Big bloke and tall – I'd say over six foot but lean with it. He had no jacket with him even though it was cold enough out. Hard to say what color his hair was at that time of night, but I'd guess it was dark brown, black even. But the weird thing that struck me at the time was the strong smell of perfume off him." Andy made a face.

Chris looked at him. "Perfume or aftershave?"

"No, I'd definitely say perfume because it was really

sweet, sickly almost. Bit odd, but of course you get all sorts these days, though in my time young fellas would get the crap kicked out of them for going around smelling of poncey stuff. But not anymore."

Weird, especially when Holly had mentioned her attacker smelling of cigarettes - a decidedly different kind of perfume...

"What about the girl, can you describe her?" Kennedy asked.

"I can actually go one better than that," Andy said, looking smug. He reached for a laptop nearby. "I can show you."

He opened the computer and the screen illuminated to show a paused image of a streetlight-lined suburban road, taken from the inside of a car.

"Dash-cam. Can't be without one in my game. Sure you've foreigners and all sorts of dodgy scum rear-ending you and throwing themselves on the bonnet and then trying to claim insurance," Andy muttered with some disgust, as he rotated the screen to face the detectives and pressed play.

*You beauty...*Chris thought, marveling at how modern technology could make their jobs so much easier sometimes. He sat forward eagerly.

The dash-cam footage - taken from the vantage point of the windscreen - complete with timestamp, showed the car driving down a road both detectives quickly recognized as Taney Road. A little way on, the headlights of Andy's taxi illuminated a young blonde woman in a short black dress walking unsteadily on the footpath in the same direction the car was traveling, her head pointing towards the ground.

They would have to get the footage over to the GFU for greater enhancement but at that point, they were both confident that the girl was indeed Holly Glynn.

"What about sound?" Kennedy asked.

"Sorry, picture only I'm afraid," Andy said apologetically. "We're not allowed record anything inside the car - passenger privacy, you know yourself."

"This could certainly prove useful," Chris said, trying to hide his enthusiasm. "Could we have a copy?"

"No worries, this is actually a copy I made myself once I knew ye were coming - you can hold onto it," the other man said, taking a portable drive from the side of the computer and handing it to Chris.

"Thanks bud, you've really been very helpful," Kennedy said.

"No worries, glad to help," Andy said as he closed the laptop. "One other thing I did forget to mention before," he continued, escorting the detectives out. "The lad I picked up - as I said, he was very quiet in the cab altogether. I only got a couple of yes or no answers out of him, so I figured he wasn't up for the chat. I was talking about the summer being terrible as usual - you know yourself, small talk - but he answered something along the lines that he wouldn't have to worry about shite weather for too much longer." The driver scratched his head as the detectives went back outside. "Dunno if that's any use to you, but sure, I said I'd tell yiz anyway."

CHAPTER TWENTY-NINE

The following day, Reilly reluctantly took the day off and spent the morning tidying up the flat to ensure everything was cleared away and ready for Todd's arrival.

As personal as things might have gotten between them in the US, she wasn't quite ready for him to see the level of outward chaos in her life.

She surveyed the meticulously cleaned room, realizing now how lonely it looked. Nobody else had sat on the couch in weeks, the table was permanently set for one person, the other spot being the place where Reilly usually spread case files out to review while she ate.

Maybe having another person in the flat for a little while wouldn't be such a bad thing?

By the time she pulled up to the Arrivals area at Dublin airport, she was already five minutes late. She'd forgotten what traffic on the M50 could be like and was momentarily appreciative of the fact that she didn't need to use the infamously busy motorway to get to work.

Battling her way through the crowds to get inside – with all the talk and notice at work about her pregnancy, the gathering crowd of travelers had no qualms about ramming their elbows into her tender stomach as they hurried by, clearly more concerned about getting to and from their flights – she made her way over toward the information screens.

She couldn't help but notice the sharp smells of the airport. The sweat of the people around her, the over applied perfume that drifted above the women, and the fresh smell of new luggage.

Some of the restaurants located just outside the arrivals area advertised some greasy all day fry-ups and Reilly felt a strange craving for the stodgy food, despite the repulsive smell.

Just as she made her way to the overhead screens to check on Todd's flight, she heard someone calling her name.

"Reilly," a voice said from beside her with a hint of impatience, as if the person had been trying to get her attention for a while. She barely had time to glance up at the smiling tanned face that loomed alongside her before Todd had engulfed her in a huge bear-hug. She winced a little as the force of his muscled body pushed against her tender middle, but she managed to briefly embrace him back before he let go.

She took a step back from him then, trying to gain some much needed distance. His sun-kissed hair and deeply tanned skin was a huge contrast amongst the mostly pale-skinned passers-by, and his attire (khaki shorts and a light blue Ralph Lauren polo shirt) made Todd Forrest stand out like the proverbial sore thumb.

He had obviously taken a moment to look her over as well, noticing that she was staring at him, because when she met his gaze, he launched that thousand-watt smile at her. "Man," he said, holding her at arm's-length, "you look so ... different."

Reilly knew what that meant – she looked *huge*. She knew that her bump continued to grow frighteningly bigger every day, but she didn't want to draw attention to that if she didn't have to.

At the sight of him now in front of her, Reilly was suddenly thrust back into memories of Clearwater– the two of them together in the bright sunlight, balmy nights and laidback gulf coast atmosphere. Vacation weather was pretty much permanent in Florida; every day you walked out your door you were met with incessant sunshine.

Although, as law enforcement she and Todd both knew well that despite the cheery, bright weather, people were just as dead just as fast there, as they were in Dublin.

"And you look exactly the same," she said, rolling her eyes good-naturedly. Despite his time under the sun, it didn't look like Todd had aged at all since his twentieth birthday. It never took much for Reilly to imagine him posing on the beach, a board under one arm and a gorgeous, swimsuit clad model in the other.

And that smell... Reilly's sensitive nose caught not only the whiff of Todd's aftershave he'd applied that morning, but some underlying scents as well. He smelled of sweat, no doubt from the long plane ride across the Atlantic, yet still the tangy saltwater smell from the Gulf of Mexico drifted off him like it lingered in his pores. Reilly thought of all the time he spent by the water at his dad's house right on Clearwater Beach, and realized that it probably did at this point. The gulf coast and sunshine was by now a part of Todd Forrest's DNA.

The two walked back out into the typically cloudy Dublin gray, though it did nothing to quell Todd's never-ending stream of smiles and optimism. He commented on everything – from the lilting Irish accents all around to the bustling travelling public. When they were back in her car, he took a deep breath and turned to her.

"So where do you want to eat? I'm ravenous. Airplane food is *not* my thing."

Reilly shifted the car into gear and laughed, "Is airplane food anyone's thing?"

She immediately thought of the pub she and the

detectives sometimes went to after too many long days pouring over case files. But she couldn't take Todd there. Her two worlds were already clashing too much with him in the city at all. And she didn't need the friendly landlady seeing her with him and asking questions.

She decided to head further in towards the city and get the worst of the airport traffic behind her while she tried to think of somewhere suitable to go. Typically, she hadn't considered that he'd want to eat after the nine hour flight from Orlando and subsequent connection through London.

She truly wasn't cut out as a hostess.

When they reached a place she thought he might like on the outskirts of the city not too far from her place, Reilly parked the car a little way down the street. Todd immediately came around to the other side and opened the door for her while she was still in the driver seat. She awkwardly tumbled out, still not quite used to the additional bulk.

When they got inside the restaurant, and took a quiet table in the back, he practically tucked her into her seat, pulling it out for her beforehand.

"So how have you been?" Todd asked, once they were both seated. They'd engaged in idle chit chat in the car but she instinctively knew that this was a more pointed question about the baby. He picked up the napkin from the table and unfolded it over his lap in a measured way that reminded her of Daniel, his father.

"I've been okay," she replied, surrounded by awkward tension. "The case I'm working has been moving along too slowly for my liking, my feet are constantly aching, my head is always pounding, and the kicks I get in the middle of the night don't make for a sound sleep." She looked up at the ceiling then, knowing she had said much more than she meant to.

Todd started laughing, "Well," he said, "besides the middle-of-the-night kicking, some things never change."

Reilly chuckled and relaxed a little after that, and the two of them caught up, filling in the details of what had happened since they'd last seen each other. The waitress came and went as Todd ate ravenously but ordered more and more, and after a couple of hours, she realized the sun was nearing the horizon.

Todd must have noticed, too, because he said, "Well, I don't know about you, but I'm beat. Guess we should head back to your place and get settled?"

"Yeah, I've got an early start in the morning," she said, grabbing her coat and belongings. Todd walked her out, his hand touching the small of her back casually enough that she couldn't say anything about it.

She drove the short distance home, and every time she started to yawn, Todd would try to tell her a funny thing that had happened so she could stay awake. It worked, but only because she realized she had missed Todd's little mannerisms, not because his stories were funny.

"You can sleep here," she said, pointing to the couch along with the pillows and blankets she had set out for him. "The bathroom is through this way, and the kitchen is over there."

Todd looked briefly around the small flat, looking huge in the tiny living space. He paused, blankets in hand and he and Reilly looked at each other for a moment, as if they were both remembering a time when things had been very different between the two of them.

A time when they might have been stumbling in the door and struggling to find their way to the bedroom without once breaking apart.

She cleared her throat, "Good night, Todd," she said, turning sharply to head to her bedroom, alone.

He called after her, just a moment too late, "Good night, Reilly," and his voice managed to carry far more than the meaning of those three words. The utterance was soft and sad, and nothing like Todd, and perhaps that's the reason the expression stood out.

As she went to close the door, she turned back briefly and watched him, her hand still on the door-frame as he spread his blanket out over the couch methodically and set his pillow slanted slightly to the right, just the way he always did.

Before he could look up and see her watching him, she closed the door and climbed into her own bed, realizing not for the first time that it was empty and cold.

She wriggled around a little, trying to find a good position in the usually comfortable bed. She fell asleep shortly after Todd stopped making the usual guest noises — brushing his teeth, washing his face, and finally tossing and turning on the couch to try to find a comfortable position himself.

Reilly's last thought before she drifted off to sleep was that he would never be able to find a comfortable position on that lumpy couch, and despite herself, she couldn't help but think of the empty spot right next to her.

CHAPTER THIRTY

She woke the next morning to the smell of something cooking.

Over the years, she had done some research into the subject of nasal sensitivity and found it no surprise to discover that smell had a nasty tendency to elicit more emotional responses than any of the other senses.

For example, a man might look right past a sweater that resembled the one his ex used to wear. He might not notice a voice, identical to hers, calling across a crowded mall. But if he smells her perfume, just for a second, drifting by in the parking lot, or puffing from a cushion months later, or being spritzed in a department store, his head will be immediately bombarded by memories and emotions before he even has a chance to think.

Because that's how smell worked – it went right

through all the detours the other senses took before getting to the brain, going right through conscious thought to the part of the brain that produced emotion before you had even fully comprehended what it was you were smelling.

That's what happened to Reilly as she woke – it wasn't often that she couldn't identify a scent as soon as it hit her, and now thanks to the wonderful odors wafting under her door, she was hit with a sudden nostalgia for the warm nights she had spent in Todd's place in Florida, only to be awoken by this wonderful smell.

"Huevos Rancheros?" she said, leaning in the doorway.

Todd looked away from the pan on the stove, and the eggs sizzling away inside it, and grinned. Reilly had forgotten that she was still in the chiffon cami she wore as night clothes and she flushed, feeling suddenly exposed.

"I know they're your favorite," Todd remarked with a wink. He looked back down at the stove for a moment, then looked back up at her quickly, taking a sharp breath, "You look amazing, you know," he added, nodding once as if to be sure of it, before focusing on the food again.

Reilly flushed again, her cheeks growing warmer than she would have liked. She went back into her bedroom to get dressed, struggling a little with each layer before she joined Todd in the kitchen again.

In truth, she didn't really have time to sit down for breakfast, not if she wanted to get to the lab early enough to make up for yesterday's day off, but she spared a few minutes to enjoy the food Todd had prepared. It was indeed her favorite and she tried not to give away how well he had prepared it, but it showed clearly on her face.

Todd knew well her fondness for Rancheros.

Soon, she pushed away from the table and moved across the living room to gather her things. She was going to be late.

"There's a bus stop just down the road and a number for a cab company on the fridge if you need one," she said, feeling like a mother preparing to leave her child alone for the first time. The thought struck close to home – in a few years time she *would* be doing just that.

With an actual child.

Todd followed her as she grabbed her bag off the floor.

"You're going to the lab today? I thought we could maybe spend the day together?" he said, crestfallen. "We have a lot to talk about after all."

"I'm sorry but I really do need to get to work. We're in the middle of an investigation and it's still early stages. You know the drill...We can talk tonight."

"Okay, see you later." He made a move as if to kiss or

embrace her, but she shut down any such action by pulling her kitbag close to her chest and moving quickly to the door.

"See you later. Enjoy Dublin."

"Wait." She turned to see Todd looking around, his expression confused. After a few more glances around the room, he looked up at her, his gaze inquisitive, "Where's the TV?"

She laughed out loud, remembering his obsession with reality TV. "I don't have one," she said, grabbing her jacket, "but there are some books in the bedroom if you get bored."

Todd feigned a horrified look just before she closed the door to her flat, and despite herself she chuckled.

ON THE WAY TO WORK, Reilly found herself thinking about the Hackett case again, as well as the latest information concerning Holly Glynn's attack.

The taxi-driver's dash-cam footage confirmed the girl was indeed telling the truth about her attack happening on the way home, and that she didn't know the guy. So it looked as though their early assumption about the two incidents being connected had been proven incorrect.

But did this realization get them any further in tracking down Graham Hackett's killer?

The details filed in, presenting themselves like files

spread out over Reilly's mind the same way she'd spread them out over a workspace.

The teenager had been beaten to death in his own bedroom, by a right-handed attacker with a hurley stick in the early hours of the morning. By then, most of the kids present at the house party had reportedly either gone home or onwards to another location. The team had isolated some potentially interesting trace from the victim's body, but were having a hell of a time identifying what most of it was, let alone whether it would be any help with identifying his killer.

The detectives had already done a reasonable job of interviewing the friends and checking out alibis, but had found little untoward thus far.

Other than Simon of course. Graham's older brother had been present at the party and multiple witnesses reported that he and Graham had engaged in a verbal spat that night, just hours before the younger Hackett boy was found murdered in what was clearly a crime of passion.

To say nothing of the fact that Simon had some beef with his brother attempting to move in on the girlfriend who'd apparently broken up with him that same week, and according to the detectives, was indeed right-handed.

Another potential suspect was Dean Cooper, the former club teammate who supplied Graham Hackett, and it seemed most of the Gaelic team, with PEDs.

Thanks to Rory's determined efforts in tracing Cooper via social media, he'd since tipped off the detectives about a gym the kid frequented, and they were due to pay him a visit today.

All the various suppositions swirled in her head as she drove, and by the time Reilly reached the lab she was more determined than ever to figure this thing out.

CHAPTER THIRTY-ONE

"I'm warning you people ..."

As she neared her office, Reilly heard raised voices up ahead outside Jack Gorman's domain. Her colleague's back was to her, but she had an all too clear view of Holly Glynn's father's angry red face, shouting at her GFU counterpart.

"You are spending more time helping a dead body than finding my daughter's attacker," Glynn was complaining. "That bastard is still out there, walking around scot-free. He could be out hurting some other innocent girl as we speak!"

"Mr. Glynn," Reilly said, approaching the two men, "did it not occur to you that whoever murdered Graham Hackett could also potentially be out there, right now, hurting someone else?"

Michael Glynn quieted as he turned to look at

her. His mouth shut as he remembered Reilly as the female investigator who'd spoken to his daughter at the hospital. He took a step back from her, and she noted the jaded look that came over his face. "There is nothing more important than finding the animal that hurt my daughter," he said, finally. "Nothing. The Hackett boy is dead and gone, but my daughter has to live in fear until someone finds the son of a bitch and throws him in a cage."

"I agree that it's essential to find the person who attacked your daughter Mr. Glynn, and the detectives are following up on recent information regarding same. Our remit here in the GFU is to help with that, and we also assist in finding countless other criminals. Though I'm sure you are quite proficient in your own occupation, you'll just have to accept that this isn't your job. My team and I will do everything in our power to help the detectives track down the person who attacked your daughter, but your showing up at our place of work and shouting at people who are only trying to help you, achieves nothing but bad will."

Glynn glared at Reilly for a moment, and she faced it head on, unblinking. Eventually, he straightened his tie before sending her and Jack another glare. "Well I've already let it be known to your superiors that I am *not* satisfied with this," he said, his voice low and thick with anger, "and if my daughter does not get some peace soon, I *will* bring the matter to the press."

"We are closing in," Reilly assured him, "we will find him."

When Glynn walked away, she turned to leave, but Jack called after her.

"Are you really closing in?" he asked dubiously.

Reilly didn't want to lie to her colleague but at the same time she needed to stay optimistic. "Yes," she told him as convincingly as she could, "we are."

Afterwards, she went to the lab to find Gary and Lucy at their workstations, both of them looking worn out.

"Good morning," Gary greeted. "Or is it? Could be afternoon for all I know. Anyway, good news boss - we've been busy. We – got it or, I should say Lucy - got it late last night. That petroleum based trace we were trying to figure out is ... paraffin."

When Reilly's apathetic expression didn't match up to the reaction he'd expected he added, "Well, not only paraffin, that's just one of the components. There are a couple of others too, but we have to narrow those down yet to truly individuate. I'm still on the strawberry soap stuff – except, I really don't think that's what it is - soap, I mean. The chemical makeup is similar, yet different.

When Reilly looked pointedly at him, he nodded once and turned back to the workstation. "Right," he said, "You are absolutely right, boss - less chat, more action."

But it was good to see they were making some progress at least.

Mid-morning, she was just about to catch up on some of yesterday's lab reports, when her cellphone rang.

Recognizing the call as coming from her own home, she swallowed hard.

"Hey," Todd said in his American drawl, which for some reason felt out of place here in her office. "I was wondering what you wanted to do for dinner later - I thought I might cook?" He paused for a moment, then said, "I could pick up some food at the store nearby and maybe some strawberries for dessert."

His casual reference to the strawberries they had shared in Florida, and the sudden craving she had for them almost had Reilly agreeing to his plan, but then she remembered something. "I'll be home late tonight," she said, adding almost as an afterthought, "I have a doctor's appointment."

Todd was silent for a moment, then he said, "For the baby?"

"Yes," Reilly replied, seeing no point in lying to him. She'd almost forgotten about it until an alert on her iPhone calendar reminded her that morning.

"Okay," he said, somewhat breathlessly, "change of plan. How about I come along and then we pick something up for dinner afterwards?"

It was more of a statement than a question and

Reilly took in a breath, not ever anticipating her baby's father attending an ultrasound with her.

But given the circumstances, how could she say no?

CHRIS AND KENNEDY pulled up outside an impressive glass-fronted building close to University College Dublin.

"A long time since you frequented somewhere like this..." Chris quipped teasingly to his partner, as they walked into the buzzing reception area of X-Treme Fitness.

Showing their detective credentials to the receptionist, they were quickly buzzed through to the gym area. The smell of sweat mixed with warm rubber from the treadmills was oppressive as the two stood in the doorway trying to suss out their intended target.

After a beat, they made their way over to the weights section where several pumped-up youngsters worked hard lifting punishing-looking iron, all the while preening at themselves in the mirrored walls.

Another similarly beefy guy was sitting on a bench filling out what looked like a time sheet, or more likely Chris realized, a weight log.

"We're looking for Dean Cooper?" he called out to no one in particular, but sure as you like, the youth on the bench looked up, eyeing the detectives suspiciously.

"That's me," he said quietly.

"We'd like to ask you a few questions, son," Kennedy said, showing his ID.

"Sure, no worries. Mind if I just finish filling in my log? Otherwise I'll forget my numbers and - "

"Actually, we do mind," the big man snapped. "Listen bud, as I'm sure you're aware, your mate Graham Hackett was murdered at a party last week, a party you attended. I think talking to us should be your only priority at the minute."

Despite the detective's tone, Dean Cooper's cocky demeanor didn't slip for even a second. "Yeah I was at Hacker's house, hanging out with some of the others for a while," he shrugged. "I didn't kill anyone though, if that's what you're wondering." He remained sitting, drying his hands with a towel and then he picked up a container holding a drink that looked to Chris like muddy water.

He bristled at the guy's laid-back attitude. There was a time kids would redden up and be automatically courteous and helpful in the presence of authority. But much like Simon Hackett, this asshole had been brought up with a silver spoon in his mouth and evidently a superiority complex to match.

"So where were you between one and five AM in the early hours of that morning, Dean?" he asked. "Anyone to vouch for your movements?"

Cooper shrugged again. "I left the house just after one, I think. Me and a few of the lads got the munchies, so I drove us up to Maccers. Anyway, Hacker's gaff got boring once he and his big bro started going off ..."

"Going off? Explain what you mean by that?" Kennedy asked above the deep base of the uptempo music being played, even though every last one of the meatheads around them seemed to be wearing headphones.

"Ah. Just the brother was being a bit of a buzzkill and they got into it a bit."

"So Simon Hackett started the argument? Any idea what they were arguing about in particular?" Chris pressed.

Dean seemed to think for a second. "The brother seemed really pissed off with Hacker, but I couldn't tell you over what exactly - some girl maybe? Like I said, it was a downer so a lot of us took off after."

"You mentioned you drove some of your friends to McDonalds," Chris asked. "Were you not drinking like the others?"

Dean seemed to think the very idea was preposterous. "Ha! No point in busting my balls in here, and then going out for a skinful - I'm very careful with what I put into my body."

Chris had to bite his tongue not to bring up the steroids there and then, but decided to continue with this line of enquiry for the moment. "Are you friendly with both Hackett brothers?"

"Well, I know - knew - Graham well enough. He

used to come in here a bit at one stage, but I don't think he could handle the weights. Dunno much about the brother, except he was supposed to be some big hot-shot hurler back in the day. Seems sound enough but I don't think he and Hacker were all that close. They certainly weren't that night any way."

"And you think the argument might have been about some girl - Holly Glynn maybe?" Chris threw the name out just in case.

Dean shrugged again as he took a deep slug of his puddle water. "I don't think so. Actually, it wouldn't surprise me if she was the one who did it though. Hols wasn't too happy that they broke up. And she definitely didn't like all the attention Hacker got from other girls."

Chris and Kennedy shared a glance – this contra-dicted what they had so far been told about Holly and Graham's relationship. From what their closest friends had said, the break-up had been amicable.

"So you play on the same club team as Graham and the others," Kennedy ventured.

"I used to, but to be honest gah's not really my cup of tea. I'm more of a lone wolf, and this is more my territory," Dean replied, indicating around the gym.

"Planning to spend a lot of time here over the summer holidays so?" Kennedy asked, leading the kid toward his next line of enquiry. "No part time jobs lined up or anything?"

"Nah, be nice to enjoy a couple of months off before

I start college. Been looking forward to the break all year."

"Okay. So how does a young lad like yourself finance a three-month holiday on top of that nice little Golf parked outside?"

For the first time since they arrived, Dean shifted a little in his seat. "I've been saving ... and the old man looks out for me too. Wants me to enjoy myself before the hard work starts in college."

"So it's not being financed by your little side business then?"

"Side business? Dunno what you're talking about."

"Strange. Word is you make a nice living providing ... supplements to some of your old teammates." Chris came right out with it.

"Yeah, I might share stuff with some of my mates now and again, but they're herbal pills, legal," the younger man said, his face blanching a little.

Chris raised an eyebrow. "Legal my ass. Tell us another one." Seriously the muscles on this kid were so buff they looked like they'd been blown up with a bicycle pump.

"Look Dean, we already know you were supplying PEDs to Graham Hackett. We found the pills, we have correspondence between you both discussing payment, and we have spoken to others about it too. Things aren't looking very good for you, bud. I suggest you start talking." Kennedy let the gravitas of the situation sink in a little.

Dean stood up from the bench then, his laid-back demeanor now completely absent. His face was flushed, even though it had been a good fifteen minutes since he'd lifted his last weight.

"Look, I had nothing to do with the Hacker thing that night, okay? I left with the others and they can vouch for me, check the CCTV at the drive-in at Carrickmines if you like."

"What's to say you didn't drive back to the house after you dropped the others off?"

"Ask my mother, I went straight home. I'm telling you, I had nothing to do with it. Should I not have a solicitor here or something?" Dean was increasingly nervous and looking around agitated. "Look, the stuff I gave the lads is harmless, just a booster and a few fat burners, it's hardly like I was flogging heroin or anything."

Chris continued writing in his notebook as Dean pleaded his case.

"Well, this is an informal chat so no need for a solicitor at this point, though I'm sure we'll be in touch again after verifying some of your claims. Also Dean, you are now going to cease using and supplying supplements of any kind, legal or otherwise. You don't want that shit messing up your body, to say nothing of your criminal record."

"Right. Okay."

With that, Chris and Kennedy made their way back towards the entrance, both pretty sure that Dean Cooper would have little energy for lifting weights for a while.

They walked out into the fresh air, glad to be away from the loud music, clanking weights and monotonous drone of the exercise machines.

"How does anybody enjoy that? It's like a feckin' torture chamber," Kennedy grumbled, glad to be getting back into the car.

Chris gave him a look. "Don't knock it till you try it." Then starting the engine, he sighed. "Well, dealer or not, I think we can knock old Deano off the suspect list."

"How so?"

"Didn't you watch him filling out that weight log?" Chris looked sideways at his partner. "He's a *ciotog*."

CHAPTER THIRTY-TWO

Later that evening, Reilly grabbed her handbag from the footwell of the passenger seat of her car, and when she turned to get out, Todd was there, holding the door open for her.

Disgruntled, she stepped out. "I can still open doors," she growled as he proceeded to shut both doors while she locked the car behind them. "I'm not an invalid."

He had picked her up from work, embarrassingly.

Reilly had been on the phone to Chris, disappointed by the news that Dean Cooper was left-handed, and thus highly unlikely to be their killer.

The security footage at the McDonald's drive-in the kid had mentioned also subsequently checked out, putting Cooper some distance from the house during the window of Graham's attack.

And so it seemed they were back to square one.

Or in Chris's mind, back to Simon Hackett. "I'm going to bring him in for another chat," he told her. "There's something he's not telling us, I'm sure of it."

When security had buzzed up to let Reilly know someone was looking for her downstairs, she had rushed away quickly, so nobody in the lab would catch on to whom exactly the cute American waiting in reception really was.

Todd had dressed up for the occasion, she noted, in a dark blue button up shirt that complimented his eyes.

Now, he walked close to Reilly as they made their way into the hospital, and every so often, his hand would brush against hers. She had the feeling he wanted to catch hold of it, so she kept it firmly by her side, the fingers curled up.

"I didn't open the door for you because I thought you *couldn't* do it, I opened the door for you because I realized all the other things you do, and I thought I might take it upon myself to relieve one of those burdens," Todd explained as they walked, shooting her one of his dazzling grins.

Reilly would hardly call opening a car door a "burden" but she accepted his explanation, anyway. There was no point in arguing with him and if she did, he would probably just blame her opposition on the pregnancy.

It was something the people around her had started

doing more and more. Any time something upset her, or she was unhappy with the performance of one of her team members, she knew they secretly chalked it down to her hormones. It seemed she wasn't allowed to have genuine concerns about anything these days; everything that affected her was because of the baby.

The smell of the hospital assaulted Reilly's senses right away. Antiseptic and cleaning supplies, mixed with the smell of infection, decay and hopelessness.

She and Todd made their way up to the antenatal department, and approached the desk. "I have an appointment with Dr. Moore at six," she said, glancing back at Todd, who was looking through some of the informational booklets a little too enthusiastically.

"Sure," the receptionist said, after hitting a few buttons, "Go ahead and take a seat, and she'll come out for you when she's ready."

Reilly found her seat, and Todd sat next to her – quite close – still holding a pamphlet he'd started thumbing through. It was ironic that he wanted to read about pregnancies and babies when it was everything she could do to try to forget about it.

"Reilly Steel?" A young nurse called out a couple of minutes later, so she stood and went through the door, Todd trailing beside her.

From the look on the nurse's face as she led them through to her obstetrician's office, she seemed quite taken with Reilly's handsome companion.

"Just come inside and we'll get you comfortable on the bed. Dr. Moore should be in shortly."

As the nurse left, Reilly climbed up on the recliner and sat back against the comfortable pillows. Instead of sitting in one of the chairs against the wall, Todd stood next to her, one of his hands braced on the back of the bed, as if she was about to give birth there and then.

She caught him staring at her stomach again, and sighed, figuring if there was any place for it, it was here. As if on cue, the baby kicked. "Give me your hand."

Todd held it out automatically, though he seemed a bit confused. She took his tanned hand by the wrist and gently guided it to her stomach, laying his palm flat against it. Soon after, the baby kicked again and Todd's hand twitched like he was going to pull it away, but then stayed.

His gaze met Reilly's. "Oh," he said simply, his face filled with awe as he stared at her.

"I don't mean to disturb anything ..." Dr. Moore said, a smile etched across the obstetrician's graceful features as she slipped into the room.

Reilly blushed despite herself, and Todd removed his hand like it had been on a hot burner, as if they were teenagers caught out by an adult.

If Dr. Moore was confused by Todd's appearance at this appointment, she said and showed no sign of it. Instead, she pulled the ultrasound machine closer to the bed and snapped on her gloves as it powered on. Reilly duly pulled her shirt up and Dr. Moore smeared some petroleum jelly over her, before grabbing the machine and bringing the wand to her stomach.

Reilly winced as the wand moved over her tender skin – she was becoming quite swollen, and pressure applied to her stomach at any point by anything was uncomfortable.

Todd's face lit up as he looked at the image forming on the ultrasound. He found Reilly's hand again and held it tight, and though it felt odd, she held on too, taken by the wonder of seeing their baby moving about on the screen.

It was only a collection of white pixels, she thought, but still, she couldn't shake the excitement welling up in her chest as the baby moved.

"Everything's looking good," Dr. Moore said, smiling at the two of them. "Did we want to know the gender?"

Reilly looked uncertainly at Todd. She was incredibly torn about finding out the baby's gender. The realist in her felt it would probably be good to know so she could perhaps personalize the situation somewhat, and make it all more real, but at the same time, what did that matter? "No, I don't think so," she said.

Todd's Adam's apple bobbed as he looked at the screen. "Yeah, let's wait," he agreed, as if they'd already discussed such a thing a million times.

After Dr. Moore finished up the ultrasound and

checked Reilly's blood pressure and weight, the two of them left the doctor's office.

When they got back to the car, Todd opened the door for her again and this time Reilly simply said, "Thank you."

LATER THAT NIGHT she tossed and turned, trying to avoid a cramp in her side, and flipped the lamp on her side table on. Her room was bathed in a soft glow, and she sighed back against her pillows with the effort.

Todd was asleep on her sofa again, though he had seemed a little put out when she set pillows and blankets on the edge of the nice couch, almost like tonight he had expected an invitation to her bedroom.

It seemed to Reilly that he was remembering their time together in a different light than she – to her, their fling had been fun and fleeting, but Todd seemed to think those nights they'd shared had meant a lot more.

She reached over the side of the bed and pulled her files onto the bedspread, opening them and looking through the notes they had gathered throughout the Hackett case. It was a habit she fell into when she was feeling down or off about something – going through the details of a case created comforting grooves in her brain, like a record track she could go over and over again.

The rest of the night passed without sleep, and she

finally pulled herself out of bed hours before she needed to be up. She went to the bathroom and drew a bath, sinking into the warm water and letting the bubbles engulf her. The scent of lavender floated through the room and calmed her frayed nerves.

She had just begun to fully relax when the door opened and a tired Todd stumbled in, so intent on heading to the toilet, he didn't even notice Reilly in the tub until he was halfway there. She should have remembered to lock the door, but she lived alone so the thought hadn't even occurred to her.

He stopped in his tracks when he saw her and rubbed at his eyes, a sleepy apology falling from his lips as he woke up more, realizing he had walked in on her. The bubbles were mostly concealing, but the very top of her bump rose up out of the water, and his eyes caught on it.

She sunk further beneath the foam. "Could you shut the door behind you?" she asked, glaring as he stumbled all the way back to the door. Her tranquility disturbed, she pulled herself out of the tub and dried off.

It took her almost twenty minutes to prepare for work whereas pre-Blob she could do it in five. She pulled on a loose fitting work shirt over her head, then slowly wiggled her pants on before sitting down on her bed, awkwardly reaching down to her feet to put her socks on.

It hadn't been nearly this hard the week before.

She had been so intent on trying to pull the sock on, she hadn't noticed a dark form slipping through the doorway and into the room.

Todd kneeled down at Reilly's feet and gently took the sock from her, pulling it up snugly over her foot.

He smelled of sleep and the cologne he had been wearing the night before, and the scent stuck in her nostrils as he pulled her other sock on for her. Then he found her brogue shoes and slipped them on, tying the laces for her, all without a word.

When he had finished, Todd rose to his feet and kissed her on the forehead, before going back to the couch.

HE WAS ASLEEP AGAIN when she walked through the living area to the front door, and Reilly stopped for a moment to watch his chest rise and fall, her mind a myriad thoughts she couldn't process.

CHAPTER THIRTY-THREE

"I already told you everything I know!"

Chris raised his eyebrows at Simon Hackett from his place across the spotless gray interview table.

Now pretty much out of options, he and Kennedy had asked Graham's brother to come down to the station that morning for another interview, hoping that some sustained pressure might reveal something they'd missed. "Really? You didn't omit anything? Like maybe about how you bought alcohol for underage teens?"

Simon let out a puff of air and threw his hands in the air, rolling his eyes, "Yeah, I bought some booze for a couple of kids celebrating graduation. Big deal. Is that it?"

Chris stood up from his seat at the table, "You also conveniently forgot to tell us about the bust-up you and

Graham got into that night. Did you really think we wouldn't hear about it?"

Simon rolled his eyes, "Oh for god's sake, we're *brothers*. We get into bust-ups all the time. Am I under arrest? Are these pathetic questions the reason you dragged me down here? Why aren't you out searching for my brother's killer instead of wasting time on this underage drinking bullshit!"

Chris sat down in front of Simon, his calm demeanor surprisingly contradictory to his inner frustration with the boy. "But this wasn't just any argument, was it Simon?"

"What are you talking about?" he asked, with another eye roll.

Chris placed his hands on the table and leaned forward, "We have several people telling us it was a rather heated argument, wasn't it? Graham brought up your failed hurling career, and your ex-girlfriend, Rebecca."

"She has nothing to do with this!" Simon snapped, finally coming out of his cool and collected composure.

Chris stopped and raised an eyebrow, "It doesn't hit a nerve to find out that she actually preferred your little brother? That Graham was the real reason she dumped you?"

Simon looked like someone had punched him in the gut. He swallowed, hard and gripped the table in front of him.

"It doesn't bother you at all that your little brother, not only a far more skilled sportsman managed to steal your girl right out from under your nose too? And after you spend so much time helping him with his exams, he disrespects you and embarrasses you in front of everyone?"

Simon shook his head and looked up, "I *didn't kill my brother!*"

Chris sat back down and leant back in his chair. "Then who did?"

Simon clenched his fists and looked up at Chris with tears in his eyes, "You think if I knew that I wouldn't have already killed them myself? You think I'm just walking around, not noticing the fact that my little brother was beaten to death in the room across from mine? You think I don't feel that every second of every day? You think I wouldn't have done everything in my power to keep him safe?" At this point Simon was near screaming, spittle flying from his mouth.

Chris narrowed his eyes, still not convinced. "What did you see that night Simon?"

"Nothing. I already told you."

Chris stood up and gathered his things from the table. "Then we're finished here."

Simon stood up, the color returning to his face. Before Chris could leave, he turned to him and said in a sorrowful voice, "You may think that I killed Graham. You may think that I'm heartless enough to beat my little brother to death like that and you may lock me up for the rest of my life for something I didn't do, but I didn't do it.   There was nobody in the world I loved more than him. Not my parents. Not Rebecca. Graham and I had each other, and that was it.   And now he's gone."

When Chris exited the interview room and moved behind the glass, Kennedy cleared his throat.

"So whaddya think?" he asked, fully expecting Chris to renounce his firm belief in Simon's guilt and finally admit that he was being too hard on the kid.

"I think he's a bloody good liar."

CHAPTER THIRTY-FOUR

When, after yet another long day of fruitless analysis, Reilly walked in the front door of the flat just about ready to collapse in her bed, Todd was waiting to greet her, smiling his thousand-watt smile.

"How was work?" he asked.

She managed a smile. "It was boring actually. We need a lead, a breakthrough, you know what it's like."

Todd laughed as he moved around, taking things from Reilly's unsuspecting hands and grabbing his coat. "Oh yeah, I know what it's like," he said, pulling his arms through the dark sleeves of his leather jacket, "So are you hungry? Ready to eat?"

She blinked at him, hoping he wasn't suggesting they go out. He must have noted her exhausted look, because then he paused.

"Too tired?" he said, "Sorry, I didn't think. I can only imagine how tiring it must be, what with ... in your condition. It's just," he continued, eyeing her in a way he must have thought to be inconspicuous, "I don't know if it's good for you or the baby, to be working so much. And worrying so much. I read that this kind of thing can really affect the pregnancy."

"Do you honestly think I would purposefully do anything to hurt the baby?" she snapped, nearly snarling, "It's *my* body too, Todd. I feel fine. Yes, I'm tired but that's nothing new. So everyone can stop telling me what to do with *my* body and *my* life. I feel fine. There's nothing wrong with the baby - we saw that for ourselves yesterday."

"You're right, sorry," Todd was saying, though Reilly hardly heard him, "it's your decision. Let's just go somewhere and kick back a little. I walked around a bit earlier, and found somewhere I think you'd like."

So Reilly found herself being led from the flat only moments after walking in, and thought again of the many reasons she hadn't had a relationship since she made the move to Dublin.

Sharing her life meant leaving her familiar routine of coming home, eating when she felt like it, pouring over casework or reading late into the night - not having to consider anyone else's wishes or priorities. The irony in that, she realized, was that very soon there would be someone that would have to be her top priority.

She glanced over at Todd, wanting to resent him for the situation they had gotten themselves into, but she found that she couldn't. In truth, she blamed herself for the outcome, knowing that she should have stopped to think about the consequences of their actions.

Todd opened the door for her when they got to the restaurant, a place within walking distance of her flat that Reilly had often noticed but never tried, and her senses were immediately assaulted by the heady scents of a kitchen – different fruits and vegetables mixed in with the smell of pasta sauce and the sweet bitterness of chocolate. It was enough to make anyone's mouth water in anticipation, but Reilly was so ravenous she was almost prepared to snatch the food from the other patron's tables as she and Todd walked by.

A waiter led them to a small intimate table in the back, and she settled into the hard chair, wishing for her soft recliner at home.

Once they'd given their orders, Todd laced his fingers together, leaned forward, elbows on the table and said abruptly, "I think you should come back to Florida with me."

She stared at him, her mouth slightly agape, and he watched her reaction carefully, trying to sense if he should continue. When she did nothing but stare at him, he took that as a cue to go on, "You know I want to be a part of the baby's life, you know that I'll do anything to be a father to our child. But I realized something when I saw you standing there under those screens at the airport. I want to be with *you*, too. I want to be a part of your life, Reilly. We can raise our baby, together. In Florida where our baby can grow up in the sunshine, on the beach, with us and his or her grandfather."

Reilly blinked again, unsure if she had heard him correctly.

This was the same Todd that had swept her off her feet, taken her by storm and made her time in the US oh so enjoyable, and now he was proposing something much more serious, though neither of them had intended anything like that when they had their fun.

Sure, they'd had some contact since then, and some flirtatious conversations, but surely he knew it wasn't going to work? And it wasn't as if he was even considering moving to Dublin. In his mind, she belonged in the United States.

Unbidden, she suddenly had an image of her and Todd sleeping in the same bed, walking with a stroller, attending parent-teacher conferences together. She saw them sitting together, old-aged in recliners on the porch of Daniel's beach house, too old to make it down to the water.

Todd wanted to take her back to the United States. Yes, it was where she'd been born and had grown up, but Dublin was home now.

Wasn't it?

The thing that mattered most to her at this point in her life was her job, and Todd wanted her to turn her back on that.

It won't be what matters most to you for long, her mind was quick to supply, and a gentle kick to her stomach reminded Reilly that her own life wasn't the only one she had to consider anymore.

"You don't have to answer me right away," Todd said, reaching across the table and finding her hand, "I'll be here till Monday. You have plenty of time to decide."

THREE MORE DAYS TO decide what to do with her life.

Wonderful.

CHAPTER THIRTY-FIVE

The lights in the GFU building were low when later that night, Reilly snuck back in.

Though technically she didn't sneak in; instead she walked right in using her key card to get through the secured doors.

Declan the security guy had nodded at her as she passed– it wasn't exactly a rare sight to see the GFU chief in the office at eleven o'clock at night, particularly in the middle of a major investigation.

But Reilly felt as though she was sneaking, because when she left the flat Todd was sprawled out on the couch, sleeping soundly. His hair was a blonde mess on his head, and his tan skin was dark against her pale couch, although it looked like mere days in Dublin's gray atmosphere had already managed to leech out some of his golden hue.

She'd donned some semi-professional clothes and tiptoed the best she could through the living room creeping past where he slept. She hadn't had a plan when she left the flat – she just knew that she needed to leave.

Though she knew Todd had the best intentions, his presence in the flat had managed to settle over her like a suffocating blanket.

He'd fretted cloyingly over her after the ultrasound appointment, and following the embarrassing episode whereby Reilly couldn't get her socks on, he had insisted she woke him up tomorrow before she went to work so he could assist her again.

Though, he had spent the longest time trying to persuade her not to go into work at all. "I'm only going to be here for a few more days," he reminded her, "I'm sure *one* day away from the lab won't kill you." She must have looked completely horrified by the idea, because he added chuckling; "How about I throw in a foot rub," he said wiggling his fingers suggestively, which irked her even more.

Foot rub aside, while a day of being fussed over and taken care of was tempting, there wasn't a chance in hell of her accepting.

There was just too much at stake. Graham Hackett's killer and Holly Glynn's attacker were still out there, and she was just going to run through the details over and over until something jumped out.

Her office was completely dark when she walked in, and she decided to leave the lights off. Too much florescent lighting made her nauseous, lately.

As iSPI booted up, Reilly's thoughts wandered back to the place they had spent most of her recent time residing. She had worn grooves in her brain, thinking and thinking about the same scenario over and over.

Todd wanted her to come back to the US with him, he'd made that much very clear. Everything pointed to that being the best option for her — it was where she grew up, where her dad had returned, where Todd's family was.

Todd himself was willing to dote over her and support her — something the old Reilly would have detested, but was gradually coming to realize would be a huge help once the baby was born. And after the baby was born, she wouldn't have a problem getting a job in the US - not with her existing FBI credentials, to say nothing of the fact that Todd's father, her former mentor, had practically begged her to join his private investigator firm in Tampa the last time she'd visited

She knew all this, but, for whatever reason, something in her gut told her that going back to the US with Todd was the wrong move. Despite all of the overwhelming evidence in favor of it, her instincts were telling her to stay in Dublin.

But why? Certainly not for the weather. Or the brutal crimes she'd already been exposed to in her time here, or indeed her trauma at the hands of a serial killer only a few months before.

She swallowed and rubbed her neck. It was one thing to think about the baby and her situation with Todd, but she didn't want to think about her recent run in with The Chef any more than she had to. She'd thought enough about that to last her a lifetime.

She considered her surroundings, imagining Rory hard at work on a laptop, or Gary expertly walking the grid at a crime scene. She thought of Lucy working diligently in the lab analyzing trace, of blustery old Jack Gorman in his secluded office, worrying about his daughter. Of Julius arguing with Kennedy sticking to his purely scientific way of thinking, as he made smart-ass remarks.

Kennedy, munching into whatever disgusting junk food he'd sought out, making a joke about something Reilly had said. Greeting her with his customary, "Blondie."

And finally, she thought of soulful dark eyes, eyes that had seen almost as much misery as her own. She thought of the single brief kiss they'd shared; and of the multitude of conversations they'd enjoyed. He'd had her back in every situation – had saved her life more than once.

Perhaps it was something more than just Reilly's gut keeping her in Dublin.

The computer roared to life before her, the lights

flashing through the dark room, and damn near burning out her retinas. She brought a hand up to her eyes and let them adjust fully before loading a copy of the iSPI rendering that would reconstruct the Hackett crime scene before her eyes.

She ran through the software's suggested point of attack, once again taking careful note of the attacker's suggested particulars as calculated by the program. Then she flipped through the detective's case notes until she found Simon Hackett's profile.

The older brother's height was certainly within the parameters of iSPI's rendering of the attacker, attributing the perfect angle and trajectory for the brutal injuries that had been inflicted. Reilly once again visualized Graham Hackett's broken body on the floor of his bedroom. There were many kids - sportsmen - at the party who would have been skilled enough with a hurley stick to swing it through the air like that and beat the kid to death.

She continued going through the simulation, stopping and starting it to compare it to the onsite crime scene reports and trace markers. The darkness closed in all around her, until it was just Reilly and the crime scene.

She caught something then that she hadn't noticed before, and was leaning in to get a better look when she heard a throat clear behind her. She was so immersed in her work, and so completely engulfed in silence, her first reaction to the presence of an unknown person was fear.

And Reilly's first reaction to fear this late at night, in her sleep-deprived state, was to strike out.

Unluckily for her assailant, her perfectly placed uppercut caught him right under the chin, and his plan to startle her succeeded swimmingly.

He grunted in surprise and brought a hand up to ward off any further attacks, while Reilly rose to her feet and took a moment to look properly at her victim, washed out in the glowing white light of the computer monitor.

CHRIS HAD THOUGHT he might startle Reilly at most, but he certainly hadn't expected a violent outburst.

He'd driven past the GFU building on his way back from dinner at Matt and Kelly's house nearby and had seen the light on in her office.

When he'd gone up to investigate, he'd immediately recognized the silhouette outlined by the monitor inside.

It was just like her to come in so late at night, he thought, admiring the soft curve of her shoulders, the way her blonde hair tumbled out of her pony tail. Sometimes Chris had the urge to reach up and pull the rest of it free altogether, and he'd had the urge right at that moment.

But he'd settled on walking up behind her. When she didn't notice his steps over the soft carpet-tiled floor, he'd cleared his throat. Which was when her small, but mighty fist had met him square in the chin.

"Damn," she said, taking a step toward him, "Chris, I'm so sorry."

He shook his head, still holding his face. She really could throw one hell of a punch.

Reilly nearly melted in embarrassment and guilt, and a few moments later, she had returned from the staff room with an ice pack and bottle of painkillers for him. She handed Chris the ice pack and he begrudgingly put it to his chin. He'd taken a seat in one of the rotating office chairs when she rushed off, disgruntled over the punch. How had she managed to take him like that?

If Kennedy got word of this, he would never live it down.

Despite himself, a chuckle swelled up in his chest as Reilly shook one of the pills into her hand. She glanced over at him as he erupted into low, rolling laughter, shaking and bringing his other hand to his eyes in his mirth.

She froze, worried the blow to his chin had knocked his brain loose, and he would never be the same. Her fear was dispelled however, when Chris's eyes met hers and his laughter passed over to her like a shared breath.

In only a few moments, the two decorated members of Dublin law enforcement were beside themselves with laughter. After a minute or so of this, their collective chuckling died down and they took those few necessary breaths of air, looking at each other the whole time.

When it was apparent the air had well and truly been cleared, Reilly pulled the chair that she had been sitting in over and sat down beside him. "What are you doing in the GFU at this time of night?" she asked him.

Chris turned the now-melted ice pack over in his hands and looked up at her, his bright brown eyes shining. "I could ask you the same thing."

She swallowed and looked down at the floor, not sure she was ready to admit to him that she had a Florida golden boy in her home, and his presence was suffocating her. With her eyes on the floor, she caught a glimpse of her hastily chosen footwear.

Chris must have noticed as well, because he asked, eyes widening, "And why are you wearing flip-flops?"

Reilly let out another short burst of laughter at this before admitting, "I can't reach my feet, Chris. I can't put my own goddamn socks on."

He looked at her, shaking his head in surprise at the admission.

"You didn't answer my question," she pressed, still curious.

He shrugged, turning and setting the ice pack on the desk behind him. "I saw your office light was on - what's your excuse?" He knew Forrest was staying with her at the moment and the very thought of it made Chris queasy.

But if Reilly was here because she was avoiding something - or someone - then that made him feel a whole lot better.

"PRETTY MUCH," she said, remembering what she had just noticed on the screen before Chris had interrupted her. "Yeah..." she said again, standing and moving over again to the iSPI unit.

He watched her walk with intent over to the monitor and waited for a moment before joining her. When he sat down next to her, she was clicking through different angles of the Hackett scene rendering, evaluating one particular part of the room - over by the desk.

He watched her curiously, certain she was seeing something he wasn't, because while Chris was fairly perceptive, she almost always managed to notice things most others didn't.

Sure enough, she paused the image and pointed at the window.

"There," she said to Chris. "Gary must have input this information after I'd examined the stuff on Graham Hackett's desk."

Chris was at a loss. She was clearly enthused about something, and felt it must be of some importance. He leaned closer, looking at the heavy oak desk and the dark blue curtains...

"The window?" he ventured.

She nodded, clicking through the simulation and checking it against the crime scene photos. "The frame is open just a crack, but obviously wasn't caught until I moved the curtain to check out the stuff on the desk and Gary scanned the room for iSPI. That's why you can see it here," she added, referring to the simulation, "but not on the photos."

Chris glanced over at her, impressed with her astute observation but he wasn't certain how this new information helped with the investigation.

Reilly was sitting back in her chair, shaking her head, "Why would the window be open?" she asked out loud, to nobody in particular.

"The room was too hot so the kid wanted to air it out a little? It was a warm enough night, remember."

"Or whoever murdered Graham Hackett came in or left through the window, Chris," she said, stating the obvious. "Which means it's unlikely to be Simon."

Graham's brother would have no reason to come in through it; he lived in the house. Which meant that the murderer must have been someone who needed to enter or exit through the window, so any others that lingered at the party wouldn't see or be able to tell anyone was even there.

Chris said nothing, but seemed disappointed.

"It could be that - or it might mean absolutely nothing," Reilly went on, biting her lip, "but I have a feeling it's related to what happened. I'm just not yet sure how."

He chuckled a little. "Pity we can't exactly base everything on feelings."

She glanced back at him then, picking up the rather unsubtle connotation to his words. His eyes were as soft and brown as ever, even under the low lights of the room, and she had to exert a lot of willpower not to say something she shouldn't.

Not for the first time, Chris and Reilly were in a situation where they both knew what the other was thinking, and also both knew there were good reasons not to act on those thoughts.

She swallowed hard and looked back to the screen whispering, just loud enough for him to hear. "Yeah, pity."

CHAPTER THIRTY-SIX

Gary reclined back in bed, absently watching TV as Lucy brushed her teeth in the other room. He was supposed to wait for her; she hated getting into the bed when he was already sleeping, but he could barely keep his eyes open.

The lights were low in the room, Gary was dozing off periodically, and when the ads came on he almost turned over, ready to fall asleep. But then something caught his attention. He sat up, rewinding the TV back to the start of the advertisement that had triggered his realization. He watched it two more times, the idea forming fully in his mind.

"Luce," he called, scrambling to get out of bed. He roughly yanked his jeans on up over his boxers as she came skidding into the room, in a pair of shorts and t-shirt, ready for bed.

"What?" she asked, her eyes wild, her toothbrush hanging from her mouth. She took it out, still assessing the room for some kind of threat as her boyfriend hurriedly dressed and reached for his stuff. "What's wrong, Gary?" she asked, worry slipping into her tone as she took in his frenzied state.

"I figured it out," he said, his voice breathless as he looked around under the bed for his shoe.

"Figured what out?" She eyed him curiously.

Gary rewound the TV to the very end of a food ad before a deep bass pounded through the speakers. Lights flashed as the camera panned through different chaotic scenes of young people jumping up and down at a club, pumping their fists and whipping their hair. The last shot, just before the advertisement for an upcoming programme on Ibiza holidays, was of a bunch of teens surrounded by foam up to their waists.

"What in the world...?" Lucy asked, leaning forward. It looked like the time her mother had let her fill the bath when she was younger - she'd put too much bubble bath in and the foam had almost flooded the bathroom.

"A foam party," Gary exclaimed, before grabbing Lucy and kissing her on the cheek. She didn't have time to react, because he was already on his way out the door. "The strawberry stuff ... I know what it is."

A LITTLE LATER than usual the following morning, Reilly headed for work, attempting to tune out the news channel on the TV behind her. The busy café close to the GFU was bustling with the usual morning custom, and it was all she could do to stand in line long enough to get her order.

"Five donuts, four coffees, and one rooibos tea," the barista said, handing her drinks over. Reilly took all of it, balancing it in her arms as she exited the café. Some of the older women looked at her disdainfully. *Caffeine is bad for the baby*; she could almost hear everyone muttering.

It took her five minutes to reach the office, and in that time she had won many internal battles over whether or not she should rip open the packaging covering the donuts.

There were a lot of things Reilly had expected to see when she eventually walked into the lab that morning, but Gary and Lucy asleep at their workstations was not one of them. Various specimen slides were laid out on the counter and the microspectrometer was still running.

Reilly took another step into the room, trying not to feel jealous of the two of them. Still, she'd had her share of young love, she knew how it went, and how it would go.

"If this is what you consider being professional in the workplace," she muttered, just loud enough to startle them awake, "I guess you'll have to brush up on your definitions."

Gary blinked a few times at her, as though he was still in a dream – and not a good one. He looked around, disoriented, then his gaze drifted down to his chest, where Lucy was still sound asleep.

His smile was immediate and genuine, and Reilly had to fight the urge to grab her phone and snap a picture of the two of them like that. Her tone softened a bit as she said, "What are you doing, did you get evicted or something?"

Gary seemed to come to his senses at the question, and his face lit up as he sprang from his seat. The sudden movement roused the sleepy Lucy, who sat up and rubbed her eyes tiredly, looking around in the same fashion.

"You won't believe this," he was saying, untangling himself from Lucy, "but we got it. We know for sure what the soap – well, what the astringent is."

Reilly looked at him, an eyebrow raised, and he grinned back at Lucy. "Drum roll, please." She shook her head and rolled her eyes. "Foam..." Gary announced theatrically.

Reilly brought her eyebrows together, not understanding, "Foam?"

"Yes," he said, moving past her and over to the machines he and Lucy had toiled over in the early hours. "Some of the clubs in town - when they're celebrating something major – New Year's, Midsummer or graduation – they throw these foam parties.

"It sort of looks like everyone is taking a bubble bath together," Lucy remarked, stretching her arms over her head.

Reilly was still confused, so Gary kept talking. "They fill the place up with foam, and people dance around in it. But the logistics aren't important. What's important is that *somebody* left traces of that stuff in Graham Hackett's room. And there was one such party celebrating the end of exams at a club in the city on the night of Graham Hackett's murder. So whoever was in Graham's room the night he was killed," he finished ominously, "was also at that foam party."

CHAPTER THIRTY-SEVEN

Chris and Kennedy were at the lab within half an hour.

"Alfalfa, soybean, wheat, and limestone," Julius was saying to Reilly, when they walked in. "I have no idea why that combination would exist, or what it relates to, but there are also minuscule amounts of it on the murder weapon. Once we know the specifics, we can dig deeper again."

"Interesting," Reilly said, nodding thoughtfully at the detectives. "The organic composition of other trace we picked up from the murder weapon," she told him. "Like I said on the phone, we've also identified the strawberry-scented substance. Seems it's foam. Some sort of party foam used at clubs."

Lucy then jumped in with another discovery, "And some other substances in that petroleum-based compound also found on the victim, are beeswax with some kind of ... tree resin I'd say. I don't know what that indicates exactly but..."

"Board wax," Reilly said, immediately reminded of her old surfing days in California. "I used to make my own all the time."

"You surfed?" said Gary, surprised.

Reilly had done a lot more than just surfed – she lived for the waves and had spent most of her free time out on the bay under the sun, her blonde hair flying behind her as she went back out, again and again, to tame the rip.

She'd been good at it too. She'd always been athletic, and the technique just came so easily to her. It didn't hurt that she loved the water, or that she loved doing things over and over until she got them right.

"Yep, all the time," she said wistfully. "I actually solved one of my very first Quantico challenges by recognizing a particular board wax brand."

"Okay, I get the foam, but why the hell would there be board wax at the scene?" Chris asked, bringing her back to the present.

"Does it relate to hurling in any way?" Lucy mused. "Would the players use it to smooth out their hurls in the way surfers do?"

"Well if they do, it's a new one on me," said Kennedy. "I can't see it somehow, can you? And you wouldn't want them all slippery and waxy in yer hand like that. Grip is what you want."

"Okay, Jimmy Barry," Chris chuckled, referring to Ireland's most famous star hurling player. Who knew Kennedy was such an expert on a so-called culchie sport?

"Also, Rory has since uncovered something more about Graham's online ... exploits," Reilly told them cryptically, and Chris couldn't help but think that it never rained but it poured.

The detectives duly followed her down to the tech room where Rory awaited.

"I was digging through some of Graham Hackett's older texts - going back a couple of months," he said, "and I found this."

(Thor, 6:55 pm) *What the hell, Hackett?*

(HACKR, 6:56 pm) *Jesus, what's your problem? Are you still pissed off about what happened in practice? Can't help it if I'm faster than you ...*

(THOR, 6:58 pm) *You know exactly what I'm pissed off about. It was a shitty thing to do to Megan.*

(HACKR, 7:00 pm) *Hey, mate, she sent those snaps to me, so* *if you're going to be pissed off at anyone, it should be her. Nice pair on her tho, dunno why anyone would friendzone a piece of ass like that... Unless maybe you prefer our mate Eddie ...*

(THOR, 7:05) *Hey, go fuck yourself, Lance, seriously.*

Chris read through the exchange then looked at Rory, who was looking absently at the screen. After a beat he sat up, the detectives' confused expressions leading him to believe he should start explaining.

"Okay, so there's an app you can get on a smartphone called Snapchat, and using this app, you can send photos that disappear after a certain amount of time. Only the thing is, almost all smartphones are equipped with a screenshot ability, so it doesn't take a genius to save a photo you've received over Snapchat, especially now that there's double play ..." he took a breath, "this is what happened with Graham Hackett and Megan Wright a couple of months ago – Megan sent Graham a photo she expected to disappear, but it didn't, because he saved it and forwarded it on to all his friends."

"Who's Lance, then?" Kennedy asked, baffled.

"Probably Lance Armstrong - a dig at Graham Hackett's juicing?"

"Well, what's so bad about a photo anyway?" Chris asked. "Don't these kids' lives revolve around sharing everything they do anyway?"

Rory snorted, then looked up at Chris when it was

clear he wasn't joking. "Think about it. What kind of photo might you *not* want shared around?"

It only took Chris a moment longer to understand his meaning. "You mean these kids are innocently sending ... inappropriate pictures to each other?"

Rory smiled sadly and shook his head, "You have no idea. Wait till you read through the rest of these messages. They might be kids but there's nothing innocent about them."

Chris shook his head. "Wait," he said, after another moment, "if they're all doing this, then why does this Thor guy - whoever he is - care that Graham does it to Megan?"

"Well," Rory said, "from what I've gathered, Thor and Megan went out together for a while. So he's obviously pissed off on behalf of his ex, and looking to defend her honor."

"But who's Thor? Can you find out?"

Rory nodded. "Already working on it."

"So it really is looking like it could be someone other than Simon..." Chris said, somewhat despondently.

It was much later in the evening, and he and Reilly were back in her office going over the new information, while Kennedy volunteered to check out the security cameras from the city center club that had held the foam party on the night of Graham Hackett's attack.

"I agree. The brother just doesn't fit. For one thing, he didn't need to exit or enter through the window and for another the nightclub he was at wasn't the one that held the foam party."

"So, who *do* you think did it, then? This Thor guy? Maybe one of Simon's older college friends? And if so, why?"

She yawned. After last night's middle of the night exploits, it had felt like a helluva long day. "I have no idea, but it looks to me like there are a number of possibilities. Especially since Graham wasn't as pure as everyone likes to make out. There's the drugs element for one - Dean Cooper may not have been his only source - and now the revenge porn..."

"Well I wish you would hurry the hell up and find us something concrete instead of piling on more theories ..." Chris harrumphed, the new information that pointed away from his preferred suspect making him cranky and disgruntled. "Maybe if there weren't so many distractions - "

"What distractions?" Perhaps it was the lack of sleep, the intensity of the investigation, as well as the emotional upheaval about the situation with Todd, but the barb really got to her. She pushed her chair back away from her desk and stood up, glaring at him. "How dare you Chris? How *dare* you suggest that I'm not concentrating properly on the job? Look at everything we've uncovered this week. What the hell do you think I was doing here at all hours of the - "

Her words were cut short as a searing pain ripped through her abdomen, and she struggled to take a breath. Her hand automatically went to her stomach and she winced, putting her hand on the nearest thing to lean on.

Which turned out to be Chris, who'd bolted out of his chair and round the desk at the first sign of her discomfort. "Jesus, are you okay?" he asked, breathless with concern, as Reilly's hand found the front of his shirt and balled it in her fist. "I can phone for an ambulance, take you to the hospital even?"

She shook her head and straightened up a bit as the pain subsided, but still heavily leaning against him. "Dr. Moore - my obstetrician said there would be discomfort from now on," Reilly said, "Cramps. Pretty sure this is one..."

Chris looked back at her tired, overworked form, feeling guilty as hell. He'd just accused her of taking her eye off the ball.

Did he ever feel like an asshole...

He stood stock still, not knowing what else to do, as she grimaced afresh, her fist still clenched around a piece of his shirt. "Hey, maybe you should sit down for a second," he suggested gently, reaching for her arm.

Just as someone made an appearance in the office doorway.

"Hey ..." said a male voice in a distinctive American twang. And Chris suddenly knew who the visitor was, even before Reilly uttered the name.

"Todd..."

CHAPTER THIRTY-EIGHT

Reilly stared, completely floored to see Todd of all people standing in her office, flanked by Declan, the security guard from downstairs.

"I remember him meeting you in reception the other day," the guard was saying. "So I thought it would be okay to bring him up." Reilly's expression seemed to be telling him otherwise. "Considering, you know..." Declan stared at her bump, as if suggesting that it was all fine and dandy to allow a member of the public access to her office simply because he was the father of her child. Not that anyone knew for sure, but she guessed they'd put two and two together. And come up with fifty. "It is okay, isn't it?" he added uncertainly.

"Sure Declan," she replied sighing. Though Todd was not her keeper and had no right coming to her place of work unannounced. What *was* he doing here anyway?

But in her office he was, striding toward Chris and putting his hand out. "Hey, I'm Todd, Reilly's - "

"Friend," she put in quickly. "Daniel's son. Chris knows your dad - he met him a couple of years back when he was here for the ... Jess situation."

Chris reluctantly took his hand, retreating stiffly. "Chris Delaney. Detective."

Todd glanced between the two of them, his gaze reserved. "Cool. So how's everything going?"

"You know we can't discuss the case, Todd," Reilly warned.

He shook his head at her, "I wasn't asking about the case, hon, I was just asking - in general. How's it going?"

She blanched at his casual (and she thought, rather patronizing) use of the endearment, and couldn't look Chris in the eye.

"Shitty actually," Chris responded. "The case I mean."

"Right - which is why I guess my girl's here so late." Todd chuckled. "How many times have I tried to tell her that work's not everything..." he joked, glancing at Chris as if for support, "Especially now, right? Hey, you promised you'd try to make it home a little earlier while I'm in town. And yet here I am - practically having to steal you away on a Friday night." He gave Chris's shoulder a friendly nudge. "Hope you're not working her too hard, buddy."

Chris cleared his throat. "Reilly works herself too hard, I think we all know that," he said smiling fondly at her. "I've never met anyone with a better work ethic or track record."

Todd raised his eyebrows at the blatantly protective tone Chris had used, but continued talking to him like they had been buddies for a long time.

"Oh, trust me, I know all about Reilly's track record," he said, flashing one of his epically white smiles.

Reilly harrumphed, aware that this was quickly turning into a pissing contest. "Speaking of work," she said, directing her gaze at Todd, "What are you doing here?"

Todd stood right in front of her, turning his back to Chris, "You weren't home when you said you would be," he said, gently putting both hands on her shoulders. "I was worried."

Reilly raised her eyebrow at this – she wasn't used to being accountable to anyone. She suspected she could disappear from the face of the earth in the evening, and nobody would notice until she didn't show up at the GFU the next morning.

"I went to the store, hoping I could pick up some avocados for dinner, but I couldn't find any, and then I was bored, so I figured it wouldn't hurt to stop by and check on you."

"You'll have a hard time finding fresh avocados in the shops around here," Chris remarked, causing him to turn back around.

"Oh?" he said, glancing once again to Reilly, "I was thinking of making us some Mexican food for dinner. Your favorite. But maybe we should do it tomorrow night instead; it's late now. Hey, you should stop by," Todd added, turning back to Chris, as if laying down some kind of challenge. "Sure," he insisted when Chris looked taken aback. "It's Saturday night - we'll have a good time. Any friend of Reilly's is a friend of mine."

Chris's expression was the exact one Reilly would have expected to see after such a suggestion. At first, he looked tense and closed off, seemingly right on the verge of finding the perfect excuse to decline, but she was surprised when he then squared his shoulders and offered a smile. "Grand," Chris said, "I will so. Tomorrow night you said?"

She stared at the two men as they shared a look she couldn't quite identify.

"So," Todd was saying as he broke Chris's intent gaze and returned it to her, "are you ready to go home now? There's a foot rub on the couch waiting for you."

After the severe cramp she'd just experienced, a foot rub sounded like heaven. And Todd was right; she had promised to try and be home a little earlier while he was in town. They had lots to discuss after all. She nodded tiredly, giving one last look at the files scattered over her desk.

Chris could only watch as she and Todd Forrest walked out the door together, something fierce and competitive brewing in his chest.

CHAPTER THIRTY-NINE

Having reviewed the new information about Graham Hackett's possible involvement with revenge porn, Chris and Kennedy decided to pay Megan Wright another visit.

This time, when Megan answered she kept the door partially closed. Her eyes narrowed and a worried look crossed her features. "What's wrong?" she asked, her eyes moving rapidly from Chris and back to Kennedy. "I thought I told you everything the other day."

"Not quite pet," said Kennedy, using his best paternal voice. "We've had some new information that we need to talk to you about."

Megan sighed and stepped outside the door, closing it behind her. "My baby brother is sleeping," she supplied in explanation, "I don't want to wake him."

"Okay," Chris said, taking a step back and letting her

sit down on the steps. "Megan, we believe there was a certain ... situation involving you and Graham Hackett recently. Something about an ... intimate photograph?"

Megan's cheeks immediately reddened and she shook her head as she looked down at her lap. "That..." she said, tears brimming at her eyes. "that was so stupid of me."

Chris felt for the girl as she continued on. "I thought... I don't know, I was flirting around with Graham a bit, to try to make someone jealous. I didn't know, obviously, that Graham would forward the photos on to everyone else."

"Thor? Why would flirting around with Graham make him jealous?" he asked. "And who's Thor?"

Megan shook her head again, sending her honey brown hair fluttering around her face, "My ex - Conor...he wanted to end things... he had just got the scholarship to play in Australia, and he thought it would be best if we broke up straight away instead of hanging on till he left when we'd have to eventually. I thought he was just using it as an excuse to see other girls, so I suppose I wanted him to know that two could play at that game. And he and Graham never really got on."

Conor Glynn, Chris realized.

"And how did Conor react when he found out that Graham had shared the pictures?"

"He was pretty pissed off about it. The next day, he

came up to me at school, and he just had this *look* on his face, like he didn't know what to say to me."

"Has Conor talked to you since then?"

A sorrowful expression passed over Megan's face and she wiped the back of her hand over her cheek.

"No," she said, her words wobbling through the air. "He got so cold after that. It was awful, as we were really close. And then I wondered if maybe he had been serious when he said he didn't want to string me along until he left for Oz. We used to confide in each other, like I knew how the other lads on the team were jealous about the scholarship and I suppose when I started that shit with Graham, maybe he felt like I'd betrayed him too."

"Did you ever make a complaint or maybe tell your parents about what Graham had done – with the photo?" Kennedy asked gently.

Megan looked horrified at the very thought. "Not for a second, why would I? It was my own stupid fault for doing it in the first place. I didn't want my parents ... or anyone else to see the photos either."

A classic case of victim blaming, Chris realized, feeling for Megan. How goddamn frustrating for the girl to have internalized at such a young age that – stupidity (or perhaps naivety?) aside – what Graham Hackett had done to her was wrong.

He resolved to ensure that Rachel would never feel that way, that he would let his goddaughter know that if any boy or man treated her with anything other than respect, he would have Chris to answer to. He shuddered at the very idea, and for once had a brief glimpse of the worries Kennedy no doubt had to face every day of the week.

"So Conor - he's Holly Glynn's brother?"

She nodded. "That's another reason I didn't want to say anything about the photos. Holly's my friend and I didn't know how she'd feel about me coming on to her ex. But it was long after things were over between them." She looked at the detectives, pleadingly. "Please don't tell anyone. I know it was stupid, believe me. It's bad enough that I pushed Conor away, but it would kill me to lose Holly too."

CHAPTER FORTY

Saturday night, the entire flat was flooded with the smell of Todd's home cooking, and Reilly knew that she would smell it long after he had gone back to the US.

She would smell it in the furniture, lingering off of the clothes in the closet, stuck to every fabric and inch of carpet in her small flat.

She sat back on her sofa and watched Todd work amongst the tiny kitchen, slicing and scooping things in pans on the stove.

If she stayed in Dublin, she thought. She would only continue to smell his cooking after he'd gone if she didn't end up following him back, hooked onto his arm like a carry-on bag.

There was a sharp knock at the door then, and Reilly knew who it was immediately. There was a door-bell but Chris always insisted on knocking. Perhaps he thought it sounded less formal, but Reilly had a suspicion he enjoyed hitting something that wouldn't hit him back every once in a while.

When Todd didn't react, Reilly pushed herself to her feet and shuffled over to the door, unlocking the deadbolt and pushing it open.

When she caught her first glimpse of Chris, she inhaled sharply and was met with the musky scent of his cologne. It was a scent she had always liked – most men opted for a more sickly chemical scent that came with most mass market brands, but Chris's skipped over being artificial, and was more like he had just walked out of a patch of evergreen trees.

He was wearing a dark gray button up shirt with the sleeves rolled up to the elbows. Reilly rarely got to see him in jeans, so she took in the sight with interest – they were black, snug-fitting, and surprisingly stylish.

Finally, her gaze moved to his eyes, which were smiling at her from under their brown hue. He held up what looked like a bottle of red wine and she stepped back, allowing him entry.

"It smells great in here," Chris commented as he and Reilly stood together in the living room.

"Wait until you taste it!" Todd piped up from the kitchen. He winked at Reilly and she offered him a cool smile. She wasn't playing along with the cozy domestic thing he had going on.

Chris rolled his lips into his mouth for a second as he observed the interaction then pushed them out in a forced grin. He held the bottle in his hands, preparing himself to say something, when Todd piped up again.

"Hey nice one," he said, flashing his thousand-watt smile at Chris like a grenade, "looks like Reilly's gonna be left out of the festivities tonight," he said, gesturing toward the bottle with an inclination of his head.

"Actually," Chris said, chuckling under his breath at Todd's attempt at conviviality, "it's sparkling grape juice."

"Oh," Todd said, sounding genuinely surprised, as if it was unheard for an Irishman to arrive bearing anything other than strong liquor. He glanced over his shoulder toward the stove, "Almost ready," he said, before turning his back to them again.

Reilly made brief eye contact with Chris, hoping to convey the weirdness of the situation, and melt some of the nervous tension fizzing in the air around them.

It's just a shared dinner between friends, she tried to tell herself, although the underlying voice, the one in the logical part of her brain, told her that she knew this wasn't the case.

"Come and sit down," she said to Chris, leading him to the small table she normally ate at. Usually, the table would be covered in case files, notes and graphs that Reilly had made, or speculations she had scribbled on spare pieces of paper. Now and again she sketched out a crime scene to get her head in the right place, and taped it to the wall.

But none of this was apparent now, as Todd had completely transformed the space into more like what it was meant to be used for. The table was covered with a tablecloth, there were three place settings with accompanying cutlery and glasses, and he had even gone so far as to pick up fresh flowers from the florist down the street.

Chris noticed her hesitant pause as she surveyed the elegantly set table – something told him it certainly wasn't Reilly's doing.

Todd came over just then with two plates of food balanced in each hand. "Let me just grab the rest," he said, after setting two servings down on the table and pulling Reilly's chair out for her.

"I'll help you," Chris said, putting down the bottle of grape juice before taking a step to follow Todd.

"It's okay," he said, "I've got it. Just make yourself comfortable."

The two men shared a look for a moment, then Chris shrugged. Todd was clearly challenging him, but he was not in the mood to play. He sat down across from Reilly and she immediately sat forward, an inquisitive look on her face. "So how'd it go earlier with Megan – "

"No shop talk," Todd called out. "You promised."

She rolled her eyes and met Chris's gaze, who smiled.

That'd be the day.

But in truth, they really couldn't discuss an open investigation in front of Todd in any case.

A moment later, he came hurrying back over, two more plates in his arms. He set them down on the table and introduced their meal before settling into his own chair. "OK first up, we've got a fresh tuna and tomato salad, with avocado on the side. Next coconut shrimp, then beef burrito with guac and cilantro."

Reilly looked incredulously at Todd. His menu for the night was clearly reminiscent of the many meals they'd shared together in Florida - this was proper Gulf Coast beach food.

Which didn't go unnoticed by Chris.

The guy seemed to be doing everything he could to throw his relationship with Reilly in his face, evidently sniffing out a rival, whereas Chris had done nothing to instigate that. Nothing that he knew of anyway. He tried to convince himself that he was secure enough in his relationship with Reilly that he didn't need to prove himself to a complete stranger.

After all the food was served, and Chris had taken a few bites of the food and (begrudgingly) found it to be delicious, an awkward silence threatened to settle over the three. Reilly, sensing the tense atmosphere, tried to think of something to say. And, of course, there was always one thing that came to her mind, first and foremost.

"There was more about the Hackett investigation on the news earlier," she commented, pushing her salad around on her plate.

"Since when do you watch the news?" Chris chuckled, as he set his glass down. He glanced around, as if trying to find the TV. "And where?"

She smiled back at him, "In the store on my way back from a run."

"I would have gone to the store for you," Todd said frowning.

Reilly waved her hand through the air. "It's fine, I was just grabbing a smoothie. Anyway it was early and you were still sleeping when I left."

Todd shook his head, "You know at some point you're going to have to let someone help you with something, or you're going to run yourself into the ground."

Chris regarded Todd in a different light for just a second, as this was a subject they could actually agree on.

She glanced over at Chris, the fire in her eyes telling him that he did not need to cement his agreement with Todd's assertion, as she already knew about his view on this subject.

The three seated at the table again fell into a terse silence. Chris was about to excuse himself for the bathroom, just for something to break the tension, when Todd swallowed a bite of his taco and shifted his weight towards him.

"So Chris, are you married buddy?" he asked, dabbing at his face with one of the stark white napkins.

"No," Chris said realizing that the guy would have known full well this wasn't the case, since he would have surely already asked Reilly about his relationship status.

"I sense some ... emotional tension in you, Chris," Todd continued, leaning forward with a bit of salad on his fork, "maybe a tricky romantic past?"

Chris tensed considerably at the observation, then recalled Todd's occupation. They were in the same line of work, noting details and missing nothing, and getting paid to do so.

He chuckled in a way that seemed good-natured, and said, after the right amount of pause, "No offence mate, but I don't think it'll do me much good to take romantic advice from you."

His comment landed right where he wanted it to, and Reilly watched as Todd's jaw visibly tensed. She shifted in her seat. Although the food was wonderful, and she would have normally enjoyed the company of either man, she found that she felt more nauseous than relaxed.

Chris took a sip of his sparkling grape juice and shook his head almost imperceptibly, but Todd was too busy glancing at Reilly to notice. He needed to gauge from her which direction to take next, but all he could gather was that she was uncomfortable.

"So what were they saying on the news?" Chris asked, looking for something that might pull Reilly out a little, get her to engage in the conversation. "About the case?"

She shrugged and fixed him with a look he couldn't place. "Mostly Michael Glynn complaining about how useless we are," she said, swirling her grape juice around, trying to convince herself it was wine, "O'Brien's already been in my ear about that - Glynn feels we're not doing enough to find the man who hurt his little girl."

"Understandable," said Chris. "But if his daughter can't remember much, what does he expect us to do about it?"

"Sex crime?" ventured Todd, picking up on the thread.

"Attempted sexual assault," Reilly told him. "Likely not connected to our murder. But we've got little by way of a suspect either way."

"Don't we?" challenged Chris teasingly, referring to Simon.

"Hah, I recognize that tone for sure," Todd put in, laughing. "Let me guess Chris, you have a hard-on for a suspect, but our Reilly is thinking 'no dice' because - evidence."

Reilly couldn't help but chuckle at Todd's blatantly

American colloquialisms but figured Chris would know exactly what he was saying.

"More or less," said Chris staring directly at her, a twinkle in his eye. "She's a hard woman to persuade."

"Yeah well, maybe she's right," Todd went on, his tone blatantly taunting. "I'm just saying buddy, carelessness is what puts innocent people behind bars. The only thing worse than a guilty man going free is an innocent man having his life stolen away for something he didn't do, wouldn't you say?"

Maybe it was a combination of the scrutiny his suspicions of Simon Hackett had garnered all throughout the investigation, and all the digs Todd had already thrown at him in the first few minutes of sitting down together, but Chris couldn't help but retort: "I don't know - *buddy*. Is it any worse than the kind of carelessness that knocks up an old friend?"

Reilly pushed her chair back from the table, and the sound of the legs screeching on the wood was startling to Chris and Todd, who by then had almost completely forgotten she was in the room.

She stood up, staring down at the mostly untouched food on her plate. "Out," she said, her tone low and serious. "Both of you. Now."

Todd and Chris tried to placate and apologize respectively but she ignored them, instead repeating herself over the sound of their voices. "I mean it. Get the hell out."

When they'd both exited the flat, stoic and apologetic, Reilly took all three plates of food and brought them back over to the sofa with her.

She sighed as she sank back down into its comfy softness. No sense in wasting perfectly good beach food.

CHAPTER FORTY-ONE

The pub was low lit and the voices were hushed in their conversation. The highlights of the day's Premiership football games were playing on the TVs overhead, but nobody seemed interested.

Chris looked at the pint of Guinness he had ordered. It sat on the counter of the bar, waiting for him. All he had wanted was to have a nice civilized dinner with a friend and the father of her child, and then leave, hopefully reassuring himself that Todd Forrest was in fact a decent guy.

He shook his head. Nice fantasy. Of course the real reason he had accepted the invite was Forrest and the blatant challenge in his eyes. The guy thought, for whatever reason, that Reilly belonged to him, and evidently suspecting a connection between her and Chris, seemed to want to lord that fact over him. A pissing contest.

Asshole.

Someone slid onto the stool next to his then, and Chris ignored the guy, taking the first creamy sip of his pint. The dark liquid hardly stung on its way down and he looked up, searching out the barman so he could have another on the draw.

"Tequila on the rocks," the man next to him drawled, "and another of whatever he's having."

Great...

Chris looked over at Todd, then looked back down at his drink and swallowed the last of it before the barman slid him another one. He shook his head at the glass as Todd said, "Pretty rough in there, huh?"

Chris turned on him, his own accent even more pronounced when he was annoyed and had a pint in him. "Would you not take the hint, dickhead? I've had enough listening to you already. Get the fuck away from me," he growled, grabbing his drink forcefully.

Todd recoiled a little, evidently surprised at this overly aggressive turn, in what up to then had been a fairly placid encounter. "Hey listen, I'm just trying to do what's best for Reilly."

Chris turned to look at him, his expression incredulous. "What's *best* for her? You thought that swanning all the way over here suddenly deciding to play happy families is best? Insisting she takes time off to entertain you while working her arse off on a case - at six months pregnant - is best? Confusing her by trying to tempt her back to Florida with you - away from the people who care about her - is fucking *best?*"

Taken aback by his own vehemence, he stopped before he said too much.

Todd calmly knocked back the rest of his drink before waving for another. "Actually, I do think going back to the US is what's best for Reilly, and our baby," he said and the words were like a punch to the stomach. *Our baby*. Up until then, Chris had only really thought of it as Reilly's baby, and Todd's phrasing had knocked the wind out of him.

"Think about it. Reilly grew up there, she trained there, she's American through and through. Mike's back now too. I'm there and the baby's other grandfather. The US is a far better place to bring up a kid, Reilly knows that. With a job like hers, how in the world is she going to cope with raising a baby in a foreign country? Alone."

Chris shook his head – Dublin was hardly the middle of the bloody Amazon.

And Reilly would not be alone.

He thought not only of himself but Lucy, Karen Thompson and the rest of the GFU team - hell, even Kennedy had offered to chip in with babysitting. They all cared about her and no matter how firm Reilly's resistance to their offers, her Irish 'family' would do everything they could to help her out.

"Question for you then," Chris asked Todd, keenly

interested in the answer, "if Reilly says no and you're so concerned about being a part of the baby's life, are you considering moving to Dublin?"

Todd looked pained for a moment. "My whole life is in the US - my dad, my job...I can't just pick up and leave everything I have there. No, Reilly is just being stubborn. She'll figure it out that coming home is for the best in the long run."

"Did it ever occur to you ..." Chris said, gritting his teeth, "that Reilly's whole life might be *here*? Yeah, Mike went back to the US, but she's built her own life over the last few years. Her work is here, her friends are here. All the things she loves are here," Chris said, his voice now barely a whisper.

Todd watched him for a second, gauging the meaning from his words. Suddenly, he let out a bark of laughter. "You and me, man," he said, clapping Chris on the back, "I think we're in the same boat here."

Chris raised an eyebrow. He hoped that if he and Todd Forrest were ever in any boat together he would have the good sense to jump overboard and make for the nearest island. "At the bar of a shitty pub in the company of a man they can't stand?"

Todd looked a bit taken aback at Chris's candor, but didn't completely disagree with him either. He usually had an easy time getting along with people, but this guy was to Dublin like Todd was to Florida.

Delaney was dark, solemn and reserved, all the

blinds drawn and doors closed; whereas Todd was bright, sunny and usually cheerful, and the two personalities seemed to clash on principle alone.

He wondered what it was Reilly liked about this guy. His gruff exterior, yet old-fashioned good manners? His reluctance to come right out and just say the things he meant? His cheery personality?

It occurred to Todd then, that Chris was probably wondering what it was about him that Reilly liked.

"Hey, I guess we both love her but..." Todd began but Chris stopped him, his jaw set as he put his second empty glass on the counter.

"Don't," he said simply, a tidal wave of mixed emotion flooding through him at the words, especially coming from Forrest's mouth.

Todd shrugged and polished off his second drink too. "You got it," he said, then standing up, asked, "Know of any good hotels around here?"

Chris, finally pleased by something the other man had said, listed off a couple of hotels nearby that were likely to have rooms on a walk-in.

"Okay. Guess we're both well and truly in the doghouse tonight." Clapping Chris once more on the back, Todd slung his jacket over his shoulder and left the bar.

Two glasses lingered at the spot where Forrest had sat, but all too soon many more were added to Chris's empty cluster.

CHAPTER FORTY-TWO

The next day, as Reilly returned a missed call from Gary the night before, she thought again about the way the teenagers in her high school had acted, and was reminded of the way Chris and Todd had behaved last night.

And to think, she had been sure she had escaped that kind of behavior for the rest of her life.

Todd had been aggressive to begin with, especially with the meal he had prepared. Of course, it had been delicious, but that wasn't the point. He was laying down a marker, trying to psych Chris out by throwing their time together in Florida in his face. She couldn't get Chris's expression when he saw the food out of her head.

Furthermore, she couldn't shake off the feeling she'd got when Chris talked about her and Todd's 'carelessness', because as much as he had intended it to be an insult toward Todd, it had hit Reilly in the gut just as hard.

Todd hadn't come home last night, which was fine with Reilly, who had gone straight to bed after gorging nearly everything on the table. Feeling sick afterwards, she'd crawled into bed, still dressed in the clothes she had worn to supper and woke up the next morning to find her flat as empty as it had been when she had told both of the men to get out the night before. As well as finding a couple of missed calls from Gary.

"I spent my Saturday night following up on that animal feed trace," her colleague said drolly. "Good thing I have an understanding girlfriend. Anyway, turns out that specific combination of ingredients is used as exotic pet food."

Reilly furrowed her eyebrows inquisitively, "Do the Hacketts have any pets? Perhaps our doer works with exotic animals?" she speculated.

It was tenuous but at least now the trace evidence was starting to help build up a clearer profile of the attacker, and perhaps more importantly rule out Chris's favorite suspect.

Reilly knew he wouldn't be over the moon to hear that this new evidence suggested he and Kennedy should widen out the investigation away from Simon, but after last night, she figured he wouldn't be over the moon about all that much today anyway.

Irritated afresh by how last night had gone, she picked up a nearby cushion, held it in her hands for a moment, then buried her face in the soft cotton and let out a frustrated scream.

When she lowered the cushion she let out a smaller shriek.

Todd was standing in front of her, an alarmed expression gracing his features.

"Reilly...?" he said, tentatively, like she might freak out again if he spoke too fast, "are you okay?"

She dropped the cushion, her heart pounding. "No," she said, finally, after a few moments of heavy breathing. "Not particularly."

He brought a hand to the back of his neck, still looking down at her. "About that, last night... I'm really sorry. It was never my intention to upset you. I suppose I just wanted a glimpse into your life here. If that guy Chris was the closest person you had in Dublin, I thought that maybe getting to know him was the first step. But I can see now that I don't fit here. I tried, but I can't. If this," he gestured to Reilly and him, "is going to work, if *we're* going to work, you need to come back to Florida with me. We need to do this together." He took a step towards her, his face open and hopeful. "And I want this to work. I want to be there for our baby. I want our baby to grow up the way any kid should, with a loving mom and a loving dad... parents that love each other. Because I do, Reilly. I'm in love with you, and the only reason I didn't tell you that before was because I knew there was nothing keeping you in the US. But this... this changes everything. This gives you – us – a reason."

He took another step forward, and his hands were on either side of her face before she could blink. His spiel had been so convincing, so captivating, she hadn't fully realized what he was doing until his head lowered down to hers.

He tenderly brushed his lips against hers, the whisper of a kiss, and then Reilly's good reason came rushing back full force. She braced her hands on his chest and pushed him back, enough that he let go and stumbled back a few steps.

His expression screamed of hurt and anger, and she struggled to her feet, her own anger building up at his attempt to kiss her. "No," she said, pushing her hands into her hair. "No, Todd, I'm not going to follow you back to the US like you want me to. My life is here. My work is here. All of my friends, all of the people I love – they're here. And I'm not going to abandon my life just because you want me to."

Stung, Todd rolled his eyes, pulling on the sleeves of his shirt. "Right. The people you love."

"What's that supposed to mean?" she muttered.

"Isn't it obvious?" He looked up, finally meeting her gaze. "You're in love with that guy – Chris. I don't know how you can claim to walk through crime scenes every day and not miss a single thing, but really - you don't know the first thing about yourself."

Reilly swallowed hard, not wanting to show how hard his rebuttal had hit. She hadn't known when she was pregnant, Chris had to point it out to her. When they were working another case and her traumatic experience with the serial killer that had almost taken her life was getting to her, she still hadn't noticed.

She cared about Chris yes, they cared about each other. Could it be possible that she was actually in love with him?

"No," she said, shaking her head, "I am not in *love* with my colleague. You're just grasping at something to make me into the bad guy. I'm not going back to the US with you because of all the things that matter to me. My job. My friends. My life. It has nothing to do with Chris."

Todd was walking from the room now, so Reilly followed him as he went. He was grabbing his things from the couch and stuffing them in his suitcase. He disappeared into the bathroom and came back out with his razor and shampoo.

"What are you doing?" she asked, venom still lacing her tone as she watched his furious retreat.

Todd chuckled maliciously, shaking his head down at his suitcase as he zipped it shut in jerky movements, "I'm getting out of here, Reilly. I'm going back to the hotel I stayed in last night to wait it out before my flight tomorrow. I'm not as stupid as you'd like to believe. I can tell when I'm not wanted."

"C'mon, Todd," she said, now softening a little, "you can stay here till then. You don't have to get a hotel."

"Reilly, I've spent every night here sleeping on your couch. And every night I've lay there, wondering why. I can remember the time we spent together can't you? I wasn't on the couch in Florida, Reilly - neither were you. And I think I've figured it out."

He stood and yanked his suitcase off a nearby chair so it hit the ground heavily, bouncing on its wheels. He turned and fixed her with a look that said no matter how much she denied it, no matter how much she lied to him, he could see it clear as day. "It's much harder for you to forget about him when we're here, in this world, isn't it?"

She shook her head, tears building up in her eyes, "That isn't fair, Todd."

He laughed mirthlessly. "Please, don't tell me about what is and isn't fair." Todd got to the front door and ripped it open, his eyes holding too much emotion when they met hers. "Have a good life, Reilly," he said, his voice soft and sad before he closed the door behind him with a resounding certainty.

CHAPTER FORTY-THREE

Chris and Kennedy approached the Glynn house for the second time in the space of a week, this time hoping to talk to Holly's brother Conor about his reaction to the photos Graham Hackett had shared of his ex, and to question the kid about his whereabouts the night Graham was murdered.

But this time there was something noticeably different about the property.

The plants lining the house were drooping, as though they hadn't been watered in days, the lawn was slightly overgrown and the gray Dublin sky hung a little lower over the Glynn's rooftop.

All of the blinds were drawn, all of the lights were off, and the house seemed to give off a feeling of emptiness. Chris was reminded of the countless abandoned properties they had searched over the years.

He and Kennedy shared a look as they stood on the front step, then his partner shrugged and knocked on the door, three solid times. The dull, bouncing sound of his knocks echoed on the other side of the door, and they could hear them through the rest of the house.

"Nobody's there," he remarked, sounding thoughtful.

"Damnit - maybe the parents took the kids away from it all - it is the school holidays," Chris said, though it would be surprising given the father's stranglehold on the investigation thus far. Then turning around, something by the neighboring fence caught his attention.

A young boy was peeking over the top of the pristine fence, watching the two detectives carefully. He had been so silent; Chris wasn't sure how he'd noticed him. It was fortunate that he did, however, because when he met the kid's eyes, he spoke.

"Are you looking for the Glynns?" the boy asked, his face dirty, a football in his hands. He couldn't have been much older than Rachel, Chris thought, immediately wondering where the kid's parents were.

Chris glanced at Kennedy before looking back at the boy, "Yeah," he said, taking a step from the path and into the lush grass, "Do you know where they are?"

The boy rubbed his eyes with one of his hands roughly, then looked back up at Chris, "No, but they left the other day - off on holidays I think."

Chris raised his eyebrows and Kennedy took a step

forward toward the boy, "Holidays? Did you see them carrying anything - suitcases and stuff?"

Yeah. I don't know when they're coming back, and I'm a bit worried because I think Sandy is in there all alone."

"Sandy?" Chris asked, his eyes widening, then guessed the kid must be talking about a pet dog.

"Their chinchilla," he said then, like that much should have been obvious to the detectives. He dropped his ball on the grass and grabbed the top of the fence, bringing his full face into view, then grinned toothily at the two men, now that he could see them clearly.

"Their chinchilla," Kennedy deadpanned, having no love for things small or furry. He wasn't completely sure he knew what a chinchilla even was.

"Thanks little man," Chris said, taking three long strides over to the boy. He held out his hand and when the boy extended his smaller, dirty one, he dropped his card into his small palm, "If you think of anything else that might help us out, just tell your mother to give us a call, okay?"

The kid nodded, looking up at Chris. He was tall enough to tower over the kid. He was still wearing his sunglasses despite the dreary weather, and the bruise that was currently spreading over his cheek told tales of exciting fights with mysterious bad guys.

"Do you have a badge?" the boy asked, recalling movies and TV shows he had seen.

Chris glanced back at Kennedy, who was gesturing for him to get on with it. Chuckling, Chris looked back at the kid and said, under his breath, "Kind of. Would you like to see it?"

The boy nodded enthusiastically and Chris pulled his detective credentials from his pocket, letting him get a good look before he folded it and tucked it away again.

With shining eyes, he looked down at Chris's card in his hand and asked, "Are you a super spy?"

Chris held back a laugh as he said, "No, I'm a detective. We're pretty much the same thing, though."

The boy nodded, folding the card and tucking it away in the pocket of his shorts, much in the same fashion Chris had concealed his ID. "Okay," he said, shooting him another toothy grin "Cool. Affirmative."

Kennedy was still shaking his head when they finally climbed back into the car. He muttered something under his breath and Chris said, "What?"

He chuckled. "Sometimes, I think you're more comfortable with the kiddos than with people your own age."

Chris thought about that for a moment, then laughed along with Kennedy against the pounding headache he had gained from his pointless drinking the night before. After the first two pints, the barman had kept them coming, and Chris had allowed himself to wallow in the hopelessness of the situation.

"That bad, huh?" Kennedy asked after a few minutes of driving.

Chris opened one eye and glanced over at the older man through his sunglasses.   "Yeah," he said, before settling back against the seat, "last night was rough."

"I'll say," Kennedy said, shaking his head. "Where'd you get the shiner? Or should I even ask?"

"Don't even ask ..."

His partner suppressed a grin. "Rightio."

Chris winced as a particularly close car horn blared in his ear, but wasn't going to say that he didn't deserve everything he'd got for his idiotic behavior.

CHAPTER FORTY-FOUR

Isn't it obvious? You're in love with Chris.

Reilly stared at her ceiling, Todd's words still ringing through her ears even as she desperately tried to push all the things he had said from her mind.

She was not in love with Chris. It was possible that she had been oblivious to other things, but she wasn't completely stupid. She was capable of gauging her own emotions.

She rolled on her side and let out a small groan. In the period of a few short months, her life had done a complete one eighty. She had been in control of everything before the pregnancy, and now it felt like there was nothing she could do to stem the unfortunate events headed her way.

Todd wanted her to give up her life and go back with him to the US, but Reilly knew now that she couldn't do that. Though she was sure Todd would be involved as much as he could - which given the distance, wouldn't be much - it looked like she was definitely going to end up raising the baby by herself, in Dublin.

What would the baby do to her work life? How much time would she realistically be able to contribute to each case when she had to contribute so much of her time to a needy child?

Her thoughts rounded back to where they always did: work.

Chris was still keen on Simon Hackett as the murderer. He had the motive, and there were several witnesses saying that Simon and his younger brother had gotten into a heated argument the night Graham was murdered.

But Simon would not have needed to come through the window, and Reilly was now pretty sure that's where Graham's attacker had come in or out, if not both.

To her, Simon Hackett had always been too neat, too simple. Then there was the animal feed trace, the foam and where the hell did the board wax fit in?

No, everything pointed to a third party - another so far unidentified person. If this person was indeed the one who had beaten Graham Hackett to death, it wasn't something they had planned. He (or she) had crawled through the window into Graham's room, maybe had some kind of verbal spat or bust up and then... lost it.

But who? Not Holly Glynn surely, though the presence of her DNA in the room raised some troubling questions...

Reilly stopped pacing and dropped her hands to her side suddenly, as her eyes fell on a pamphlet Todd had left on the side table from the doctor's office. It was an educational pamphlet about twins. The likelihood, how twins developed, and the different kinds of twins that existed...

The thought struck her so suddenly and surely, her thoughts racing through her head, piecing everything together faster than she could move around the room, finding decent clothes to wear to the lab. Then Reilly was yanking on her clothes, becoming disgruntled when she found that - incredibly - they seemed tighter than they had been the day before.

She was stumbling out the door, grabbing her phone from her bag with clumsy fingers as she locked up behind her.

"Julius?" she called out, her voice shrill with excitement. He'd picked up after her third call, and Reilly imagined him sitting at home relaxing after a hard week, hearing the buzz and knowing that three rings meant it was truly important and she wouldn't stop until he answered.

"Boss," Julius said, his voice heavy, "Just once, why

can't you have your shocking revelations during work hours?"

She laughed, a sound so light and cheery it surprised him. "You're very funny Julius. It's great that you're in such good sprits though, because I'm going to need you to meet me at the lab in ten minutes."

Julius grumbled something unintelligible into the receiver and Reilly said, "Twenty max, then," before hanging up and jumping in her car.

It took her less than ten minutes to get to the office in the light Sunday traffic, and she grabbed her bag and hurried in, flashing her ID at Declan, the same guard who'd let Todd up to her office a couple of days before.

The thought of that, of Todd being worried enough to come looking for her, sent an ache through her heart, but she shook it off and kept walking. She was too close to a breakthrough now to let her personal problems get in the way.

THE LAB WAS dark and cool, and it took a moment for the fluorescent lights to power on, flickering slowly over the expensive equipment.

Reilly put her hands on her hips and took it all in. Hopefully, with the evidence already here, they had enough to get their guy.

"Fancy seeing you here, Goldilocks," a familiar voice

said, and Reilly turned to see Kennedy standing in the doorway of the lab, two Styrofoam cups in his hands.

She shook her head at him, shocked. "What are you doing here?"

A nonplussed Julius pushed past Kennedy into the room. "I called them. I figured whatever amazing revelation you've had will be confirmed as soon as I work some magic, and then we'd be calling the detectives anyway. Getting them here early saves me the trouble and gets us refreshments while we wait."

Chris came in just then and handed Julius a cup of steaming hot coffee. He took a sip and sighed, then glanced briefly over at Reilly. "Afternoon..."

Kennedy chuckled under his breath as he handed the cup to Reilly. She took it and looked dubiously at the three of them, before taking a careful sip.

"Hot chocolate?" she said, raising her eyebrows indignantly, "you got me *hot chocolate*?"

"Well, you can't have caffeine, so..."

Reilly frowned at him – he was right, she couldn't have caffeine, but drinking hot chocolate while the rest of them drank coffee made her feel like a child. Not to mention jealous at the extra boost they got while she felt like she had been run over by something four times her size.

And speaking of which, what the hell had happened to Chris's cheek?

Well, no time to think about that now. She set down

her cup and clapped her hands together, making all three of the men jump, "C'mon Julius, let's get to it," she said, trying desperately to avoid Chris's hangdog gaze.

Chris for his part, felt like a heel. After walking in and seeing Reilly – her tired posture, her red-rimmed eyes, and the frown that had jumped on her face as soon as she saw him – he had felt a whole new rush of guilt over what had happened the night before. But this wasn't the time to apologize to her, not when she was in her fevered frenzy, and certainly not when Kennedy and Julius were around.

He glanced over Kennedy's shoulder to see her moving around the laboratory equipment with Julius, extracting things and putting slides through analysis. Just once, Chris wished he could be there when she had a brilliant epiphany. He wanted to see that look on her face when it all made sense.

On the other side of the room, that self-same look was plastered on Reilly's face. Julius was analyzing a blood specimen while a report printed out nearby. She snatched it and read through the results, lowering the paper at the same time Julius stepped back from the machine, a startled look on his face.

"What?" Kennedy was saying, as he and Chris pushed up from the table and walked over to Reilly and Julius.

"Twins," Reilly said, softly, under her breath.

Chris and Kennedy looked at each other for a moment, extremely confused.

"No," Julius said, shaking his head at the results, "I can't believe I didn't think about it. It didn't even cross my mind that the epithelial DNA didn't belong to the girl."

"Will one of you geniuses please explain to us what the hell you're talking about?" Kennedy pleaded.

"Holly and Conor Glynn are twins, yes?" Reilly explained, "but we didn't ever consider that they might have been *identical* twins, because identical twins come from the same egg, and are almost always the same sex."

"But in some cases," Julius jumped in, the excitement in Reilly's voice transferring over to his, "an egg can have three chromosomes, instead of the usual XX for a girl, and XY for a boy, it has two X's and a Y. When those eggs split to make monozygotic twins – or twins that come from the same egg – it can be a boy and a girl. Thus, identical twins."

"And the epithelial - skin - trace found at the crime scene that we just analyzed - reports as an XY chromosome."

"So..." Kennedy said, still confused as to what the two of them were getting at.

"So the DNA can only belong to a male," Chris said slowly. He licked his lips and looked down at the floor. "The brother. Conor."

"We already know he was angry at Graham Hackett," Kennedy said. "Those pictures of his ex. But that played out long before ..."

Reilly had the answer right away. "Holly's attack. Conor somehow found out about what happened to his sister. Someone told him, or he saw her when she got home or something."

"But he was supposedly elsewhere when she was attacked, and nowhere near the party," Chris pointed out, "how could he have found out?"

She shrugged, "I don't know, maybe he came home early. Or maybe ... maybe we got this all wrong. Maybe *he* - not Holly's attacker was the one in the cab that night and got out when he saw her stumbling down the street."

Chris stood up. "The taxi driver mentioned something about his fare smelling of strong aftershave. But maybe it was foam, and maybe like you say, it wasn't her attacker at all, but Conor on his way home from the foam party. He stopped to check on his sister when he saw her on the street."

"Okay," Kennedy said, "so one way or another Conor finds out about what happened to his sister. She's upset and in shock and was just at Graham Hackett's house, who he dislikes anyway. So he puts two and two together ..."

Julius sat down on one of the lab chairs, draping his arm over the back and spinning it so it faced them. He took a sip of his coffee. "He dislikes Graham Hackett because of the revenge porn?"

"That and the fact that Conor was a bit of an outcast amongst the other lads on the team. They were jealous of him and Graham was a sort of ringleader. Glynn doesn't join in on the juicing and still he gets this big Aussie scholarship," Kennedy continued, putting the pieces together.

"So Conor decides to confront Graham about what he *thinks* he did to his sister," Julius took up the baton, "he goes to the house - but the party's finished and everyone's gone home. So he gets in through the window. And when he gets in the room, Graham is in there. Asleep, passed out maybe?"

"I'd say not," said Reilly. "I'd say Graham's awake and he grabs the hurl - likely his own as we never found any others in the room.

And there's a scuffle, with Conor shedding trace we later mistakenly identify as belonging to his sister. Maybe Graham has a few choice words about Conor's sporting prowess or something about his ex, Megan like he did in those online messages, not knowing that he's there for a different reason altogether."

"But eventually Conor grabs the hurl off Graham and turns it on him. He grabs it, transferring foam residue from the nightclub. Either way, Conor goes off at something Graham says, and continues moving through the room, coming at him until Graham backs off and then becomes scared."

"He falls back and then, when Graham's down, Conor lines up the last shot to his head like a winning puck in the net," Chris said, his voice low as he stared at the tiled floor, recalling Conor's prowess on the hurling pitch when they'd interviewed Edward.

"Then realizing what he's done," Reilly continued, "he goes back out the window and gets rid of the murder weapon in a neighbor's trash nearby."

"But where does the animal feed come into it?" Julius asked, finishing his coffee.

"Animal feed?" Kennedy asked, remembering Chris's conversation with the Glynn's young neighbor earlier that day. "What kind of animal?"

"Exotic animal feed," Julius said, moving the chair back and forth with his foot. "But the Hacketts don't have pets."

"No," Chris said, recalling with a shudder the cage that had been present in the Glynn house when they had gone to interview Holly and her mother. "But the Glynns do."

"Would chinchillas - whatever the hell they are - be considered exotic?"

Reilly looked up at Kennedy. "The Glynns have a chinchilla? Why the hell didn't you mention anything like that before?"

"Because we just found out today," he shot back.

"And in fairness, if we told you about every little thing we saw every time we went to interview someone, it would get very annoying. In any case, I don't even know what a chinchilla is, let alone what the feckin' thing eats."

Reilly ignored him, one last thing niggling at the back of her mind, "The board wax... that fits too," she said, eyes widening with excitement.

"How?" Chris was already standing up and tugging on the ends of his jacket. He tossed his coffee cup in the bin and inclined his head at Kennedy.

"When you think of surfboards, where else in the world, other than California do you think of?"

"Bloody hell," Kennedy said, understanding dawning. "It is the Glynn brother - it has to be."

CHAPTER FORTY-FIVE

The room filled with an air of expectation as the four of them understood that finally, they had their man.

And that Holly Glynn's attack had indeed been connected to Graham Hackett's murder all along.

Chris was on the phone to O'Brien the second they'd identified enough to take Conor Glynn in, and while the chief was dubious - especially given the kid's solicitor father had recently been in his ear so much - reluctantly, he gave his blessing.

Reilly grabbed her jacket from the table, "I'm coming with you," she said, struggling to pull it on. Kennedy reached around and found the other sleeve for her, and she thanked him, quietly seething that now it was starting to look like she couldn't even manage to put her own clothes on.

"When we went to the Glynn house earlier today," Chris was saying in a rush, as he hit the elevator buttons, "there wasn't anyone at home. Like all of them had rushed off in a hurry."

Reilly raised an eyebrow, "So, what makes you think they're back? What if the parents figured out what Conor did and decided the best option was to just up and leave the country? The father's a solicitor - he'd work all the angles to protect his son."

Chris called ahead to another officer to meet them at the house with the warrant for Conor Glynn's arrest while they exited the GFU building and got in Kennedy's car.

The cool midsummer air blew in through a crack in the window as Reilly put her head against the glass. Finally, *finally*, they were getting there.

Her mind swung back round to Holly Glynn then, and the dull feeling that had occupied her stomach for the duration of the case flooded back in. While she was pretty sure they'd managed to find Graham's killer would it bring them any closer to finding Holly's attacker?

And what of that attacker - had it been Graham all along? Was Holly pretending that she didn't remember anything about it in order to protect her brother?

But if it wasn't Graham, and Conor had lashed out at the other boy mistakenly assuming he'd hurt his sister, then it made an already troubling situation even more difficult.

Reilly was stuck, unsure right then if she preferred that her child be a girl - always vulnerable to that kind of opportunistic sexual attack - or a boy incapable of controlling his revenge impulses?

"We're here," Chris said, eventually.

A soft rain had just started to fall, drifting through the wind, more mist than raindrops. It spattered the windshield in front, accentuating his quiet voice. And sure enough, when Reilly glanced to her right she saw the Glynn house.

On the outside it seemed like the patrons of the house would be happy, perhaps settling down to enjoy a relaxing Sunday afternoon together?

But every single one of that family was now broken in some way, she realized, as she stepped out of the car.

And it was about to get a whole lot worse.

"DETECTIVES!" Chris called out, banging on the front door.

This time, Michael Glynn opened the door, his face grim, "What the hell is this - "

Chris flashed a copy of the arrest warrant in his face and pushed past him, into the house, "We're looking for Conor," he said, loud enough that if the boy was in the house he would hear.

Reilly, Kennedy, and the other uniform moved into the house. She read a decorative plaque resting on a shelf to her right.

When it's raining, look for the rainbow. When it's dark, look for the stars.

She looked away from the sign and into the face of Susan Glynn whom she had briefly met in the hospital. Holly's mum looked incredibly jaded and worried, and Reilly wanted to reach out to her to say something, but instead she just looked at her shoes.

She saw Kennedy heading toward the stairs and followed him up. He moved through the bedrooms, peeking in each one before moving on to the next. She followed him into the last room in the hallway and had to note how startlingly it resembled Graham Hackett's bedroom.

The posters taped on the walls were exclusively that of famous sports stars, domestic GAA players and international soccer heroes. The walls were dark blue, the bed unmade and messy.

Reilly took a few steps over to the dresser. The drawers were hanging wide open, most of the clothes missing and in disarray, as though they had been ripped from their spots suddenly.

She moved over to a shelf laden with sports trophies and very quickly spotted a familiar looking white cylinder. It looked like soap, except it was circular and waxy. Alongside the shelf, stood a full-length surfboard.

She snapped on a pair of gloves and slipped the board wax container into an evidence bag.

When she and Kennedy were coming down the steps, Chris met them in the hallway.

"He's not upstairs?" he asked, and when Kennedy shook his head the other officer said, "he's not back there, either."

They all moved into the family room, where Holly Glynn and her parents had taken up defensive positions on the opposite side.

"Where is your son?" Kennedy demanded of Mrs. Glynn.

"You leave her out of this," Michael said, stepping between his wife and the detective. The man's trademark anger was missing this time, and instead it seemed as though the father was jaded and worn.

Chris squared his feet, looking the man up and down, trying to determine if he was a threat to them. Something about this entire situation felt wrong.

Behind him, Reilly had sighted the chinchilla cage, as well as a bag of food open next to it. She produced another evidence bag, taking a small scoop of the food for them to analyze and compare against the trace they had found at the Hackett crime scene.

But by now, she was pretty certain everything fit. All they had to do now was locate their killer.

"Where is Conor?" Chris demanded again, this time a near growl.

"Out training probably. Why?" the father said, his tone low and even, while his Adam's apple jumped and bobbed.

Chris raised a single eyebrow. Surely, as a solicitor, Glynn understood the costly consequences of lying to the detectives. "Fine," he said, "take him in."

The officer moved forward and asked Michael Glynn to turn around so he could cuff his hands. Glynn did so, slow and controlled, like he had been practicing all his life.

"Daddy ...!" Holly rushed from the other side of the living room, where she had been sitting quietly before. Her hair was wild, and tears streaked down her face. She looked around the room frantically, and when her eyes caught Reilly's, she took another step forward, her tone pleading, "You have to help him," she said, gesturing toward her father, who was being escorted from the house. "He didn't do anything wrong," she cried, her words laden with hysteria.

Susan Glynn was sobbing hard, and she moved to embrace her daughter, who pushed her away. "Tell them!" Holly implored of her mother, "Don't let them do this!"

Kennedy and Chris were busy with Michael Glynn, but Reilly didn't miss the words Holly had uttered.

Tell them....

She followed close behind Chris and Kennedy, her

gaze lingering on a portrait above the mantelpiece of the Glynn family in much happier times.

Reilly looked down at her shoes as she shut the door on the two women, her heart laden with sorrow and guilt for the force that had whirled through this family and torn them apart.

CHAPTER FORTY-SIX

Chris walked into the warm interview room and pulled a chair out roughly, sitting down and leaning back in it.

After a minute or two of silence in the stagnant interview room, he laced his fingers together and leaned forward. "Did your son attack and kill Graham Hackett in his own home on the night of Wednesday 18th of June?"

Michael Glynn looked up calmly, "Did *you* attack and kill Graham Hackett?"

Chris sat up in his chair, his jaw visibly tensing. He laced and re-laced his fingers together, "No, Mr. Glynn, as a matter of fact, I didn't. My DNA wasn't found at the crime scene, nor was there any other trace evidence putting me there. I wasn't the one who had an existing beef with Graham Hackett, nor believed him to have assaulted my sister."

At this, Michael Glynn looked unnerved, "You have really put a lot of work into this murder investigation, haven't you? Let me ask you again: where is the devoted team looking for Holly's attacker? Where are the men barging into homes, looking for the bastard that hurt my daughter? Does it only matter to you when the victim is dead? If the bastard had killed Holly, would you be looking a little harder?"

"Well, based on your son's actions, it seems we already have Holly's attacker..." Chris began.

"You don't."

"What?"

"You don't. Holly says it wasn't Hackett."

"Then why did your son take off on a vengeful rampage? Beat the shit out of Graham Hackett before practically caving his skull in with a hurl?"

Glynn recoiled a little then, evidently unaware of the severity of the attack.

"Michael, I understand your family has been through a difficult time – and that you are only trying to protect them. But I need to talk to Conor. If he did believe Graham Hackett was his sister's attacker, then there are mitigating circumstances. You as a solicitor know this. But until we have him in custody and find out the real story, we can't help him or you."

"I have nothing to say to you," Michael Glynn said,

disdain clear in his rough voice, "you barge into my home, scare my already traumatized wife and daughter, and drag me here in cuffs. People like you think you can walk all over everyone simply because you've got a flashy badge tucked away in your belt. You know, solicitors get a bad rap, but the guards are the real arseholes. You guys don't care about anything but locking people up on the flimsiest of evidence. I've seen innocent man after innocent man rotting in cells, because a guard was too lazy to get off his fat arse and find out the real truth."

Chris rolled his lips into his teeth and gripped his file with an intensity that turned his knuckles white, "You're really not going to tell me where you're hiding him?"

Glynn scoffed, "No."

"Well then there's nothing I can do. Irrespective of what you think, I have responsibilities too. Jim and Tara Hackett lost their son. Holly's alive."

"And what about my son? What chance does he have once you lot get to him?" Glynn spat.

"That's the thing, Michael," Chris finished. "We will get to him. And soon."

But as he watched two officers walk Michael Glynn out of the room and down to a holding cell, Chris couldn't be sure if that was the truth.

REILLY REACHED the station just as Chris was exiting the interview room with the officers and Michael Glynn in tow. She watched as he disappeared down the hallway, and as he went, she caught a glimpse of the solicitor's salt and pepper hair.

The man was doing so much to protect Conor: was giving up everything he had – his family, his job, his life - sacrificing his own freedom for a crime he hadn't even committed.

All to protect his son, who had yet to take responsibility for his actions. Surely as a solicitor he knew coming clean now would stand Conor in better stead.

Though perhaps being a father trumped being a solicitor.

A flash of panic flared in her mind then. Would she be willing to make that level of sacrifice of herself for her child? Would she be willing to give up her own life for her son or daughter? Was she capable of that?

Holly Glynn and her mother arrived at the station just then. Holly wore a light blue sweatshirt that climbed up her neck and ran all the way down to her wrists. Her hair was pulled back in a simple pony-tail, and she wore jeans that covered her legs but were not tight.

When she saw Reilly she made her way over with intention.

"I need to talk to you," she said, her voice breathless and teary.

"Okay," she replied cautiously, "what is it?"

Holly shook her head and glanced back in the direction her mother had gone to find out where they were holding Michael.

"No," she said, her voice low, "I need to talk to you... officially."

CHAPTER FORTY-SEVEN

The room at the station Reilly found for them to talk in was small and washed out, but on such short notice she couldn't do much better.

Holly sat still in the seat across from her, her sky blue sweatshirt pulled down over her wrists. She was shaking, but Reilly couldn't be sure if it was because she was cold, or because of something else.

"Okay," she said, "what did you want to tell me?"

Holly looked her in the eye and said clearly, her voice free of the tears tracking down her cheek, "I think ... I think Conor did kill Graham."

"Okay, Holly," Reilly said softly. "Tell me everything, right from the beginning. The truth this time."

The girl took a deep breath. "Most of what I already told you and the detectives was true. The girls and I got to Graham's house sometime after ten and the party was already going strong. After a while, a couple of us went out to the back deck. Graham and I started chatting. You know, how when you break up with someone, there's that awkward period of time where you can't talk? Graham and I had gotten over that, and we were just talking. He was telling me about this other girl that he really liked actually. But he wouldn't tell me who she was."

"I felt a bit sick and went to the bathroom upstairs, and when I came back out I saw Megan and some guy pass by. I told Graham that I was going to go see what was going on. He was going to come with me, but I didn't want to embarrass Megan, so I told him to leave it. I followed her, like I told you, but then I lost sight of them at the bottom of the garden. So like I said, I didn't feel too well, and it was late so I decided to just go home. Not long after that, there he was walking along with me. He said he'd walk me home."

Reilly held her breath. "Who?"

She looked tearful. "It was creepy from the moment he came up to me, but I didn't want to make a fuss so I just let him walk me home..." Holly trailed off, wiping her face with her hands clumsily.

I didn't want to make a fuss.

It was an almost innate female trait, Reilly knew, that came from physically being the weaker gender.

"Then about halfway to my house, near the green, he started trying it on, started kissing me and stuff. I told him to stop, that I wasn't interested ... but then he got mean ... angry. He's strong, and he pushed me down on the grass like I was a feather. I kept saying no, tried to push him off me and then he started saying how I was stuck up, thought I was too good for him. A snowflake. Like Conor."

Reilly frowned, her brain racing through the various witness reports as she tried to figure out who Holly was talking about. Was it Edward, her brother's teammate - who seemed to have some kind of unrequited crush on Conor? But if he was homosexual why would he be interested in Holly? Though who knew with kids these days - especially in the teenage experimental phase. But more to the point, why would Holly protect Edward?

"He tore at my clothes and I tried to fight him off then, but he got his body between my legs and held me down. Like I told you before, it was only when he was ... unbuckling himself that I managed to raise my knee and get him in the groin.

So I ran off and he screamed after me, calling me a frigid bitch and swore that I'd better not start accusing him of anything or he'd tell everyone that Conor was stacking too - mess up the scholarship for him."

"I don't understand. Why would Edward want to mess up Conor's scholarship?"

"Edward? Edward Lyons? No, God no, he adored Conor − he' one of his best friends. I'm not talking about Edward - I'm talking about - "

A snowflake... Tell everyone that Conor was stacking ...

"Dean," Reilly said, suddenly recalling those same distinctive phrases the teen had been using in his social media exchanges.

Holly nodded ashamedly. "I should have told him to piss off, but he's mean ... I know what he's capable of too. He hated Conor - all the other lads did. And it would be just like him to try to ruin my brother's future out of badness."

"So presumably you told Conor what happened?" Reilly asked, realizing that Holly's attack must have been the trigger for her brother's murderous rage.

But why did he go after Graham, when Dean was the one to blame?

Holly started to cry again. "After I got away from Dean, he walked back in the other direction toward the house, and I continued on home. I was shocked, upset, and still a bit woozy, and I stumbled on through the streets, without anyone noticing me, I thought. But then a taxi pulled up, and it was Conor. He'd seen me walking on my own and asked the driver to stop. When he saw my torn dress and that I was in a state, he started freaking out, asking me what had happened. It was stupid, but I couldn't tell him about Dean then because I was scared he'd make good on his threat. So I was telling Conor that I was at Graham's house, and Conor just ... took off. He looked so *angry*... I don't know what I thought was going to happen, but I never thought he was capable of ...that. He didn't know it was a party - didn't realize there were loads of us there. He thought it was just me and Graham in the house and that Graham had ...." She was crying outwardly now, heavy sobs. "And by the time he got to the house everyone else must have gone."

Reilly fished through her purse and produced a tissue for her. Holly accepted it gratefully.

"Conor told me to go straight home and I did. I didn't know what to do - wasn't sure what he was doing, so I just went upstairs and waited in his room until he got home. I don't know how long I sat there ... it must have been at least an hour, maybe?

When Conor did get home, he opened the door, and he was covered in blood. He came over and hugged me, told me everything would be okay. But he looked ... I don't know sort of ... spaced. A bit like some of the guys when they do poppers. But Conor doesn't do drugs - he never has. So I just assumed he'd got in a fight, that he'd caught up with Dean on the way and maybe figured out what had happened. Like I said, Dean is strong, one of those muscle-heads. So I asked him where he'd been, but he didn't answer. He just hugged me quickly and then said he needed to take a shower.

But some of the blood got on my arms, so I went back to my room and climbed into the shower, to get it off and I don't know - I guess to get ... Dean off me too. I felt tired and dirty and I was worried about what had happened with Conor. I don't know how long I sat in the shower, just letting the water run over me, but then the next thing I remember is Mom pulling me out and taking me to the hospital. She saw my ripped clothes and the bruises between my legs and..."

Holly sobbed again as she ran through the events of that night, the impact of her mother and brother's assumptions - but mostly her failure to explain the details - weighing heavily on her.

She took a deep breath when she had finished her story, then blew her nose into the tissue. "You must think I'm a terrible person," she said, finally. "But I really, honestly had no idea that Conor would do something like that to Graham - to anyone. I cared about Graham, he was my friend and yes, it didn't work out between us but I would never in a million years ..."

"So what did you do when you found out Graham had been killed?" Reilly asked. "That morning at the hospital when I spoke to you - you must have known then it was Conor."

She shook her head. "I was still in shock and confused ... but to be honest I really wasn't sure if it had anything to do with Conor. The thought crossed my mind, particularly with the blood, but I truly, honestly didn't think my brother could do something like that. And for a day or two afterwards when I got home, Conor wouldn't admit it either. It was only when I told him he'd got it all wrong - that it wasn't Graham who'd attacked me, that he broke down and admitted what had happened. He didn't mean to kill him, honestly he didn't. My brother's a good guy, but Graham taunted him, made him angry ..."

"Where is he Holly? Where is your brother now?"

The young girl's face was pale and scared. She had just given up her brother - her own twin - and Reilly couldn't imagine the decision she had to make next.

"It's not that I don't love Conor," Holly continued, "I do. But I can't let my Dad go to *prison* for him."

"Where is Conor, sweetheart?

Holly swallowed and glanced around the room, then fixed her eyes back on Reilly. She could see the chaos behind her eyes, the turmoil she must have suffered to get to the decision where she would give up her twin.

"He left for Sydney on Friday morning," Holly said, finally. "He left as soon as Mom and Dad figured out what had happened. The clothes from that night were still in his room. Mom was tidying up and found them in a rubbish bag under his bed."

"Do you know where those clothes are now?"

Holly shook her head, "No. I've kind of been staying in my room a lot. I only know about the clothes because Mum and Dad were arguing about it before they confronted him."

"Okay," Reilly said. "Holly, you've done an excellent job. I know this was hard and I'm sure your cooperation will help your dad too. What about

Dean?" she asked then. "Do you want the detectives to - ?"

"There's no point," she said, shaking her head resolutely. "Even though he scared me, he didn't actually do anything. And I think enough people have paid."

"It doesn't matter that he wasn't successful in doing what he wanted to, Holly. He still tried to overpower you, force you to do something against your will."

Holly shrugged as if it was the kind of thing she already understood she'd have to get used to in life. Men would always have the upper hand.

And maybe that's the way it had always been Reilly thought, but it didn't have to be. Men - boys - like Dean Cooper needed to be answerable, needed to know that their superior body strength didn't mean they could automatically impose their will on women.

Maybe it was too late for Holly's generation, but she'd make damn sure that her kid - whatever gender it turned out to be - took those things for granted.

Mrs. Glynn pushed through the door then, rushing to her daughter and wrapping her arms around her. She looked up at Reilly, her expression furious and hurt, "Don't you think she's gone through enough today without more questions? She's already told you everything she knows."

Holly pushed back on her mother's chest and shook her head, wiping her eyes with the sleeves of her light blue sweater. "No, mom," she said, "it's okay. I wanted to talk to her. I told her ...everything. It's not fair to Dad."

"You told her everything ... oh love," Susan Glynn's face fell, as she was torn between her daughter's distress, her husband's predicament and her son's guilt.

Reilly moved to the doorway then, wanting to say something, but not knowing what she could say. She just watched as mother and daughter embraced, both equally distraught.

CHAPTER FORTY-EIGHT

"The Glynn kid is on a flight back from Australia," Kennedy announced the following afternoon, tucking his phone in his pocket as he entered the lab. "Gave himself up in Sydney."

The GFU team looked up at him, silence filling the room when really there should have been some sort of jubilation over catching their guy. But they all knew that the endgame was a lot less fun when you knew that families were going to be torn apart.

There would be no winners in this case.

"Conor Glynn is facing murder charges," he continued, "and his father is facing charges for trying to cover it up. There's a suggestion that the mother did something to cover it up, too – they still can't find the clothes he was wearing on the night of the murder – but it looks like Glynn is taking the fall for his wife."

Reilly came in then, a box of case files in her arms. Gary stood up at once and took the box from her, setting it on the counter.

"I'm not incapable of carrying stuff you know," she remonstrated, but at this point, she was worn out from arguing about special treatment.

"Clearly," he said, giving her midriff a significant glance, causing the rest of them to chuckle.

"Oh, you think that's funny now? You wait until we're a couple of days into getting this stuff in order for the prosecutor's office."

As expected the laughs died out quickly.

"Well," Kennedy said, putting his hands on his hips, "seems like that's my cue to head away."

"Wait," Gary said. He glanced at the others. "It's been a long slog, lots of overtime - weekends and everything. We should go out and celebrate now that it's over. We can always start that stuff tomorrow."

There was complete silence in the room as everyone watched carefully for Reilly's reaction. He was right though; it had been a long hard slog and some of them had even worked through the night. They deserved a break.

"Fine,' she said, hefting the box up off the table. "Better put this back in my office then."

Gary stood up and again eased it from her hands, an apologetic smile on his face. "Sorry," he said, "I just can't let you carry it. It's how I was raised."

Lucy rolled her eyes but Reilly was smiling. "O'Grady's then?" she said, referring to the nearest pub.

The team left the office and made their way to the pub nearby.

The interior was low lit and surprisingly loud for a Monday afternoon. A darts match was playing in the corner and a few guys were watching it - shouting and yelling at the screen.

Reilly made her way to the bar to take care of the order. She knew the others' individual poison almost by heart. The barman came over, his eyes wary as he took in her form. "What can I get you?" he asked, polishing the inside of a glass.

"A tonic water with lemon for me please," she said, after rattling off the team's order, somewhat tickled by the notion that she would get anything other than a non-alcoholic drink. But that was Ireland for you.

From where she stood, she watched the gang chatting effortlessly, having fun and laughing with each other. Even normally stoic Julius was getting in on the fun, playing a round of darts against Gary, whose competitive nature was getting the best of him.

"Fancy a game of pool?" Chris asked, suddenly appearing alongside her, mirth lining his voice.

Reilly looked at him in surprise. He held up his hands. "I called Kennedy and he mentioned the whole gang had clocked off early for the afternoon - you included. I had to shake my ears out, make sure I wasn't hearing things."

She chuckled. "The guys deserve it. And I doubt I'll have much of an opportunity to join them from now on."

The barman slid back over. "What can I get you mate?"

Chris glanced at Reilly, "I'll have what she's having," he intoned jokily.

The barman nodded and Chris took the others' drinks over to their table while he waited for his own.

Reilly remained at the bar, so he did the same, taking a seat alongside her. When his drink arrived, he took his glass and removed the lemon, setting it down on a beermat nearby.

"So are you going to tell me what happened to your face?"

Chris looked sheepish. "Honestly, it's nothing sinister. Believe it or not, I fell and tripped on a curb on my way home from the pub the other night. Gobshite."

Reilly exhaled a little. She'd wondered ...

"Look..." He glanced over at her GFU colleagues, who were laughing on the other side of the pub, then back to Reilly. "I'm so sorry for the way I acted the other night. At your place."

"Chris - " she started, but he held a hand up, cutting her off.

"No," he said, gripping his glass in the other hand, "it's not okay. I should have behaved better. With everything going on in your life, you didn't need all of that shite piled on top of it."

Reilly stared down at her water for a moment, trying to process Chris's apology. Finally, just barely audible over the sound of the sports fans in the back shouting, she replied. "Thanks. It means a lot. But Todd was ... well, I think we both know what he was doing."

"Is he still ..."

She shook her head. "Flew out this morning. It's okay, we got some things straightened out before he left." She glanced sideways at him but didn't elaborate.

Chris took a sip of his water and grimaced, "Never did like it with lemon," he explained, seeing the puzzled look on her face.

"You know, after the week we've just had, I'm beat. I think I'm going to go," she said, gathering her things.

Chris finished his water in one swallow, like it was the last sup of Guinness. "I'll walk you out," he said, and when Reilly didn't argue, he turned and followed her out.

A late afternoon Dublin bay sea fog had descended outside, causing Reilly to pull her jacket closer around her. The two walked side by side back to the GFU car park as they made small talk about the case, their words billowing out like the fog around them.

"Do you want to come back for a while?" she asked as she paused by the car, her voice barely above a whisper. "I could do with the company."

His face was impassive and then he nodded. "Okay, I'll follow on."

CHAPTER FORTY-NINE

When they reached her flat and Chris stepped inside, he was once again flooded with the memory of what had happened the last time he'd stepped over this particular threshold. He recalled uneasily the uncomfortable atmosphere, the terrible strain that had existed between him and Todd and the way Reilly had reacted to it.

She noticed the expression on his face and shook her head. "You can stop feeling sorry for yourself. That was Todd's fault, too. And mine, for thinking it would be okay to have two alphas together in the same room. So I think it would be best if we avoid the subject from now on," she said, a smile on her lips, "you'll just keep apologizing, and as much as I love to hear it, I'm starving."

She moved to the kitchen, and Chris followed her

tentatively. He watched uselessly as she gathered the ingredients from the fridge and the cabinets.

"You know I'm not much of a cook ..." he confessed, recalling Todd and his easy expertise in the kitchen.

"All the better," she said, moving around the kitchen gracefully, despite her extra bulk. She had almost gotten used to being pregnant at this point. Almost.

She felt a sudden twinge in her stomach and was reminded that it wouldn't be long until she was herself again. "My experience with men that can cook hasn't been the best, as you know."

Chris smiled at her attempt at making a joke, but the recollection of what had happened the night she went rushing in to stop The Chef felt like a knife in his own chest. If he closed his eyes and imagined it was happening again, he could still feel the immense panic that had come over him when she had left that frantic message on his phone before rushing in to go head-to-head against a killer.

"I'm thinking a spinach and chicken pasta?" Reilly said, not noticing the faraway look in his eyes. It hadn't occurred to her that Chris had his own memory of that incident, and it hadn't been pleasant, either.

He watched her turn on the stove and grab a pot for the water, then he asked the thing that had been sitting on the tip of his tongue since they'd spoken earlier "So how'd you guys leave things?"

Reilly looked at Chris, and, despite herself, heard Todd's words ringing out in her brain.

Isn't it obvious?'

She shook her head and tried to defeat the confusion crowding her head.

Chris shifted a little, uncomfortable with how long it was taking her to reply. "You don't have to answer," he said, "if you don't want to."

Reilly was startled by the naked vulnerability in his voice. She appraised him then, standing in her kitchen. He looked weathered and worn from the investigation, but handsome as ever in the suit that he seemed to wear every day. He was still watching her with careful eyes, as though he was trying to figure out what she was thinking.

You're in love with Chris...

"I'm not going back to the States," Reilly blurted, her cheeks reddening as she realized that she had been staring at him for far too long. He raised an eyebrow at this but said nothing for a little while.

"Oh," he replied eventually, swallowing and glancing around the flat, "I'm sorry."

"You're sorry?" she repeated, her voice skeptical, "Why are you sorry?"

Chris cleared his throat, "I don't know. I'm sorry it didn't work out with Todd. I mean, I just assumed. Is he... is he coming back soon?"

He'd called Reilly from the airport that morning,

apologizing for the way they'd left things, and the conversation had been ... difficult to say the least.

"Hey, I just wanted to apologize for the assumptions that I jumped to," Todd had said contritely. "I still think we can work this out ... maybe figure things out as we go along, just as long as we're together. I've even been thinking about possibly moving over to be with you. I had some time to really think about the things that are important to me, and I still think we should raise the baby together. And if the only way to do that is for me to move to Dublin to be with you, then I'm willing to do that."

"Todd..." she said, swallowing hard. "You were right."

He seemed to sense that she was not talking about their relationship, or the way that they needed to raise their child. "About what?" he replied, his voice terse and jarring, "what are you saying?"

"You were right," Reilly said again, her voice small and tired, "I can't be with you. I'm sorry, I care about you, but I don't love you. I just...can't."

Todd cleared his throat on the other end of the line, and Reilly could visualize his Adam's apple bobbing, could imagine the expression on his face as she said that to him. Perhaps he was smug that he had it all figured out before she had, or perhaps he was in disbelief. Whatever it was, she pushed on through the silence, "I'm not saying that I don't want you here for the baby. You can do whatever you want Todd, your level of involvement is up to you. But I can't move to the US, I can't be with you."

Now, she looked down at the onion she was chopping intently, and said to Chris, "No. I don't think he'll be coming back soon. When the baby's born maybe, but just for a visit."

Chris stopped the conversation there, choosing to let things unspoken remain that way. If she was uncomfortable talking about Todd, he wasn't going to push it. He'd already been kicked out of the place once and he didn't want to risk it again.

Reilly made pasta, and Chris stepped in every now and again to help her with something simple, but he mostly stood off to the side, watching her work her way through the kitchen.

When the food was ready, she dished up two plates and gestured for him to follow her to the table. When they reached it however, they were stopped by the piles of paper on the table.

Chris looked over the paperwork, charts and books, some of it pertaining to the Hackett investigation, but a lot designated to other ongoing cases. There were countless articles about recent forensic discoveries and a few textbooks sat amongst the clutter, their brightly colored covers sticking out through the manila and white of the paper and folders.

"Why does this not surprise me?" he asked, smirking.

"We can just eat on the couch," she said, her mind working through the problem quickly and coming up with a viable solution. She re-routed immediately, heading toward the sofa. If she was embarrassed by the mess she didn't show it. The only part that bothered her was how quickly Chris must have discerned that she rarely ate at the table. Truthfully, Saturday night with him and Todd had been the first time in a significant period that she'd broken bread at her table with someone else.

Usually case files were her company.

Reilly kicked off her flats and reclined back into the couch, sighing as the cushions padded around her aching back. Carefully, she balanced the plate on her rounded stomach, maneuvering her fork so she could eat it without the inconvenience of dropping the food.

Beside her, Chris let out a snort. She looked over at him, confused, until she realized the idea of her sitting her dinner on her protruding stomach must look pretty funny. Chris mimicked her, putting his feet up on her coffee table and setting the plate on his chest.

"Hey," she said, between his snorts of laughter, "I do what I can."

Chris shook his head, still laughing, "Is this a bit like the sock thing? You've had to reroute your life to accommodate dinner, too?"

Reilly laughed again, but as the thought blossomed in her mind, she quickly sobered up. She was going to have to accommodate a lot more, real soon.

She felt, suddenly, like she had the first few weeks she was in Dublin. Confused, afraid, and uncertain about her decision. What Todd had said was right. She was only just about used to the Irish culture - how on earth was she going to raise a baby here?

"Hey," Chris said softly, sensing her change in mood. He set his plate down on the coffee table. "Are you okay?"

She shook her head, tears suddenly springing to her eyes as once again the fear and anxiety she'd recently been holding back, flooded forward, pushing at her heart on their way to her eyes.

She started to lean forward, forgetting about her food, and he snatched the plate away, gently placing it on the table.

"I really don't know if I can do this, Chris," she said quietly.

It was so unlike her to be unsure about anything, he didn't think about his movements as they happened, he just scooted over and put a comforting arm around her.

At his touch, she unraveled with a sob. Chris ran his hands up and down her back in an attempt to comfort her, the same way his own mother used to do for him when he was upset or angry, but it didn't seem to have much of an effect, so then he wrapped his arms around her and pulled her close as Reilly cried into his chest.

He held her against him for what seemed like a very a long time, lightly caressing the top of her head, in an attempt to comfort her.

Some words were on the tip of his tongue but he couldn't say them to her.

Not now, and perhaps not ever.

At the moment, she was far too fragile for Chris to add to her worries. She had already made it clear that she didn't want to be with him, and the guilt of unreciprocated feelings would only weigh her down.

But that didn't mean he couldn't be there for her as a friend, like he'd promised. He tightened his arms around her, determined that while he couldn't be everything she needed, he would give her as much as he could, starting with a shoulder to cry on.

Once she had collected herself, Reilly stiffened a little and pulled away from him, her cheeks red with embarrassment. "I'm sorry ..."

"Hey," Chris interrupted, his words soft. "I'm here for you, you know that. We've been friends for a long time, remember?"

She shook her head, nodded, then looked around for something to wipe her eyes. She was sure that her face was puffy from crying. Man, she was an idiot.

Chris reached over the other side of the couch, plucking two tissues from the box that rested on a side table. "Here," he said, brushing her hair away and offering her the tissues.

She wiped her eyes and blew her nose.

"So, how did you figure out that it was the twin thing, anyway?" he asked, his eyebrows furrowing, as though he was actually interested in the answer. Reilly appreciated his effort even if it was completely transparent. He knew that the one thing that always made her feel better was thinking about a crime scene and puzzling it out.

"It was because of some antenatal booklet Todd brought home from the doctor's the other day. On the front was this picture of two babies in the womb - twins - and I got to thinking about the Glynns, which led me to consider the epithelial DNA left at the crime scene. It struck me that the trace we automatically assumed was from Holly could also belong to her twin."

Chris looked at her with something akin to awe, even as his stomach clenched at the idea of Todd with an educational booklet about their baby.

"Can you imagine that?" she mumbled, her voice now low and tired, almost delirious.

"What?" Chris asked, his mind still preoccupied with the idea of Reilly and Todd attending an antenatal appointment for their baby together. He glanced down at her stomach. Had Todd felt the baby kick? Had he introduced himself as its father?

"Giving birth to twins," Reilly said, yawning openly

now, "not only would it be incredibly painful, but you'd also have so much more responsibility. Two more mouths to feed instead of one, and as a parent you'd have to keep a close eye on two - as if one isn't bad enough ..."

Chris stayed still as once again, Reilly leaned gently against his shoulder. Ever so slowly, he draped an arm over her again, wanting to make sure he wasn't crossing any boundaries. But she didn't pull away.

"Some people have more than one kid on purpose you know. And having twins would be considered a miracle for some couples."

"Yeah," Reilly said, her voice sleepy. She could barely keep her eyes open.

They sat there silently for a while in the late evening light.

After a while, she glanced up at Chris, who was staring out the large bay window facing the street. His jawline was sharp and defined, and he clearly hadn't shaved since Saturday.

He was thinking, thinking, thinking, the tick in his jaw giving away his racing brain. Whatever thoughts were running through his mind just then weren't making him happy.

Reilly thought of how he was with Rachel, his goddaughter. He knew exactly how to act with children, though he had none of his own. Whereas she didn't know the first thing about them and she was going to have one soon. She was going to have to remember to feed it, take care of it, and she couldn't even manage to keep a houseplant alive.

He closed his eyes as she continued to rest her head on his shoulder, feeling more comfortable than she'd been in months. She was aware that how they were sitting now, so close together, violated the idea that they were simply friends, but no part of her wanted to move away from him, so she stayed right where she was.

The next time she looked up at Chris, his eyes were still closed but his head was resting against the back of the couch. He had dozed off.

She stared at this man, who was holding her so tenderly, encircling her in his strong arms in sleep, and was reminded of the time he had saved her life, the many times he'd had her back since she'd come to Dublin.

And when the words that encapsulated exactly how she felt about Chris Delaney suddenly materialized on her lips - just like Todd had insisted - it was all Reilly could do not to whisper them out loud into the darkness.

THE END

ABOUT THE AUTHOR

Casey Hill is the pseudonym of husband and wife writing team, Kevin and Melissa Hill. They live in Dublin, Ireland.

TABOO, the first title in a series of forensic thrillers featuring Californian-born CSI Reilly Steel was an international bestseller upon release. It was followed by subsequent books, INFERNO (aka TORN) HIDDEN, THE WATCHED, TRACE, AFTERMATH and ENDGAME.

A prequel to the series CRIME SCENE, is also available.

Translation rights to the series have been sold in multiple languages including Russian, Turkish and Japanese.

www.caseyhillbooks.com

Forty miles south of Washington, D.C. lies the small town of Quantico. Situated among lush greenery, the 547 acre property is where FBI recruits run obstacle courses, engage in firearms training and participate in mock hostage scenarios in Hogan's Alley.

It's the world budding forensic investigator Reilly Steel was born for.

During her first student semester at the Academy, a fatal accident occurs at a student party off-campus, and a fellow recruit is under suspicion. But by the behavior of the other students and the forensic evidence at the crime scene, Reilly guesses that there is more to the story than meets the eye.

Will her instincts, and everything she's learnt at

Quantico so far help Reilly uncover the truth behind the victim's death?

Forensic investigator Reilly Steel, Quantico-trained and California-born and bred, imagined Dublin to be a far cry from bustling San Francisco, a sleepy backwater where she can lay past ghosts to rest and start anew.

She's arrived in Ireland to drag the Garda forensics team into the 21st-century plus keep tabs on her Irish-born father who's increasingly seeking solace in the bottle after a past tragedy.

But a brutal serial killer soon puts paid to that. A young man and woman are found dead in a hotel room, the gunshot wounds on their naked bodies suggesting a suicide pact.

But as Reilly and the team dig deeper and more bodies are discovered, they soon realize that a twisted murderer is at work, one who seeks to upset society's norms in the most sickening way imaginable...

CSI REILLY STEEL SERIES

Printed in Great Britain
by Amazon